STARGATE
ATL

ENTA

The jumper spun sideways and then end over end. The inertial dampeners didn't go out, but the view flipped crazily in the port, the ground changing places with the sky. John heard the collective gasp, but the rumble was already dying away. He felt the yoke ease up and brought them smoothly out of the spin, taking them up and away into the upper atmosphere.

John let his breath out, feeling sweat break out all over his body. He looked back at the others. Teyla was gripping the arms of her chair, Rodney's hands had left permanent dents in John's shoulders, Zelenka looked faint and was holding hands with a very pale Miko. Ronon just looked impressed, but he was gripping the hatchway tightly. John said, "Everybody okay?"

"We were upside down," Zelenka said weakly. Miko patted his arm.

"I think we are well." Teyla looked up at Rodney, her brow furrowed in concern. "What was that?"

John twisted around to see that Rodney's face was white with shock. Rodney's throat worked and he said, "It's unstable. That sensor spike, right before the blast—

"It's not a Stargate."

Miko stared at him blankly, then gasped in horror. Zelenka took a sharp breath, shaking his head, saying, "No, no, Rodney, it cannot be."

STARGATE ATLANTIS™

ENTANGLEMENT

MARTHA WELLS

FANDEMONIUM BOOKS

An original publication of Fandemonium Ltd, produced under license from MGM Consumer Products.

Fandemonium Books
PO Box 795A
Surbiton
Surrey KT5 8YB
United Kingdom
Visit our website: www.stargatenovels.com

STARGATE
ATLANTIS™

METRO-GOLDWYN-MAYER Presents
STARGATE ATLANTIS
JOE FLANIGAN   TORRI HIGGINSON   RACHEL LUTTRELL   JASON MOMOA
with PAUL McGILLION as Dr. Carson Beckett and DAVID HEWLETT as Dr. McKay
Executive Producers BRAD WRIGHT & ROBERT C. COOPER
Created by BRAD WRIGHT & ROBERT C. COOPER

ISBN: 1-905586-03-5   ISBN-13: 978-1-905586-03-5
Printed in the United States of America

CHAPTER ONE

John Sheppard lowered the binoculars. Even now that he had had a few days to get used to it, this view was still incredible.

They were on a moon that orbited a gas giant, and the shape of the huge planet was always visible in the sky, banded with the red-brown clouds of perpetual storms. It made a brilliant backdrop for the Ancient ruined city spread across the plateau.

The city went on for miles, a roofless maze of tumbled walls and pillars of indigo stone, with interconnected rooms, halls, dry fountains and pools, open courts. It stood above a barren desert plain, and the strong cool wind carried sheets of dust that washed up against the city's walls in continual waves. It was alien and exotic and beautiful; everything that made stepping through a Stargate worthwhile. John said wearily, "There's got to be something here besides rocks."

"No. No, there really doesn't." Rodney McKay climbed up the last few steps to join him on the terrace, looking over the acres of rubble-filled ruins with a grimace. "Rather like Charlie Brown at Halloween," he added sourly, folding his arms.

John let his breath out, resigned. "Did you figure out what—"

"No."

"Why the readings were—"

"No."

"Or the—"

"No."

John stared at him, depending on his sunglasses to convey the full depth of the extent to which he really wasn't in the mood. Rodney, impervious to hints, demanded, "What?"

John tucked the binoculars back into the pocket of his tac vest deliberately, and did not push Rodney off the platform. It hadn't been a good day, or a good six days. One of the most promising Ancient sites they had found in the entire time the expedition had been in the Pegasus Galaxy was turning out to be a huge dud. Maybe the biggest dud since that intriguing room on the twentieth level of the southeast tower of Atlantis had turned out to be for making fruit ripen really fast and not recharging the Zero Point Modules. The only saving grace was that nothing here had tried to kill them yet.

The Stargate address had come out of the Ancient database in Atlantis, and the view of the ruined city on the MALP's fuzzy camera had made the entire science team dizzy with excitement. John's 'gate team had done a survey by jumper a week ago, and the extent of the ruins and the energy signatures Rodney had been able to pick up had seemed to confirm that this was a spectacular find. John had thought they had hit the jackpot here, that they were going to turn up more Ancient tech than they knew what to do with and maybe even a second ZPM. The first one that the relief mission from Earth had brought had saved their asses, allowing them to raise the city's shields and defend against a hiveship fleet, but it had to be used sparingly.

Since then, the team's enthusiasm level had dropped

drastically. The energy readings that had seemed so encouraging at first just became scattered and erratic the further they got into the ruins. Even bringing in a team of archeologists and more Ancient technology experts from Rodney's lab hadn't helped. The extra personnel had come up with various ways to boost the sensors and made elaborate attempts to triangulate the source of the energy, all with no luck.

Rodney squinted up at the planet filling the sky, the big red swirling cloud of a storm dominating it now. "We're coming up on the eclipse," he pointed out.

John took a last look around at the empty city. "I know." He started down the battered stone steps that wound down through this square tower. Technically it was night right now; this side of the moon had a night phase when its orbit took it between the gas giant and the sun, but due to the reflected light from the planet, it wasn't so much dark as slightly overcast. The only time it actually got dark was when the moon's rotation took it around the far side of the planet, and John needed to finish his check of their security points and patrols before then.

The steps wound down a central column to the ground level, to the walkways between the crumbled structures. A ruined city of this size, with its narrow streets and overhanging structures, should have felt oppressive. But the gas giant provided a constant ever-changing show, and the translucent quality of the blue stone brought light down to even these lowest levels.

They hadn't found any signs of recent human habitation here, which at least meant that the Wraith were unlikely to visit this moon any time soon. That was important right now, and not just in the usual sense of not being eaten; the Wraith currently believed that Atlantis had destroyed itself in a nuclear blast and the expedition had to keep it that way.

In the open court at the bottom of the steps, they met Teyla, who was walking her patrol circuit. "Any trouble?" John asked dutifully.

Teyla tended to take most situations with trademark Athosian equanimity, but from the tired edge to her expression, John could tell she was bored out of her skull, too. She said wearily, "At lunch there was a small altercation over rations among Dr. Chandar's technical assistants."

Rodney snorted. "Spoiled bastards. I did without coffee for six months last year."

John gave him a look. "We know. We were there." He asked Teyla, "What rations?"

"The packages of snack cakes. Apparently there are only a small number left, and Petersen was accused of taking two. They would not stop arguing, so I took the disputed package and ate it myself. I confiscated the remainder from the supplies and concealed them under the emergency medical kit in Jumper One. Dr. Beckett assisted me so I gave him several." She frowned a little. "I fear now that extreme annoyance led me to overreact."

John regarded her solemnly. "Did you punch anybody?" He thought in her position he would possibly have punched somebody.

Teyla shook her head regretfully. "I did not."

"Then you're fine." And Jumper One was full of the confiscated goods, so he figured there wasn't a downside.

Teyla accepted that with a nod. She looked at

Rodney, hesitated, and added, "I don't suppose you have found—"

"No, we haven't found a damn thing!" Rodney snarled, teeth gritted. He turned abruptly, heading up the street.

John lifted a brow, watching him stalk away. "I think he's starting to take this personally."

Teyla's mouth quirked. "And we are surprised by that?"

"Not really," John admitted.

Teyla continued her patrol. John didn't have anything better to do for the next few minutes since he had his security check routine timed to the last second by now, so he followed Rodney.

The big building at the end of the street was mostly intact, with a few soaring spires still stretching toward the sky. The entranceway with triple archways and heavy doors still in place had been a tempting distraction, until they discovered that there was nothing inside except dust. Pulling his sunglasses off, John caught up with Rodney at the little archway to one side and the steps that led down.

The stairs were wide and spiraled down around a central column, and were lit by an array of battery lamps. They led to a mostly open room, with empty corridors leading off from each wall. Like everything else here, it was made of the smooth blue stone, glossy and reflective where it wasn't marred by cracks or gouges where Ancient equipment had been removed when the city was abandoned. In the center was pretty much the only thing they had found so far: a circular bank of consoles set into stone pedestals. There were side panels that opened to reveal a confusing mass of crystal and clear conduit, the

usual materials that the Ancients used. Right now it was
hooked up to half a dozen laptops, and a large collection
of portable and not-so-portable monitoring equipment.

On the third day of the mission, when they had tracked
the intermittent power signatures to this room, Rodney
and the other members of the Ancient Technology team
had gone nuts, certain it was a major find. But the three
members of the archeology team hadn't been enthusias-
tic. "It is either very, very dangerous or very, very useless," Dr. Baroukel had said, studying it grimly.

So far it was the second option all the way.

Now Radek Zelenka glanced up from an array of
laptops spread out on a folding table, wiping sweat off
his brow wearily. "Hello, Colonel, Rodney." He waved
around at their equipment. "Still nothing."

Dr. Chandar, tinkering with the connections of one of
the laptops, added, "There haven't been any new fluctuations in the signature, so we haven't been able to test the
new triangulation method." He was one of the new scientists who had come out on the *Daedalus*, and this was his
first offworld mission. Unlike the science team veterans
who had come to Atlantis with the original expedition,
the new people had never been through an attack by a
hiveship fleet, never seen their friends turned into empty
husks by Wraith, never lived for months with the fact
that they were out here on their own and might never see
Earth again. Even now that the Wraith thought Atlantis
had self-destructed, and the *Daedalus* ran regular support
and supply missions between galaxies every few months,
this still wasn't a safe mission, and John preferred to go
offworld with expedition veterans, people who knew
that in their bones. Just because nothing had tried to kill

them yet in this apparently empty city on this uninhabited moon, didn't mean it wouldn't happen.

"Yes, I actually didn't need the word 'nothing' translated." Rodney sourly eyed Chandar, the equipment, the chamber, and the scientists and techs studying the monitors. "I wasn't really expecting anything to have changed in the past half hour."

Miko Kusanagi, young, Asian, with most of her face dominated by coke-bottle glasses, looked up from her laptop, waving shyly at Rodney. "Dr. McKay, I have the new analysis of the readings—"

"Right, fine, yes." Rodney stamped over to peer at her screen. "Not that I suppose it's any different from the old analysis." This was Dr. Kusanagi's first time offworld, though John wasn't too worried about her survival skills. She had been with the expedition from the beginning, and had survived a year in Rodney's lab, so she had to be much tougher than she looked.

John wandered over to the Ancient consoles, looking at the crystals set in the smooth metal surfaces. The archeology team had pointed out the places where other devices had been attached, the spots on the floor where they thought other equipment, long since removed, had once stood. "So we still don't have a clue, huh?"

It was a rhetorical question, but Chandar said earnestly, "I still think it's a monitoring device of some sort." He threw Rodney a wary look. "McKay, I know you and Zelenka do not agree—"

Zelenka leaned back in his chair, and shrugged amiably. "We would agree perfectly, if we could find some hint of what it could be monitoring."

Rodney waved a hand in weary resignation. "Yes, if

Archeology would get off their collective asses and find something—anything."

John knew Archeology had to be bitching just as hard about Ancient Tech, but at least they had the courtesy to keep it among themselves. In the interest of fairness and not just to relieve boredom by messing with Rodney, he pointed out, "Archeology wants you to get off your ass and find the location of the power source, so they know where to dig."

"Yes, thank you, Colonel Obvious, I'm aware of that," Rodney said with acid emphasis, gesturing so sharply he nearly hit Miko in the head. With the ease of long practice, Miko leaned out of the danger zone. "If you have any other earth-shaking revelations—"

Zelenka interrupted, "But Dr. Corrigan has told me that he now believes most of this installation was dismantled at the same time as the city was abandoned. You would think that the Ancients would also have removed the power source, whatever it was, but—"

"But something keeps doing that!" Rodney shouted, stabbing an angry finger at the console.

There wasn't a big light show or anything else impressive, just a faint glow from the crystals and a low bass hum that John could feel in his back teeth. But every laptop in the room went crazy, beeping, flashing, displaying rapidly-scrolling screens of data. Rodney snapped, "Move." Miko scrambled out of the way, and Rodney sat down at her monitor as the others bolted frantically around the room.

Used to this by now, John smothered a yawn and checked his watch. During the eclipse they shut down operations everywhere but here, since the Mystery Power

Source Room needed constant attention in case it did something explicable. "Rodney, you coming or staying?"

Rodney waved a hand vaguely, and John correctly interpreted that as a dismissal.

John finished his pre-eclipse security check, and in the wider passage that led to the Stargate platform, he ran into Carson Beckett and a couple of the Marines assigned to help him. All three men were covered with dust and blue smudges, and they smelled a little like rotting lettuce. The two Marines looked sour and Beckett looked blissfully happy. "How's it going?" John asked him. "Find some good fungi?"

"Aye, we've been very successful," Beckett said, contentedly patting the specimen case slung over his shoulder. "There's a lovely new species under that big slab Archeology is digging out."

Beckett was the only one happy with this moon. The Ancient database had hinted that there were some species of fungi here that had been used to make some of the medicines mentioned in the Ancient medical records, and apparently it had been right. Beckett checked his watch, adding, "They've found what might be a sewer entrance a couple of streets over. I'm going to take a look down there first thing after the eclipse."

"Great." The two Marines looked a little desperate, and John made a mental note to switch them out and let somebody else have a turn.

They parted ways and John headed up the passage, climbing the smooth steps to the Stargate platform.

The 'gate stood on a flat-topped pyramid in the exact

center of the ruins. It had the best vantage point in the city, with a good view of the only open ground with enough space to land the puddlejumpers, a large roofless enclosure nearly the size of a football field that might once have been an arena or theater.

The naquadah ring of the Stargate gleamed faintly in the reflected light from the gas giant. Off to one side, out of the path of an initiating wormhole, was the MALP they had first used to test the address. Sitting on the platform and leaning back against the MALP was Ronon Dex.

"How's it going?" John said, and sat down on the sun-warmed stone.

Ronon shrugged slightly, apparently having learned by now that that was a question that didn't necessarily need an answer.

It was helpful that Ronon had volunteered for the most boring guard duty post, but after seven years of being hunted for sport by the Wraith, John got the idea that he found it restful. It wasn't a bad post; it was quiet, the gas giant and its satellites put on a continual show in the sky, people stopped by occasionally, and there were regular breaks for meals and sleep.

And an Ancient ruin, abandoned for ten thousand years, was a far cry from a human city destroyed by a Wraith culling, with burned ruins and bomb craters where science centers or weapons emplacements had once stood, desiccated corpses in the streets and recently orphaned children scrounging for food.

John leaned back, propping himself up on his elbows, tilting his head back to catch the last of the failing sun. "You want to be relieved?"

Ronon shook his head. It was too dark during the

eclipse to make this post practical; they would depend on the life signs detectors and the instruments in the three jumpers for a warning of anything approaching. Instead of taking a break during the dark period, Ronon usually patrolled with the Marines on shift, making a circuit around the camp.

They sat there in silence for a time, then Ronon stirred a little and asked, "They find out why the Ancestors put this here yet?"

"Nope."

Ronon nodded, unsurprised. "Think they will?"

John started to give him the same answer, but he had a weird feeling, so he just said, "You never can tell."

John was used to scientists having conversations while he was trying to sleep. On missions that required long hours in the jumpers or camping on alien planets, it was impossible to avoid. Unfamiliar noises would wake him instantly and have him reaching for his pistol, but familiar voices didn't disturb him, and if they did, the conversations were usually easy to tune out. In this camp site, where the scientists were sleeping in the jumpers and John, Teyla, and the off-duty Marines had put their sleeping bags near the open ramps, it was unavoidable. This particular conversation seemed to be about energy signatures, and distances, and triangulation, but it also seemed to be taking place at very close range. Unusually close range. John opened his eyes to see Rodney and Zelenka in the faint light from the dimmed battery lamp. They were crouched over him on opposite sides of his sleeping bag.

Zelenka was saying intently, "—if the source is intermittent, and the calculations are correct—"

"Of course the calculations are correct!" Rodney broke in. "This could explain—"

"What the hell?" John asked evenly.

Rodney waved impatiently for him to shut up. "—all our anomalous readings—"

"—everything that has puzzled us, the consistency of the signal yet the inability to determine direction—" Zelenka waved his hands excitedly.

"Exactly!" Rodney finished. He looked down at John. "Now what did you want?"

"I want you to get off me," John said, and thought he sounded very reasonable under the circumstances.

"The jumper," Zelenka reminded Rodney. "We need you to take us up in the jumper," he explained to John. "Quickly, before we lose signal."

"Right, right, the jumper," Rodney agreed. He prodded John in the side impatiently. "What are you waiting for?"

"I'll give you a thirty-second head start," John promised him. "And I won't use the P-90."

"What the hell is wrong with you?" Rodney demanded, outraged. "We've been looking for this energy source for days, and you want to—"

"Wait, what?" John pushed himself upright, fully awake now. "You found it?"

"The crystals beneath the central complex, the ones we thought were drained," Zelenka tried to explain, "they are a relay, the source is intermittent—"

"It's on the other moon," Rodney hissed, prodding John again. "Now will you get up and get the damn jumper ready?"

"Why didn't you say so?" John asked him, reaching for his tac vest and gun belt.

"I will come along as well," Teyla's voice said from the next sleeping bag over. "I am quite awake now."

"Immediately" wasn't possible, no matter how loud and imperative Rodney got. The jumpers only required a brief pre-flight, but there was a rule on all offworld missions that anything essential, or that could be identifiable as Atlantean if found by the Wraith, had to be stored onboard when not in use, so it wouldn't have to be abandoned in an emergency lift-off. Since that described pretty much everything they had here, that meant there were several cases of equipment and tools that had to be shifted out of Jumper One to Jumpers Two and Three, in case it was needed while they were gone. The five cranky scientists sleeping in Jumper One also had to be shifted to Jumpers Two and Three to join the equally cranky scientists sleeping there. It all took under twenty minutes, despite Rodney's insistence that this was an emergency and they should just take off with the equipment and extra passengers aboard.

Rodney had wanted Zelenka, Chandar, and Kusanagi to accompany them, but Chandar had volunteered to stay here and monitor the device on this end, rather than leave it to the techs. John felt compelled to point out, "Kusanagi and Zelenka don't have much offworld time. And it was hard enough to get him to come here." This was only Zelenka's second offworld mission, and he wasn't exactly a natural at it. The first one had been a brief foray to a culled planet, to try to get Rodney and Lieutenant Cadman out of the storage buffer of a downed Wraith dart. It hadn't exactly gone well.

Rodney waved the objection away. "Yes, I know.

But he needs to get over it, and if Kusanagi's going to advance, she needs field experience." He hesitated uneasily, rubbing his hands together. "Are you thinking about Irina?"

And about every other scientist John had taken through a Stargate and not brought back. "You're not?"

"We all know what the risks are." Rodney looked away, grimacing. Just then, Ronon came walking down the ramp with a crate, and Rodney jerked his head toward him. "And speaking of which, why are we bringing him?"

"Because he needs more mission experience if he's going to be on the team." John knew Rodney was still holding the whole "hanging upside down from a tree" thing against Ronon. It was hardly surprising, since John had stolen a handful of Rodney's popcorn ration once last year, and Rodney was still holding that against him.

Rodney said pointedly, "Nobody thinks that's a good idea but you."

"I think it is a good idea," Teyla said, calmly sorting through her pack.

"We're not voting," Rodney told her. "We—"

"That's right, we're not," John cut him off. What they were really arguing about wasn't bringing in Ronon, but replacing Ford, and he didn't want to hear about it. It had been hard enough to make the decision; he wasn't going to reconsider it now.

John had put off adding a fourth member to their team, put off even thinking about it, about anything but getting Ford back. Until they had found him on P3M-736, out of his head from the enzyme, and John had watched him jump into a Wraith culling beam.

There hadn't been a lot of options to replace him at first; John had wanted to make certain that all the teams had at least one, preferably two, Atlantean veterans to go along with the new personnel, and now they were all assigned and working together comfortably. And he just hadn't wanted to put a shiny new Marine in Ford's place. Ford had been young, but he hadn't been inexperienced, and it still hadn't saved him. Ronon had survived seven years running from the Wraith with no support network whatsoever; he was ideal for a 'gate team, if they could just teach him how to work and play well with others again. "We're bringing Ronon," John said, and Rodney flung his arms in the air and stalked off.

John also took the time to arrange a check-in schedule with Major Lorne. "Think you can handle the excitement?" John asked.

"Yes, sir," Lorne said, his expression wry in the light from the battery lamps. Lorne was Air Force and John's newly assigned 2IC, and John had been a little surprised that he was fitting in so well on Atlantis. But then Lorne had been in the SGC for a few years, and was probably used to the crazier aspects of offplanet life. He also had the Ancient gene, so he could fly the puddlejumpers if necessary. Lorne added, "If the scientists start fighting again, I'll just use the Wraith stunners."

"Fire a warning shot first," John told him. After that, they were ready to leave.

"Finally!" Rodney snarled as the jumper lifted off. He was in the left hand jump seat, connecting his laptop into the jumper's systems. "If we lose this trace—"

"Did you lose it?" John asked, guiding the jumper rapidly up through the dark sky, the sensor image of the gas giant outlined by the holographic Heads Up Display.

"No, but—"

"Then shut up."

"Everyone moved as quickly as possible," Teyla pointed out from the co-pilot's chair, her tone placating. She had called the shotgun seat before Rodney, which John suspected was also pissing him off.

"How long will it take to get there?" Zelenka asked warily from the other jump seat. Miko was sitting in the back with Ronon. She seemed more excited than nervous, while Zelenka seemed mostly nervous.

The HUD popped up a projected ETA in response to John's thought. John mentally converted the figures from Ancient. "About forty-five minutes, give or take."

Rodney nodded, his mouth set in a grim line. "I just hope the signatures are still traceable by then."

John rolled his eyes. "Why don't you get the cakes out from under the medical kit?"

Zelenka looked up, startled. "Is that where they are? I thought they had run out."

"Chandar's techs were eating them," Rodney explained darkly, standing up to head into the back.

"Bastards," Zelenka muttered.

The other moon looked red from orbit. When John took the jumper down toward the surface, following the energy signature, they skimmed over a wide open plain with pink and brown soil studded with patches of tall grass and scrubby bushes. The light had an odd quality; bright but tinted by the gas giant filling the sky, unchangeable and undimmed by the few wispy clouds.

"The jumper's detecting a low oxygen content in the

atmosphere," Rodney said, sounding preoccupied. "The levels vary between twelve and fifteen percent. Being out on the surface unprotected would be like trying to jog around the top of Mount Everest." He looked up, his mouth twisted. "That's odd."

"Why is that odd?" Ronon asked, standing to look through the cabin doorway.

Miko, sitting on the floor between the two jump seats with her laptop, pushed back her glasses to look up at him. "We've never found an Ancient occupation site on a planet or moon that couldn't support human life."

"I think perhaps what atmosphere is there is artificial," Zelenka said, studying his own laptop.

Teyla twisted around in her seat, startled. "That is possible?"

"Very much so, with Ancients' level of technology," Zelenka assured her. "If it was done here, there was perhaps not enough plant life and bodies of water to sustain the atmosphere, without whatever mechanism that supplied or created it. Since this moon was abandoned, the atmosphere would have gradually leaked away, until it reached a stable level that the surface could support."

"It's a distinct possibility," Rodney added, studying his own data. "The jumper's orbital scan picked up few open bodies of water, minimal plant life, small amounts of ice at the poles, but no sizable life signs, which means no humans, no aliens, no large fauna—"

"No Wraith," John put in, though he wasn't sorry to hear about the lack of large fauna, either. Since the planet with the thing that looked a lot like a Tyrannosaurus Rex, he was sensitive on that point.

"No Wraith, always a plus," Rodney agreed. He

looked up, wide-eyed. "Oh, oh, oh, here we go."

The jumper's HUD was picking up a group of man-made structures, standing out against the flat terrain. Despite the lack of life signs, John kept the jumper cloaked.

As they drew nearer, John slowed the jumper, bringing it down for a closer look. There were several large low buildings, with flattened domes, surrounded by stretches of pavement that were mostly covered by sand. One dome was partially open, showing that at some point it had been able to retract, allowing access to the building for air or space craft. "I think we found the spaceport," John said, and had to think, *I love it when I get to say things like that*.

Rodney was on his feet, gripping the back of John's seat and pointing over his shoulder. "Get closer!"

John lifted a brow. "You think that's a good idea? If that thing snaps shut—"

Rodney snorted. "Oh, right. This from the man whose last words were almost 'hey, I want to get a better look at the big thing with the tentacles down there.'" He waved a hand. "This dome must operate like the outer doors in Atlantis' jumper bay, and it's probably been stuck open for ten thousand years."

"Okay, fine. But I get to say 'I told you so' if the building eats us," John said, though he thought Rodney was probably right.

"I will make note of that," Teyla commented dryly.

"How comforting," Zelenka added, sounding uneasy.

John guided the jumper down toward the half-open dome. This close, it looked reassuringly stable; red lichen or moss had crept up the sides and was growing in cracks in the dark material. Still, he didn't intend to go all the way in. As he hovered over the dark opening, the jumper's outer lights came on, playing over the building's interior, illuminating a metallic floor and another set of bay doors leading to a lower level, also wedged partly open.

"Look," Teyla said softly, pointing. "The far wall."

John adjusted the angle, tilting the jumper downwards for a better view, and the lights swiveled to better illuminate the area. He saw the racks and walkways for a jumper bay, all empty. Now this was a cool find. "This is the spaceport, all right."

His voice tense with excitement, Rodney said, "We need to check those other domes. If they left even one jumper behind, or if there's a repair facility, or spare parts—"

"It would come in handy," John finished. They had lost a few jumpers over the past year. With the *Daedalus* making regular supply runs, it wasn't as desperate a situation as it would have been before resuming contact with Earth, but it wasn't like they could manufacture them yet. He thought this was a damn good day's work.

"But there is no city here, no Stargate as far as we know. Why would they put the jumper bays in the middle of nowhere?" Teyla wondered, her brow furrowed slightly.

"The city could be underground." Rodney stepped back to study his equipment again. "And actually that makes more sense. If this power source is shielded—"

"Rodney, I don't think it is here," Zelenka said, shaking his head at his laptop's screen. "These readings are

almost identical to those on the other moon." He looked
down to check Miko's screen, then turned his chair,
watching Rodney intently. "I think this is also a relay."

Snarling under his breath, Rodney lunged over Miko
to look at Zelenka's screen. Zelenka leaned sideways to
avoid being shoved out of his seat and Miko smashed herself back into the doorway. John looked earnestly at Teyla
and said, "It's like a scavenger hunt."

She lifted a brow and her lips quirked. "I hope that is
not what it sounds like."

Rodney turned back, stabbing a finger at the port.
"He's right. Keep going, that way!"

"What, you don't want to stop and explore the spaceport?" John protested. From the readings, they wouldn't
even need to use the awkward environmental suits, just
the SCBAs that were part of the jumper's standard equipment.

"You have a spaceport at home. Right now we need
to find the energy source." Rodney leaned between the
seats, nearly elbowing Teyla in the head as he pointed
at the HUD. The jumper's longrange sensors were bus-
ily assembling a rough map display. "Now go that way,
toward the mountains."

"We can always come back," Teyla pointed out practically, fending Rodney off. "The spaceport does not
appear to be in any danger of vanishing."

John began, "Yeah, but—" Rodney was turning red
and Zelenka was waving erratically toward the readings on his screen, and Miko was gazing up at him in
mute appeal. Ronon stirred restlessly but didn't weigh in
on either side. "Okay, fine." Disgruntled, John lifted the
jumper out of the dome and guided them away toward the

distant mountain range. "But next time we stop and look at the thing I want to stop and look at."

After about fifteen minutes of flight, the mountains were beginning to loom larger in the port.

"Dr. McKay, Dr. Zelenka!" Miko said suddenly. "These readings—"

"Rodney, Miko, do you see this?" Zelenka demanded. Rodney snapped, "Yes, yes, shut up, I'm trying to—"

"It's spiking!" Zelenka yelped.

"Kids." John kept his voice calm. "Share with the rest of the class. I'd kind of like to know what I'm flying directly into."

"It's a power signature." Rodney, who was obviously in the midst of a science-gasm, laughed a little erratically. "It has to be something enormous. It's showing fluctuations, as though it's in use—"

"How enormous?" John could see something on the horizon, a shape too regular to be part of the low mountains. He squinted, trying to make it out. Then the jumper's sensors picked it up, creating a three-dimensional shape in the HUD. Teyla leaned forward, staring intently at the image. According to the sensors, it was a round structure, open in the middle, with a flat roof. It looked like nothing so much as a big stadium, at least a 100,000 seater. John said, "This enormous?"

Everybody was staring at the HUD now. The jumper wasn't finding any life signs, just the power signatures that were making the scientists frisky.

"Get closer," Rodney whispered.

John gained a little altitude and dropped a lot of speed, approaching cautiously. They could clearly see the dark stone walls now, indigo like the city on the other moon,

streaked with the red dust. The building wasn't fea-
tureless, there were lines and squares embossed in it in
abstract patterns that were probably just decoration, but
there were no windows on this outside wall. Moving
slower still, John took the jumper up over the roof.

The open well in the center of the building was big
enough to accommodate at least two football fields.
Inside it was a giant silver ring, framing...something. *An
energy field,* John thought, baffled. It was black and oddly
mottled as energy fluctuated across it. "What the hell?" he
said aloud. There was pavement around the outer ring and
a few other structures standing out from the main building. He knew what it looked like, but it couldn't be.

Startled, Teyla said, "Is that some sort of—"

"A giant Stargate," Rodney finished, sounding caught
somewhere between awe and pure avarice. "It could be.
That energy field—"

"If it's a 'gate, it's active." John looked from the energy
readings the HUD was displaying to the dark fluid surface. *How the hell can it be active?*

"A ship nearly the size of the *Daedalus* could pass
through it," Teyla said, fascinated. "Surely that must be
its purpose, to transport large ships."

Zelenka waved a hand wildly. "Yes, yes, it has to be for
large transports, probably without hyperdrives, to send
them to—"

"Yeah, right, but why is it active?" John thought that
was the important point right now. "Who the hell dialed
it?" There were still no life signs, so whoever had activated it had to be on the other end of the wormhole.

Rodney shook his head. "It's been active intermittently
for the past week, or we wouldn't have detected—When

we found the crystal relay chamber, that might have triggered some sort of automatic—But the intermittent activity suggests—" He stared out the port, his expression turning fraught. "We're cloaked, right?"

"Yes," John said, drawing out the word and giving Rodney a look.

Rodney nodded to himself, his face uneasy. "Then we should be fine. Try to get down a little closer."

Keeping one eye on the HUD, and wondering at Rodney's definition of "fine," John brought the jumper in low over the roof, following the curve around. There was no way in hell he was going to take them over the giant wormhole, if that was what it was.

The ring itself was thick, maybe as wide as a boxcar, but it was bare of any symbols. "I do not see chevrons, or 'gate symbols along the rim. How does it dial?" Teyla wondered, echoing John's thought. "It must be completely different from—"

The field rippled as if a wave had crossed it, silver edging the black. Interference suddenly fuzzed out the HUD, leaving only an Ancient blinking error message. Rodney's fingers dug into John's shoulder, almost to the bone, and he gasped, "Go, go, go, now, get away from it—"

The jumper was already swerving up and away, responding to Rodney's urgency and John's startled thought, even before John could give it a new heading with the physical controls. Then John heard a rumble reverberate through the jumper's metal and the readouts went crazy. Suddenly an explosive concussion hit them like a giant hand; the jumper shivered and John fought the controls.

The jumper spun sideways then end over end. The inertial dampeners didn't go out, but the view flipped crazily in the port, the ground changing place with the sky. John heard the collective gasp, but the rumble was already dying away. He felt the yoke ease up and brought them smoothly out of the spin, taking them up and away into the upper atmosphere.

John let his breath out, feeling sweat break out all over his body. He looked back at the others. Teyla was gripping the arms of her chair, Rodney's hands had left permanent dents in John's shoulders, Zelenka looked faint and was holding hands with a very pale Miko. Ronon just looked impressed, but he was gripping the hatchway tightly. John said, "Everybody okay?"

"We were upside down," Zelenka said weakly. Miko patted his arm.

"I think we are well." Teyla looked up at Rodney, her brow furrowed in concern. "What was that?"

John twisted around to see that Rodney's face was white with shock. Rodney's throat worked and he said, "It's unstable. That sensor spike, right before the blast—It's not a Stargate."

Miko stared at him blankly, then gasped in horror. Zelenka took a sharp breath, shaking his head, saying, "No, no, Rodney, it cannot be."

Teyla threw a bewildered look at John, and he shook his head. He didn't have a clue. His first impulse had been to make a "that's no moon, that's a space station" joke, but he didn't think anybody would appreciate it at the moment.

Rodney stepped back over to his seat, bringing up a screen on the laptop there. "Look at the readings," he grated out. "They're distorted because of the intermittent power source, the instability, the energy bursts—That's why we couldn't find the damn power source, it doesn't need one! It's drawing it off subspace; it is the power source! That's why it's up here and the city and the 'gate are on the other moon, why the jumper port is kilometers away!"

"Okay," John said warily. "What is it?"

Rodney said, "It's a Quantum Mirror."

CHAPTER TWO

They needed a place to land so they could run a systems check and they needed to make a transmission to base camp, so John took the jumper back to the spaceport dome. It was far enough away to shield them from any discharges the Mirror might make, and he felt a pressing need to find a bolt-hole at the moment, even if it was just a powerless Ancient port with a broken roof.

Teyla and Ronon hadn't had the benefit of reading the SGC reports about the more portable-sized Quantum Mirror discovered in the Milky Way, so Rodney launched into an explanation. The Mirror could access a huge number of other realities, all alternate versions of this one. They could run into Atlantises that had been destroyed by the Wraith, or that had collapsed from explosive decompression on the bottom of the ocean, and those were just the good options. There was also the strong possibility they would run into realities where the Wraith had taken the city and forced the expedition to reveal the location of Earth, or where Atlantis and then Pegasus had been colonized by the slave population of a Goa'uld-controlled Milky Way. Rodney went on and on, coming up with one horrific scenario after another, until Miko looked sick, Zelenka pale, Teyla was wide-eyed with dismay, and Ronon just looked like he thought they were all insane. As the domes of the deserted spaceport appeared in the jumper's port, John finally shouted, "Rodney, stop, we get it! Going through the Mirror is asking to be screwed!

We'll all be evil and you'll have a beard! Now calm down!"

"I just want to make certain everyone completely understands the unimaginable danger!" Rodney shouted back, red-faced and upset.

Teyla leaned across the cockpit to squeeze his arm soothingly. "It is all right, we understand."

"Yes, Dr. McKay, we do," Miko told him gently. "Do you need an aspirin?"

"Dammit, no, I don't need an—All right, give me the damn things," Rodney grumbled, grudgingly accepting the tablets and a water bottle.

"You are preaching to choir, Rodney," Zelenka added. "No one can imagine the unimaginable danger like we can."

Leaning in the cabin hatchway, Ronon said, "I don't understand."

John gritted his teeth. He really wasn't in the mood right now for Ronon's caveman act. "Ronon."

"I understand what it is," Ronon clarified. "I don't understand why we're still here with it."

Rodney sighed and pressed the water bottle to his forehead. "Because we have to find out if there's the slightest chance that it could lead us to living Ancients. If it can't, we have to try to shut it down before the Wraith find it."

Zelenka buried his face in his hands. "Oh, God."

You can say that again, John thought grimly. As they reached the spaceport, he slowed the jumper, directing it into a hover above the broken dome. The HUD popped up, telling him the immediate area was still negative for life signs and energy signatures, and that the terrain sensors detected no instability in the floor below or the structure itself. He eased the jumper down, past the curved surface of the dome.

The jumper's outer lights came on, revealing blue-green metal walls and multiple levels of empty landing racks. Below, the stone floor was covered with wind-blown sand, and a half-open hatch led deeper into the structure. The others were quiet, watching as the spot-lights illuminated the giant space, so much larger than Atlantis' jumper bay.

John let the ship settle to a gentle landing and switched all the systems over to standby. He leaned back and stretched, but his spine refused to unknot; he suspected that wasn't going to change for the next few days. He eyed Rodney, who sat slumped glumly in the jump seat, his expression set and grim. Worried about him, John asked, "You okay?"

"Oh, sure, yes, I'm fine." Rodney rubbed a hand over his face. "We need to call Elizabeth."

John raised Lorne on the jumper's comm system quickly enough, though there was a few seconds of trans-mission lag. John briefly outlined the situation. Lorne, who had been in the SGC, obviously didn't need Rodney to tell him about Quantum Mirrors. He said, "Colonel, that's... Damn."

"Yeah, that's what we said," John agreed. "Dial Atlantis and patch me through to the gateroom."

That took a few minutes. By the time the connection was made, Miko had connected a laptop to the outputs in the rear cabin, running through a full system diagnos-tic, while Zelenka was opening panels to do the manual checks. The others were sitting on the bench in the back,

passing around the selection of packaged snack food from
the jumper's supplies. Tied to the comm system, John
waved at them, trying to get them to bring him something.
He was saying, "Dammit, there is a vanilla one left, I can
see it in the box," when Elizabeth's voice came over the
comm: "This is Weir. What's going on up there, John?"

"Well, the good news is, we're not dead," he told her,
swinging the chair back around again.

"Always nice to hear," Elizabeth responded, a wry
note in her voice. "The bad news?"

Rodney came forward hastily, dropped a package of
cupcakes into John's lap, and sat down in the shotgun
seat. He said, "We found the source of the power signatures. It's a gigantic Quantum Mirror."

There was silence on the other end that had nothing to
do with the brief transmission lag. "How gigantic?" she
said finally.

John ate the cupcakes, while Rodney outlined their
little adventure so far. Zelenka came forward to listen,
leaning on the back of Rodney's chair.

Rodney said finally, "It comes down to this. The
Ancients could have built this thing as an alternate
method of evacuating Pegasus at the end of the Wraith
war. If they were able to find another reality where
Pegasus was uninhabited, where it had never been colonized by the Ancients, where the Wraith never existed,
it would have been a viable option. The Mirror's circumference isn't nearly large enough to accommodate
a city-sized craft like Atlantis, but you could move an
enormous amount of people and supplies through with
smaller cargo ships. It would be much more efficient
than dialing the Atlantis 'gate back to Earth multiple

times. But we have no idea if they were successful, whatever they were trying to do with it."

Sounding thoughtful, Elizabeth said, "We've certainly never seen any indication in the Atlantean database that the Ancients had an evacuation route other than Earth. And do we know if this thing has been active all this time, or if these power fluctuations you're seeing are recent?"

"Well, yes, that's the problem." Rodney waved a hand in agitation. "One of the problems. We have no way to tell without exploring the installation to look for monitoring equipment. But I find it hard to believe this thing has been sitting here for ten thousand years releasing massive bursts of energy and activating the monitor on the base moon, without the Wraith ever noticing. I think it was dormant most of that time, that this activation is recent." He drew a sharp breath. "I think we've been lucky."

John had to agree. Except for the lucky part.

Elizabeth asked, "How do we know the Wraith haven't already found it?"

"I think it's safe to say that if they had, they'd be here right now, exploring through it for new feeding grounds." Rodney flattened his hands on the jumper's console, frustrated. "The Quantum Mirror at Area 51 was unimaginably dangerous. Two seconds after Dr. Jackson discovered the thing it dragged him into another dimension where the Goa'uld were in the process of invading Earth. This Mirror has the bonus feature of being big enough to allow an invasion fleet to fly through it, as well as being unstable. But if it was used for evacuation and it's still set for the same destination, there may be living Ancients on the other side we could apply to for information or help."

"I don't think that is strong possibility." Zelenka took off his glasses and rubbed his eyes. "If a group did use it to escape, their first act once they were safely through would be to shut down the Mirror on their side, changing the setting, so no Wraith could follow them. It would not prevent another Mirror in yet another reality from finding them—the Mirror in Area 51 was kept shut down, but that certainly didn't prevent other Mirrors from accessing it."

"Yes, yes," Rodney agreed impatiently. "That's why Hammond ordered it destroyed. But there is a small chance that this Mirror is still set to the reality the Ancients fled to. If it isn't, I agree that our chances of stumbling on it among the countless numbers of other realities is infinitesimal. And attempting to look would be unimaginably dangerous." Rodney's mouth twisted sourly. "Judging by the SGC's experiences, any reality we access is likely to be far worse off than we are. Far worse off."

"You keep saying 'unimaginable,'" Zelenka grumbled. "I told you, we can all imagine it perfectly."

"Hold it." John eyed Rodney. It had always been obvious that the Stargate networks, here and in the Milky Way, would have been built by interstellar spaceships. John felt like he was missing something as far as building the Mirrors was concerned. "So they had to go through first and build a Mirror just like this one in the other reality? How does that work? How do you get there in the first place?"

"No one knows," Rodney told him impatiently. "Quantum Mirrors exist in all realities simultaneously. Building one is a logical impossibility, but yet they exist."

John looked at Zelenka, who nodded and shrugged. John said, "Okay," and decided to go back to imagining the unimaginable danger.

"Let me sum this up," Elizabeth said, obviously trying to bring them back to the point. "You want to take a closer look at this installation, see if there's any indication that we could use it to contact the Ancients, and if not, shut the Mirror down."

Rodney leaned forward. "Exactly. We'll need to enter the structure around the Mirror. The jumper's sensors couldn't get accurate readings with all the interference from the Mirror itself; the installation could hold anything from a new Ancient database to a working ZPM." He added reluctantly, "I wouldn't count on the ZPM. Quantum Mirrors don't need external power sources; they are power sources, drawing the energy they need directly from subspace. I'd be surprised if the Ancients didn't have a way to tap into that, to use it to power the auxiliary systems in the building."

"What about the discharges?" Elizabeth asked pointedly. "Didn't the one you just experienced nearly damage the jumper?"

"I was kind of curious about that part myself," John admitted.

"Well, obviously, we'll have to land outside the installation." Rodney huffed in exasperation. "And I don't see that we have a choice. It's either leave the Mirror and chance the Wraith detecting it, or find out we've left open a portal to an invasion fleet from another reality, or—"

"I understand that, Rodney," Elizabeth reminded him. "Dr. Zelenka, what do you think?"

Zelenka folded his arms, looking uncomfortable. Sounding reluctant, he said, "This is too dangerous to ignore, Dr. Weir. If nothing else, we must try to shut it down."

"John?"

John shrugged. He didn't see they had a choice either. "They're right."

The SCBAs, or self-contained breathing apparatus sets, each had an hour tank and a couple of spares, which could be refilled from the jumper's environmental system with a setup Zelenka had jury-rigged last year. Ronon had never used one of the breathing sets before, and John wanted to make certain Zelenka and Miko remembered their training with them, so he had everybody put a set on and they did a brief twenty minute sweep outside.

Also, everybody really wanted a look at the spaceport. They could have spent a couple of days here, and John just hoped they would have a chance to come back. The place had been built to hold hundreds of jumpers and larger craft, the shape only teasingly hinted at by the landing slots high in the walls. They found passageways leading to two other domes, and even if all were empty, it would still be worth it to send a team back to look for tools and equipment in the repair bays.

Standing with the others at the edge of the hatch that opened into the broken dome's lower levels, John shined his P-90's light into the depths. He could see it was mostly filled with the reddish sand, with a few straggly plants growing in it. "That's kind of depressing," he commented, his voice muffled by the breathing mask. It fit over the mouth and nose, and the tank attached to a standard pack.

Teyla nodded, frowning. "So much work went into this place. I hope it was not in vain." She looked up, directing her light over the empty racks. "I hope some of them escaped."

"I don't know." Rodney sounded grim. He turned around, looking up at the cracked roof far overhead. "The fact that this dome was wedged open isn't a good sign. Whoever was here last had to leave in a hurry, and lost power in the process."

"There is no sign of blast scars," Zelenka pointed out, obviously trying to sound optimistic.

"If the dome was stuck open the Wraith could have used the culling beam," John pointed out. Miko made a little choked noise and Zelenka stared upward nervously. *Yeah, probably shouldn't have brought that up,* John thought with a wince.

"Thank you, Colonel," Rodney said, witheringly. "On that note—"

"Right." John nodded. The Mirror wasn't getting any less dangerous. "Let's go."

John brought the jumper in low this time, barely skimming over the ground. The HUD stayed active without him having to think about it, the sensors scanning for stray energy that might mean another discharge, as if the jumper was as nervous as they were. As they neared the building, Rodney leaned down to point over John's shoulder. "There. There's a door."

"Saw it." It was triangular, and set into the base of the structure above a short flight of steps. John put the jumper down about fifty feet from it, stirring up a small cloud of dust.

When John got the board locked down and stepped into the back, everyone was gathering their packs and fumbling with the breathing sets. He clipped his P-90 to his vest and asked, "Now what's rule one?"

"Ah, I know this one," Zelenka said, looking up with his brow furrowed earnestly. "That would be to not scream, unless something is eating us, and we need your attention immediately."

John slung the pack with the air tank across his back. "Okay, that's a rule, but it's not rule one."

"Oh, ah...everybody stay together?" Zelenka tried again.

"The rule is 'don't be stupid!'" Rodney said with an irritable grimace, checking his tablet one last time. "That's the only one that matters."

Teyla interposed, "The rule is to stay with us at all times, do not rush ahead no matter what the temptation, and always let us examine an area first before you enter."

"I don't think you have to worry about that with us." Zelenka consulted Miko with a look. She nodded earnestly.

"Yeah, that's one of the reasons I agreed to bring you guys," John told him.

When everybody had their breathing sets on and their packs ready, John opened the ramp. The air released from the cabin caused another dust cloud, billowing out and away from the jumper. John went down the ramp first, Teyla with him. The ground felt weird under his boots, the fine powdery dirt shifting over the more solid rock, and he paused to take a long look at their surroundings. There was nothing they hadn't spotted from the air; the dusty

pink plain, patchy with dry grasses and a few scrubby
bushes, stretched away for empty miles, toward the foothills and then the mountains that rose in the north. The gas
giant hung low in the sky, the red-brown bands a familiar
sight now. John signaled the others to come out.

Rodney strode down the ramp first, his eyes on the
life signs detector except for one wary glance around.
Zelenka and Kusanagi followed him, with Ronon on their
six. John used the jumper remote to close the ramp and set
the cloak. Each team member had their own remote to get
back in, and if something happened to John, both Rodney
and Kusanagi could fly the jumper, though Rodney had a
lot more experience at it than she did.

They moved toward the door, Ronon facing away from
it to keep watch as John examined it thoughtfully. It was
made of blue-green metal set into a stone frame, with
square patterns embossed into the surface. Studying the
detector, Rodney said, "Huh. I'm getting readings suggesting that the power is on inside." He sounded intrigued
rather than worried. "This isn't a ZPM signature. I was
right, it must be drawing power from the Mirror."

It meant they might not have to manually pry the door
up. "Can you get it open?" John asked him.

Rodney eyed it, then stepped to the side, touching
a small square set deep into the stone wall. The door
started to slide upward, moving a little sluggishly.
Rodney looked at John, chin lifted. "Of course."

Teyla stepped to John's side to cover the growing
opening, but their lights showed the chamber inside
was empty. John moved to the doorway, and soft white
recessed lights came on in the ceiling, revealing a
space that would have been just big enough to slide

the jumper into, if the door had been large enough. The walls were tinted the same blue-green as the outer door, and the floor embossed with strips of dull silver metal. There was another sealed triangular door just opposite, and a steady breeze.

Rodney held out a hand to feel the air flow, frowning. "It's pressurized." He looked at his tablet. "I'm reading close to twenty-two percent oxygen."

"Well, we knew the power was on." John stepped cautiously into the room, signaling the others to stay back. This was the part where he made sure the inner door was going to open and the outer wasn't going to shut and trap them inside. He crossed the room, pausing to hold a hand up in front of a silver disk set into the wall. Close up it still looked solid, but it was emitting a strong flow of air. "This is a vent."

"But the power should have been on standby," Rodney objected from the doorway behind him. "That's how Ancient systems work. And there hasn't been time to pressurize this entire structure."

Zelenka added, "Perhaps the system detected the jumper's landing, and restored atmosphere to this section only."

"But why should it?" Rodney waved a hand, still frowning. "This isn't a landing pad, it's a foot entrance. If there's a jumper bay, it should be accessed through the roof."

"Atlantis was pressurized when we arrived," Miko pointed out hesitantly.

"Well, yes, I know that," Rodney said acidly, "But—"

John tuned out the debate, touching the wall console

next to the inner door. It slid open to reveal a corridor, gently curved to follow the shape of the building. The lights came smoothly up, giving the dark blue stone a soft glow. John stepped in, feeling the strong flow of air as the open door behind him created a breeze, the lower pressure sucking out the air inside. The rounded ceiling was about twelve feet high. "Looks good so far."

The others followed him in, Rodney pausing to shut the outside door. John eyed him. "That a good idea?"

Rodney shook the tablet at him. "I have no idea why, but this building appears to be pressurized. We can save the air in our tanks for emergencies and exploring outside."

"Okay." John drew the word out, making Rodney glare at him, but John had to admit he had a point. An hour wasn't a long time to explore a building this size, and for all they knew it could take them that long just to find a lab or monitoring equipment.

John shut off his breathing set, pulling his mask down as the others followed suit. The air didn't smell dusty or musty or of anything except empty stone hallways. "So where to now?" he asked.

"Good question." Rodney glanced up from his detector with a thoughtful frown. "Let's try this way."

John put Ronon on their six again, and took the lead with Teyla, following the curve of the corridor. After a few minutes walk, John could see a section ahead where the cool white light took on an unhealthy red tint. "Rodney, do you see that?" he asked warily.

Rodney peered down the corridor. "The quality of the light? Yes, it's probably not a good sign."

"A good sign of what?" Zelenka asked a little nervously.

"How the hell should I know?" Rodney said in frustration.

They reached the edge of the red shadows and John stopped, shining the P-90's light over the floor. Nothing seemed different. Ronon, who was tall enough that his head was almost even with the bottom of the nearest light fixture, stepped close to the wall, frowning. He said, "It's a plant. It's grown over the light."

He lifted a hand and John said sharply, "Don't touch it!" He realized a moment later the entire group had shouted the same words practically in unison. He shook his head. It was a good thing they hadn't been trying to sneak up on something.

Ronon stopped, looking back at them with a lifted brow. "It's just a plant."

Rodney rolled his eyes. "Yes, well, when your skin falls off, let us know."

"Alien plants can be very dangerous, and not just if you ingest them," Zelenka added more reasonably. "There were the flowers on PX5-237, that gave Sergeant Bates those nasty bites."

Miko nodded. "Yes, the mold on PX3-581, that tried to chase Sergeant Stackhouse through the Stargate."

Teyla winced. "I remember that well."

Ronon frowned at the fuzzy growth and stepped back carefully.

John moved forward, his light revealing more patches of the stuff. "It's like that algae we keep getting in the city, in the rooms below the waterline." The lowest levels of Atlantis had been flooded in the early stages of the catastrophic storm that had hit the city in their first year there.

Even with all the repairs they had been able to make and the restored power from the new ZPM, those sections were still uncomfortably damp and subject to occasional weird growths.

Teyla nodded. "Very like. And it seems to be all over these walls. Should we take a sample for the botanists?"

"Screw the botanists," Rodney said impatiently. "The gigantic Quantum Mirror that could kill us where we stand is our top priority at the moment."

"Rodney, just calm down, we're getting there," John said pointedly.

After about fifty more yards, Rodney said suddenly, "Stop." His voice was tight with tension. John halted in step with Teyla, scanning the corridor ahead. Rodney continued, "I'm getting a life sign flicker. Something small." He turned the detector, then pointed, his eyes still on the screen. "On that wall."

In another instant their lights found it. It was a dull red lumpy knobby thing, about the size of a dinner plate, flattened against the wall. P-90 raised, John took a cautious step toward it, squinting, trying to get a better look. He could tell it had short stubby tentacles that it was using to cling to the wall; it looked a little like an octopus that had suffered multiple amputations. He said, "That's...ugly."

"Shouldn't you be shooting it?" Rodney wanted to know.

Watching it carefully, Teyla pointed out, "It is not attacking us. I do not even think it knows we are here."

"Yes, but it might attack," Rodney said in exasperation. "Granted, it doesn't seem to have any legs, or arms, but—"

"What if we kill this one and that antagonizes the

whole herd or whatever, and they attack us?" John said, taking another cautious step closer.

Rodney huffed in annoyance. "Oh, fine. I see your point."

The wall here was thickly covered with the algae-like reddish growth, and the octopus had attached itself right in the middle of it. John didn't want to kill the thing if it was harmless, but he needed to find out if it was safe to just ignore it.

He stepped close enough to the wall to get a better view of its head, staying well out of the short tentacle range. It looked like its mouth was a big pad, which it was using to suck the red growth off the wall. As John watched, one big purple eye opened and rolled to study him. Its stubby tentacles tightened protectively on its stretch of wall and it edged away from him a little. "It's sucking up the algae," he reported, stepping back. "I think we'd be a little much for it."

Teyla frowned, playing her light over the walls. "But if this building has been sealed since the Ancients departed, how did it get in?"

"There could be a door open somewhere," Ronon answered, still watching the corridor behind them.

"But this section must be sealed, or it couldn't stay pressurized," Zelenka told him. He looked a little jumpy, and was clutching his tablet protectively to his chest, but other than that he seemed to be doing okay so far. "Even if the air system was somehow activated by the jumper's arrival."

"No, this building was open at some point." Rodney squinted uneasily at the creature. "Maybe the Mirror's energy discharges triggered some sort of reactivation of the installation's systems, and it sealed and pressurized itself."

"Let's just leave the wall-octopus alone," John concluded, and they kept moving.

A little past that section, John almost walked by the tall triangle embossed into the inner wall, thinking it was just decorative. Rodney stopped abruptly. "Wait, wait. Does this look like another door?"

"Not really." John came back to contemplate it. It had a narrow blue-green metal frame, and there was a smaller triangle set in the center panel.

"I wasn't talking to you. Well?" he demanded.

Zelenka was already examining the edge of the embossed area, shining his flashlight into the minute cracks. "These are seams, so this whole piece may lift up, but why no wall console?"

His face intent, Rodney laid a hand flat on the center triangle. There was a faint pop of displaced air as the door started to slide upward. Rodney flinched back, then caught Zelenka by his jacket and pulled him out of the way. John jerked up his weapon to cover the opening, Teyla and Ronon stepping up behind him. But the space inside was empty, a stairwell with a wide set of steps spiraling upward. "This is interesting," Rodney said, preoccupied.

Still covering the corridor, Ronon asked, "Why?"

It was Miko who said, "There is no wall console, so only someone with the Ancient gene could open the door."

"It's probably security feature," Zelenka added, a little uneasily. "They didn't want just anyone to access the Mirror controls, perhaps."

John stepped into the stairwell, looking up. The lights had come on, but he couldn't see anything but stairs. Teyla stepped in to look, pointing out, "It would also keep out the Wraith."

"Good point." John glanced at Rodney. "Up? Or keep going around?"

Rodney had taken the tablet away from Zelenka and now waved it and the life signs detector in frustration. "I have no idea. In this one instance, your guess is as good as mine."

John lifted a brow, exchanged a look with Teyla, then said, "Right. Let's try up."

On the first landing there was a doorway that opened into what seemed to be an empty shaft. It had tiny blue lights set in narrow silver bands running down the sides, and seemed to lead straight down to the floor below. "The elevator's broken?" John suggested, leaning out to look down. Teyla stretched around the other side, shining her light down the shaft.

"Ah, better not to put your heads in there," Zelenka said, studying the tablet. "I'm getting a low-level energy signature."

As John eased away from the opening and Teyla stepped back, Rodney snatched the tablet again. "Wait, wait, wait. This looks like..." Brow furrowed thoughtfully, Rodney pulled a pen out of his tac vest and tossed it through the opening. It hung in midair for a moment, then vanished.

Rodney and Zelenka had their eyes on the tablet's screen, watching it analyze the readings, with Miko craning her neck to see over Zelenka's shoulder. John and Teyla stared at the spot where the dematerialized pen had been. "Hope you didn't need that," Ronon commented dryly.

"Why would this be on the stairwell where anyone might stumble in?" Teyla asked, sounding mildly horrified.

"It's not a walk-in disintegrator, if that's what you're thinking," Rodney said, still thoughtful. "Hold it, let's try this." He took out a small pocket flashlight, clicked it on, and tossed it into the shaft. It vanished. Rodney leaned cautiously out to look down. "The energy signature is almost identical to the transporters on Atlantis, and this is the right location for a safety shaft. See, there it is."

John looked. Down at the bottom, right about the level of the first floor, was the gleam of the flashlight. "Cool. So it's a transporter-safety exit." And the fact that the Ancients had seen a need for it...probably didn't mean anything good.

Going up, they found three more levels, though the topmost wasn't nearly high enough to be at the top of the structure. There were obviously more levels that this stairwell didn't access, that there had to be another way to get to.

Looking at the interior rooms, John could see the walls were unusually thick, much thicker than they had to be to support the weight of the building. "They built this place to last," he commented to Rodney, as Zelenka and Kusanagi scanned a room they had found off one of the landings. Every piece of equipment seemed to have been removed, like the ruined city on the base moon.

"Yes, I suspect they anticipated frequent quakes from the discharges," Rodney said, mouth twisted as he studied the readings on his tablet.

John's brows quirked. "So...the Mirror was probably unstable even back when they built this place?" They had heard another couple of low rumbles, but nothing close to the size of the first discharge.

"Yes. Doesn't bode well, does it," Rodney said with a grimace.

Zelenka rejoined them, tucking his equipment back into his pack. "They certainly didn't leave in a hurry," he said tiredly, wiping sweat off his brow. "Everything was removed, very carefully."

"Except the Mirror," Teyla put in. Ronon was watching the corridor and she was standing on the landing, keeping a cautious eye on the stairs.

"And either the instability caused it to activate," Rodney said, his eyes on his tablet screen. "Or another reality accessed it."

"So something could come through that thing anytime," Ronon asked, flicking an uneasy look at Teyla.

"Yes. Anything, at anytime," Rodney said, snapping his tablet shut. "Did I not make that abundantly clear before?"

"You did," John told him. "But standing next to it and knowing that adds a little extra drama."

As they continued, they found more empty rooms that could have been labs or control areas, and a section of transparent wall filled with bundles of crystal conduit. John saw the seams in the floor by accident, his light catching one when the others had stopped to take readings again. It was just to one side of a broad blue-green band that he had thought was just more floor decoration. The bands lay about every ten yards along the corridor. Signaling the others to halt, John went back to look at the last two bands, checking for seams. As he returned, Rodney came over, asking, "What the hell are you doing?"

John knelt beside a band, shining his light on the seam. "What does that look like?"

"That's just a decorative—Oh, wait." Rodney dropped to a crouch, frowning as he ran his fingers along the little gap. "This is a door, a blast door. It must come up from the floor—"

Teyla stepped closer, eyeing the floor uneasily, as John said tightly, "They're all along this corridor, and from the size of the bands, the doors are a good foot thick. We don't have any tools that could cut through this. And yeah, we have C-4, but the space we'd be trapped in is too small; we couldn't blow the wall without killing ourselves. If they close for some reason, like another explosion, we'd be screwed."

"Of course we'd be screwed, we're always screwed," Rodney said, annoyed. "What do you want me to do about it?"

"I don't know," John snapped. "You tell me."

Rodney said rapidly, "Look, there's been minor discharges since we discovered this structure and the doors are still open. Either it takes a bigger energy burst to activate them, or after the danger is past, they open automatically." His mouth twisted as he thought that through. "If the power failed temporarily, we would...probably have enough air to survive."

"Right." John considered going back. But if they did that, they might as well pretend the damn Mirror didn't exist at all and just leave. It wasn't going to get any safer to do this. He said reluctantly, "We'll keep going."

"Good," Rodney said, though his expression showed he knew exactly how wrong this could go. John looked up to see Zelenka and Kusanagi looking down with anxious faces. He suppressed the impulse to tell them it was going to be okay. He had said that too many times when the outcome had been anything but okay. He just said, "We need to move faster."

Zelenka said, "Of course, yes." Kusanagi just nodded sharply, though she looked terrified.

After that they stopped checking the empty labs, just glancing in and scanning briefly to make certain nothing useful had been left behind. They had passed two more open stairwells and John estimated that they had traveled three quarters of the way around the structure's circumference when they came to a sealed doorway in the inner wall. "I have a good feeling," Zelenka said, scanning it thoughtfully. "All the other empty labs were left open."

"Try it," John said, hoping this was it. "We're due a little luck here."

"Hold that thought," Rodney muttered darkly. He took one last look at the life signs detector, waved Zelenka out of the way, and touched the triangle in the center of the door.

It started to slide up and he stepped quickly aside so John and Teyla could cover the opening.

Bingo, John thought, as the door revealed a stretch of wall with floor-to-ceiling windows looking out at the Quantum Mirror. He stepped inside cautiously, Teyla following. It was a long room, curved to follow the inner wall, and there were three banks of consoles set in the center of the floor, all of them blue-green metal with the familiar crystal touchpads and controls. "Yeah, this could be it."

"Finally," Rodney growled, striding in. As the others followed, John stepped to the window. It was curved outward into a bubble, the outside streaked with red dust. He didn't have much perspective on how big the structure was from this vantage point. The dark curve of the building was like a stadium, the Quantum Mirror the playing field.

The black surface of the Mirror itself wasn't visible, which was kind of a relief. The dull silver-gray wall of the naquadah frame was high enough to block any view of it. John could see the frame was jointed, as if it had been laid down in sections, each about the length of a train's boxcar. Surrounding it was a large open plaza of dark blue pavement. Rodney stepped up beside him. "Yes. Yes, yes, yes. This could be the control center." He turned back toward the banks of consoles.

"No, no, this is for monitoring," Zelenka was saying, pacing back and forth between the consoles and the port, as if torn between which he wanted to examine first.

John noticed that the roof of the structure had some kind of narrow projection sticking out over the inner area. He put a hand on the top edge of the port and leaned out into the bubble, trying to get a better view. It looked as if it was just an extension of the roof. He thought he could see silver ribbing embedded in it and wondered if it was recording data of some kind from the Mirror, or if it was somehow part of the energy shielding. He made a mental note to direct Rodney's attention to it once Rodney was done exclaiming hysterically over the consoles.

Then Ronon said, "What's that?"

John pulled himself out of the bubble. "What?"

"Right there." Ronon leaned over to point, so John could sight along his arm.

It was a structure, standing on the plaza about midway around the Mirror, a couple of hundred yards from the frame. It was dark-colored like the stone, making it hard to spot. It had curving sides, the walls shaded from black to blue to near purple at the round base; John judged it was about the size of a two story house. It looked like a giant inverted tulip. He shook his head. "I don't know. Some kind of observatory?"

Miko stepped up beside him, adjusting her glasses to peer at it. "It could be, but it doesn't resemble the main structure. The shape is very...and..." She trailed off, leaning forward to stare intently at the little building. "Dr. McKay, Dr. Zelenka, please, look at this."

John's brow furrowed. "What?"

Zelenka stepped up beside Miko, peering uncertainly. "That...is a spaceship."

"What?" Rodney's annoyance fled as he stepped up to the port. "Right, those are drive pods. It's just hard to tell because they're vertical and——" He stared, his jaw dropping. "Wait, wait, what?"

"But it doesn't look anything like the jumpers," John said. He was beginning to get that feeling, that feeling that things were about to take a very bad turn. "How do you go from square box to giant tulip?"

"There could be variations, among different Ancient cultures, as there is between Atlantis and some of the other sites we have found," Zelenka said uncertainly. "Corrigan or one of the other archeologists might be able to say."

"Or it could be alien," John said. Yeah, he had a bad feeling about this. Rodney was still staring at the ship, his face rapt.

Teyla was trying to listen while keeping an eye on the corridor. "But it has been here since this place was abandoned." No one answered her and she added with some concern, "Has it not?"

Rodney, Zelenka, and Miko didn't answer, and Ronon was watching John, a wary line between his brows. Then something flashed along the Mirror's frame, and the port suddenly grayed out into an opaque metal shield. John stepped back, startled. "What—"

"That was a discharge from the Mirror," Rodney said, looking toward the consoles. "The port must be responding to it. But it doesn't seem to be—"

John looked up at a muted rumble, like thunder; he felt it roll through the structure, shaking the stone and metal underfoot, vibrating through his bones. Ronon twitched uneasily.

Nervously, Rodney finished, "—serious. On the other hand—"

"Okay, that's it," John began, "We're—"

An alarm klaxon blared and John jerked up his P-90 in pure startled reflex as everyone else flinched. "—leaving," he finished. "What the hell?"

"It's a security system," Rodney bellowed over the noise, looking around the room in frustration. "Did one of you touch something?"

Teyla shook her head, wincing at the noise, and Zelenka and Miko held up empty hands. Ronon was staring back down the corridor. John had been facing away from the port, and he knew none of the others had moved. He said, "Nobody touched anything. We need to get out of here, move, now!"

Teyla headed for the corridor as John swept out an arm to herd Zelenka and Kusanagi after her. But Ronon stepped into their path to stop them, his face urgent. "Do you hear that? That crashing?"

Teyla's face went still with concentration, her head tilted as she listened. Rodney was looking at the detector, saying, "Still no life signs. The system must have been on some kind of delay. Opening the outer door should have triggered—"

"Shut up for a second!" John told him. In another moment he heard it too: in between each deep blare of the alarm, there was a heavy metallic thud. "Oh crap," he breathed.

Rodney was looking at him, eyes wide in alarm. "Blast doors. The blast doors are closing!"

John ducked out into the corridor. The nearest blast doors hadn't shut, but the metallic thuds were closer, the echo carrying all through the building. "Ronon, which way is it coming from?" he shouted. If the doors were closing sequentially in one direction, they had a chance.

Ronon went still and cocked his head. "That way," he said a moment later, pointing to the right, the direction they had come from. The direction of the nearest stairwell. That really wasn't what John wanted to hear.

He yelled, "Run the other way, go, go," and gave Ronon a shove to tell him to take the lead.

Ronon bolted and John waved the others after him. He took their six, wanting to make sure Miko didn't fall behind. But she took off like an Olympic sprinter, keeping up with Teyla and Rodney easily, and it was only Zelenka that John had to worry about.

Another discharge shook the floor underfoot, slowing them down. They made it about fifty yards down the corridor when John heard the metallic thuds become exponentially louder. He threw a glance over his shoulder in time to see a green metal blast door slide up to hit the ceiling, just at the curve of the corridor. He swore, turning back, and Zelenka panted, "What?"

"Just run," John said, but he didn't hear the next thud until ten seconds later, and that was just after Ronon shouted, "Stairs!"

We can make it, John thought, and grabbed Zelenka's arm, urging him along.

Then a green wall slammed upward just in front of Ronon, so abruptly he bounced off it before he could stop. The others slid to an abrupt halt, and John whirled around in time to see the blast door just behind them thumping into place. Rodney was shouting, "They closed out of sequence! Dammit—"

"Rodney!" John said through gritted teeth. "Think of something."

Breathing hard, Zelenka stepped to the blast door, pulling out his tablet again, studying it intently. "Door is solid mass. This is not good."

John looked back. Miko was frantically running her hands over the other door. She said, "There are no controls here—" Ronon growled and slammed his hand against the stone.

"Wait, wait, wait!" Rodney bellowed. In the immediate silence, he pressed a hand to his forehead and said thickly, "This is a safety feature."

"Yes, but we did not know what to do, where to go,

when the alarm went off," Teyla said, turning to study the walls uneasily.

Exasperated, John began, "It trapped us here—"

"It stopped us here," Rodney snapped. "We were nearly to the stairs and it stopped us—" He halted abruptly, his eyes narrowing.

Getting it an instant later, John said, "Because there's a closer exit in this section."

Zelenka and Miko were already converging on Rodney, Zelenka saying rapidly, "It should have opened automatically—"

"The mechanism could be damaged—" Miko added.

"Look for seams in the outer wall," Rodney finished.

John scrambled with the others, running his hands over the stone, down the metal bands. It felt like forever but it must have been only a few moments before Teyla said, "Here!"

Rodney practically flung her out of the way, running his hand down the band. "It's not responding. Colonel—"

John stepped forward, pressing his hand to the band, but he didn't think this was a natural Ancient gene thing. The doors below had responded easily to Rodney's artificial gene, and there was no reason these should be different. The band didn't budge. "No, nothing," he said tightly.

"The crystals must be damaged," Rodney snarled, elbowing John out of the way.

Miko dropped to the floor, unslinging her pack and pulling out tools to hand Rodney and Zelenka as they pried at the band.

John felt another low rumble travel through the building. He saw Rodney throw a worried look at the ceiling. *It would be just our luck that this place picks now to collapse,* John thought sourly. Then a section of the band popped open, revealing the Ancient control crystals set into the deceptively simple matrix. Zelenka pointed, agitated. "There, there!" Rodney said, "I know, I know!" and rapidly switched around three of the crystals.

A section of the inner wall next to the band slid sideways, releasing a puff of stale displaced air. Inside was a circular shaft like the one they had found in the stairwell. The blue and silver light strips flickered on.

"The readings say the transporter effect should be working," Miko reported tensely, studying the tablet's readout.

Rodney fumbled in the pockets of his tac vest. "Hold on, I'll test it."

Ronon said, "I'll do it," and stepped into the shaft. Rodney gasped in alarm and John and Teyla both lunged for Ronon, but he had already vanished. "Ronon!" John yelled.

"It works!" Ronon's voice echoed up from below. "There's a door down here."

John swore, Teyla rolled her eyes incredulously, and Zelenka and Miko exchanged an appalled look. Rodney clapped a hand to his forehead and said, "That was not what I had in mind."

"Just go, come on, one at a time," John said. Miko went first, gripping her pack tightly, then Rodney shoved Zelenka in and jumped after him. John gave Teyla a nod, telling her to go next. He had one hand on the edge of the doorway, ready to step in, when a gleam of light caught his eye.

There was a small silver disk high up on the wall, standing out and angled so it was pointing at him. He froze for an instant, because he was damn sure it hadn't been there a few minutes ago when they had been frantically searching for the way out.

He took a half-step toward it. Then from the transporter shaft, Rodney shouted, "Colonel!"

John shook himself, recalling that he didn't have time for checking out mysterious objects, and stepped into the shaft.

CHAPTER THREE

John suddenly found himself standing at the bottom of the shaft, facing Rodney. Rodney yelped and flinched backward, then shouted, "What the hell took you so long?"

John shook his head; they used the transporters constantly in Atlantis, the size of the city made it impossible not to. But without the cushioning effect of the chamber it was just as disorienting as being grabbed suddenly by the *Daedalus'* Asgard transport beam.

This part of the shaft opened up into a larger well, with a darker green circle on the floor, which probably marked the space it was a bad idea to stand in if more people were coming down. The others were backed against the wall, watching Zelenka and Miko work on an open panel. John stepped out of the circle, just in case the transporter decided to reverse abruptly, and said, "I thought I saw something." He jerked his chin toward the door. "Can we get out of here?"

"Working on it!" Rodney snapped, turning back to the panel. He took Miko by the shoulders and shifted her out of the way.

"What did you see?" Teyla asked John, brows lifted.

"Something came out of the wall," he told her. "A little thing, angled like it was pointing at us."

Ronon looked up toward the top of the shaft. "A weapon?"

John shook his head. "No way to tell. Could have been

a camera, too." All three of them pivoted, checking the walls. John couldn't see anything like it down here, but with the blue-green lights and the strips of embossed metal that might be decorative or something to do with the transporter function, there were too many places for a tiny device to hide. He added, "Whatever it was, it could've just been automatically tracking our movements."

"Or something could be watching us," Ronon added.

Teyla shook her head, though she still looked uneasy. "The life signs detector showed nothing."

"But this structure is very large," Miko put in, glancing back at them and adjusting her glasses. "And the shielding is unusual. If someone was several sections away, I'm not sure the detector would find him."

They all looked at her. "Oh," John said, turning that unpleasant thought over. Considering they had no idea if the ship near the Mirror was Ancient or not, if it had been here since the Mirror had been abandoned or since yesterday, it wasn't encouraging. "Great."

Zelenka was saying, "Ah, here, relay is damaged—"

"Got it!" Rodney stepped back from the panel, lifting the mask part of his SCBA unit. "Everyone put your breathing gear back on. This system was designed to get people out of this structure as quickly as possible if the Mirror destabilized. We could run into something that might pop us right outside."

"Important safety tip. Thanks, Rodney." John adjusted his breathing unit, made certain everyone else had theirs on, then gave Rodney the nod to open the door.

Rodney made a last adjustment to the crystals and the door slid sideways. The first thing John noticed was that the door itself was nearly a foot thick, as heavy as the blast doors. The second was that the large room it opened into was not the ground floor corridor he had been expecting to see.

The ceiling was lower and instead of the dark indigo stone, the walls were the metallic blue-green, with more strips of the tiny blue lights. Most of the illumination came from square pillars, set with blocky white glowing fixtures, not unlike the ones in Atlantis. But the lights toward the back of the room weren't on, leaving most of it in shadow.

John stepped through the doorway cautiously. He really didn't like not knowing where they were in relation to the jumper. "Rodney?" he said. "Any thoughts?"

Rodney stepped up next to him, saying uncertainly, "I have no idea. I thought we were on the first level."

"Yeah." John thought, *we jumped into a strange transporter and we have no idea where it took us. Good one, John.* "But we could hear Ronon when he called up the shaft. If this isn't the ground floor, then it has to be above or below it. It couldn't have taken us to another building." He added uneasily, "Or, you know, planet." *Don't let it be another planet.*

"Unless there was a communications device in the shaft that was transmitting his voice back to us," Rodney said. John stared at him, appalled. Rodney added hurriedly, "But what's more likely is that we're a level or two below ground. Think about it: escaping a massive energy discharge by running outside the structure into the open is not the best option. It's more likely that there's a protected escape route down here." He looked around, brow creased in worry. "Somewhere."

"Okay, that is more likely," John admitted. He glanced back at the others. Teyla and Ronon had stepped out behind him, and were gazing around the room suspiciously, flashing their lights into the shadows. Zelenka and Kusanagi had put their tools back in their packs and were anxiously watching him. "It's okay. This happens all the time," John told them, judging this was a good time to throw honesty out the window and concentrate on reassurance.

"It does?" Ronon commented skeptically.

"Yes. Yes, it does," Teyla said, spearing him with a look. She turned to give Radek and Miko a reassuring smile, adding, "We need only look for the way to the surface."

"Right." John turned back to the shadowy room. "Stay together."

There was an open triangular archway at the back of the chamber, leading to an almost identical space, but unlit. John had thought the lights would come on once they got into the darkened section; they did in Atlantis, responding to any movement now that they had been initialized by the Ancient gene. But the pillar-lights here stayed dark. "That's not good," John commented, carefully examining the walls with his P-90's light while Zelenka and Kusanagi got out flashlights. He didn't see anything like a console to turn the lights on manually, either.

"This area must have taken some damage," Rodney agreed sourly, looking from the life signs detector to his tablet. "Everybody turn on your breathing units; there's a strong flow of air, but this section isn't holding pressure." He tucked the tablet under his arm and switched on his own unit, looking up with a wince. "I hope our hypothetical escape route doesn't need power."

"Great," John muttered, switching his unit on. He caught a worried look from Teyla. Yeah, they were potentially in a lot of trouble here. They had about an hour's worth of air in each tank, which had seemed like a lot when they had had a clear path back to the jumper.

Rodney said uneasily, "At least the chamber at the bottom of the shaft is pressurized, if we, ah..." He tapped the strap of his breathing tank significantly.

John just said, "Right," and picked up the pace. The air at the bottom of the shaft might keep them alive, but staying there didn't exactly offer a lot of options for searching for the way out.

They went through three more rooms and a couple of corridors, all unlit. Then the escape route stopped being hypothetical, but might as well have been mythological for all the good it was going to do them. Their lights had started to find cracks in the walls and the floor had become grainy with dirt and pebbles. Then they found the tumble of rock blocking the end of the next large room. Rodney swore, and John agreed, "Yeah, this sucks."

"But look at this," Teyla said, directing her light toward the far wall. There was a narrow silver track set into the floor, partially concealed by dust and rubble.

"Huh, that's intriguing," Rodney muttered, starting toward it. John used his longer legs to get there first, sweeping his light around to check the ceiling for any sign of imminent collapse. It looked like the wall had buckled, the rock pushing through the metal panels and piling up on the floor, but the roof hadn't given way and didn't look inclined to it. Rodney moved back and forth, his flashlight flickering around impatiently, picking out a large rounded shape buried under the rubble. "There's something under here, some kind of small underground vehicle. It must use that track—"

"What, like a little subway?" John asked.

Rodney waved his hands. "Yes, that is what an underground vehicle would be called, yes. But it's obvious this is—"

"Perhaps it goes to the spaceport," Miko said, standing on tiptoes to see as she stood next to John. She had apparently taken the order to not get ahead of the military personnel literally, and he sure as hell wasn't going to fault her for it.

"Yes, exactly." Zelenka crouched with his flashlight, trying to get a better look at the smashed metal and glass under the rocks. "If this is escape route, it would make the most sense for the subway to head directly there, at very high speed. And it could have a self-contained power source, like a jumper, and wouldn't be affected by power loss in the main complex, as a transporter would."

Rodney glared. "Of course! That's what I was trying to—"

"So how do we get out?" Ronon asked.

"We're working on it," John said easily, before Rodney's head exploded. They were still finding stuff; it wasn't time to start the real worrying until they had exhausted all the possibilities. "Right, Rodney?"

"Yes, yes." Rodney turned away from the crushed subway car, flicking his light around. "There should be alternate entrances, if this was a regular method of transportation to and from the port. In which case, there could be something nearby..." He stepped over the rubble, moving toward the wall.

They spread out a little, searching, their lights finding more rubble and dust and buckled metal. John kept a close eye on the time, thinking about their air tanks.

Finally Zelenka halted, shining his flashlight toward the ceiling. "Wait, Colonel, Rodney? What is this?"

John stepped over the rocks to reach his side, squinting. "That...looks like a hatch." It was a door-sized panel set in a recess in the flat stone ceiling. From the chunks of metal still attached, there had once been a stairway or ladder to access it. John saw with relief that it had a little console, which meant Rodney could trick it into opening for them if there was any power left in this section at all. "Good job, Radek."

"Yes, you get a gold star," Rodney added, joining them.

It was too high for even Ronon to reach while stretching up and standing on his toes, but fortunately there was no shortage of rocks. They piled up enough to make a small platform for Rodney to stand on and reach the console.

Zelenka stood below, handing Rodney tools and kibitzing. Ronon offered to hold Miko up so she could see too, but she declined. After a few minutes of work and trading insults with Zelenka, the console popped and the hatch groaned, starting to slide open. John stepped back as dirt and pebbles poured through the growing opening, a red landslide. Rodney hastily jumped down as everyone else backed away. Tucking his toolkit back into his pack, Zelenka said fervently, "Don't be blocked, please—Hah, I see light!"

He was right; wan daylight was visible through the

cascade of dirt. There were murmurs of relief. "Looks like we're in business," John said, trying to get closer, squinting to see through the dust cloud. The slide trickled to a halt and he stepped up onto their awkward rock platform, looking up through the opening. It led into a metal-walled shaft about eight feet long, and he couldn't see much beyond that but the curve of the planet dominating the sky.

He still couldn't see anything when Ronon boosted him up, but he could tell the edges of the hatch were set securely in some kind of stone platform. Ronon half-shoved, half-flung him, and John scrambled for a moment, sending another small landslide down. The walls of the shaft were crusted with dirt, but he finally got a grip on a set of handholds forming a ladder in the wall. He hauled himself up enough to brace his feet on the metal of the shaft, then climbed the rest of the way to the surface.

Poking his head out cautiously, he saw the shaft opened into the bottom of a semi-circular pit with sides too regular to be anything but manmade. Dirt was still trickling down the opening, and it looked like whatever covering that had originally shielded it had been torn away, and the whole thing buried under weather-shifted soil, most of which was now down on the floor of the chamber below.

John climbed out and struggled through the loose sand toward the side, finding a set of steps by luck when his boot caught on the first one and he smacked into the side of the pit. They were still mostly buried, but provided enough purchase to make the climb easier than trying to swim upward through a sea of shifting sand. His headset came on and Rodney's voice demanded, "What are you doing? What do you see?"

"I see sand. Lots of sand. Give me a minute." At least the SCBA kept him from having to breathe in the dust. John reached the top of the pit, and swore in relief. The outer wall of the installation was about five hundred yards away. The distance didn't quite add up; he didn't think the series of belowground rooms had covered that much ground. Rodney must have been right about the transporter; it hadn't been a straight shot down the shaft. It had taken them further outside the building, and Ronon must have called to them over an automatically activated comm system.

But however they had ended up out here, they were on the right side of the building. John could see one of the triangular doorways as the structure curved, and the rock formation not far to the south looked familiar. He fished the jumper's remote out of his tac vest. "Well hello, baby," he muttered as the readout told him the cloaked jumper was within close range. That must be the doorway they had used to enter the building, and the jumper was waiting only a short distance from it. "What, what?" Rodney was yelling in his headset as in the background, Teyla said, "Dr. McKay, please calm down," and Zelenka added helpfully, "You are using up all your air, Rodney."

"We're near the jumper," John reported, ignoring all the commentary. He shoved off from the dirt-encrusted stairs and went back to the shaft. His arrival caused another small cascade and some grumbling exclamations from below.

He dropped to his knees beside the open hatch, unslinging his pack to get the rope out. He figured Teyla,

Miko, and Radek would need it, all being too short to reach as far up as John had been able to, and Ronon could only fling them so far up the shaft. There was no good spot to tie it off; the ladder set into the side just had handholds, not actual rungs he could wrap it around. John settled for anchoring the rope by bracing his body across the shaft, planting his butt and his feet against the stable stone and metal rim. He said over the radio, "Teyla, you're next."

She managed it with some scrambling, and another small landslide as more crusted dirt was dislodged. She struggled out, shook a spray of red sand out of her hair, and looked around. "We have been lucky for once," she said, her voice wry.

"Hey, hey, watch it," John told her seriously. "Remember, we talked about that." He said into his headset, "Come on, McKay."

Teyla lifted a skeptical brow at him, taking up the slack of the rope and bracing herself to help anchor it. "Yes, you believe if we speak of luck, it goes away. I do not share your superstitions."

"You were willing to humor the people on P6S-221 who thought wearing hats kept the Wraith away—" John leaned back, steadying the rope as Rodney started his climb. "You can humor us."

Teyla shifted to take more of the weight. "Wearing a hat because our hosts asked it was simply courtesy. I am not going to encourage your primitive—"

Rodney's head appeared near the top of the shaft and John reached down to give him a hand up. Rodney was looking down, apparently addressing Zelenka, "I can't tell if it's a power access port or not, do I look like I can make a complete assessment while hanging in midair?" John and Teyla heaved and Rodney dragged himself up, scrambling out of the shaft to thump down heavily on the sand. Breathing hard, he told John, "If the jumper's nearby, I don't see why you couldn't have gotten the winch and saved us the trouble of—" Rodney froze, eyes going wide, and that was when the shadow fell over the pit.

John threw a look over his shoulder and got a heart-freezing view of a big dark shape hovering over them. He twisted around, jerking up the P-90. It was a ship.

He heard Teyla take a sharp indrawn breath and Rodney gasp, "It's—It's—"

Gritting his teeth, his whole body tight in anticipation of a culling beam, John whispered tensely into his head-set, "Ronon, fall back, get them away from the hatch, now, do it now."

But it didn't look Wraith; it didn't look like anything John had ever seen before. It was larger than the jumper, curved into a conch shell-like spiral, dark purple shaded to pink... *It matches the tulip ship,* John thought in shock. This thing went together with that ship like Lego bricks. A faint flush of cool air came from it, smelling of ozone; a cloud of dust rose slowly around it. John registered Ronon's terse, "Come on," a murmur of alarm from Zelenka, Kusanagi's breathless, "Hurry, Doctor."

"I sense no Wraith," Teyla was whispering, her P-90 aimed at the thing looming over them. "This ship is not of the Ancestors?"

"I have no idea," Rodney managed. He winced. "It's not killing us yet. That's probably wishful thinking."

John couldn't see anything that looked like the muzzle

of a weapon. Since it had been maybe thirty seconds and they still weren't dead, he added, "Rodney, when I say go, grab the rope and get back down there. Teyla, you're right behind him."

Teyla flicked a worried look at him, but nodded. "But, I, it's—" Rodney swallowed noisily. "Right." He edged back toward the shaft, his eyes still on the ship. "What about you?"

"I'm going to be right behind Teyla," John assured him. "Go!"

Rodney swung his legs into the shaft and grabbed for the rope. John shifted, bracing his leg against the edge of the hatch, but Rodney let go of the rope, grabbing onto the dirt-encrusted ladder and half-climbing, half-falling down. "Teyla, go," John snapped.

She twisted around and grabbed the rope, and just as she swung down into the shaft, the ship moved. It rolled with a sudden rush of air, dust sheeting over the pit, and John twisted his face away. He felt Teyla's weight leave the rope and he rolled to crouch on the edge of the opening, trying to disappear into the dirt and sparse tufts of grass. He couldn't go down yet; if he fell he would slam Teyla and probably Rodney into the rocks at the bottom of the shaft. Then he heard Rodney yell "Go, go, we're clear!" and Teyla's breathless confirmation. John swung his legs over the side, scrambling for purchase. Then the shadow and the looming weight overhead were suddenly gone.

His heart pounding, John looked up. The ship was lifting away from the pit. It rolled gracefully, with a sound like wind rustling through pines, then moved out of sight toward the south.

John slid down another foot before he managed to stop himself. He couldn't hear the ship anymore, but he watched the edge of the pit warily. *So did it leave?* Wraith ships didn't have cloaking technology, but it sounded like the consensus had been that this wasn't a Wraith ship. And John had to admit that the evidence was in favor of it; if it had been some new kind of Wraith ship it would still have a culling beam, and he, Rodney, and Teyla would be well on their way to getting stuck to the wall of a hive-ship as future items on the dinner menu. John winced as his headset crackled and Rodney's voice whispered furiously, "What the hell are you doing? Get down here!"

"It left. I'm trying to figure out where the hell it went." John dragged himself out, getting another ton of sand down his pants in the process, kneeling in the dirt to untangle himself from the rope.

Teyla's voice overrode Rodney's to ask, "Are you all right?"

"I'm fine. Rodney, just out of curiosity, when did you last check the life signs detector?" John kept his head down as he made his way to the half-buried steps at the edge of the pit.

Rodney was saying to someone else, "Oh please, I have no idea what it is and unless you've got a copy of *Jane's Fighting Intergalactic Spaceships* hidden in your pack, neither do you." He answered John, "When you first climbed out, there was nothing on the screen but us. The ship must have been out of range. Or it's shielded against the detector, which frankly would be just our luck. And if it's still out there, I'm not getting a reading. So basically it could be anywhere so be very, very careful!"

John scrambled to the top of the steps and took a cautious peek over the edge of the pit. "Oh, crap."

"What?" several different voices demanded.

"I found it. It landed." John cautiously eased back down, digging his binoculars out of a tac vest pocket. "Guess where."

John could hear Rodney thumping himself in the forehead. "It's next to the jumper, isn't it?" Rodney said bleakly.

"Yeah. Maybe about twenty yards from it." John wiped sweat and dirt off his forehead and lifted up enough to focus the binoculars on the alien ship. "That's not an accident. It has to be able to see through the jumper's cloak."

"An Ancient ship would have that ability," Radek put in, sounding unnerved.

Teyla said, "But if they were somehow Ancestors, they would see we are human, and try to contact us."

"They could be like us, humans who have found and learned to use Ancient technology," Miko added cautiously.

"Maybe they are trying to contact us," John pointed out. With the binoculars he could see more detail on the ship, including bulbous projections that might be sensor devices or weapons, and a curved depression in the hull that could be a hatch. He put the binoculars away, checked his watch, and grimaced. They didn't have a lot of time left on the air tanks, and all that climbing and suppressed hysteria had to have used up an extra share of oxygen. "If they wanted to lure us out into the open, all they had to do was fly behind the building and wait till we came out."

Then Ronon said, "Maybe they just want to make sure we're good to eat first."

John shook his head wearily. There was a moment of silence, then Teyla said, "Ronon. That was unnecessary."

"We have fifteen minutes of air left," Rodney added, his voice grim.

"I know." John didn't see that he had a lot of choice. "I'm going to get the jumper and bring it over here. If I'm not back in seven minutes, get back to the building. Teyla's in command."

Rodney was already sputtering, "What? Alone? Are you out of your mind?"

Easing up to the top of the steps, John didn't see how company would help if the ship decided to fire on him. "Yeah, alone."

"Sheppard, I'll go," Ronon said as Teyla began, "Colonel—" and Rodney started, "We could try—"

"Ronon, stay with the others and do what Teyla says. That's an order. Everybody shut up now. That's also an order." Wincing, John stood cautiously, already feeling like he had a target painted on his chest. But there was no sign of movement from the ship.

The others interpreted "shut up now" as "continue to argue in furious whispers" but it kept John company as he crossed the suddenly endless stretch of open ground between the pit and the cloaked jumper. He moved at a jog, because he just didn't have time to take it slow and cautious. He gave the other ship as wide a berth as possible.

The argument was still raging in his headset. He heard Rodney say, "You're discounting the possibility that it could have come through the Mirror!" and Radek reply, "I am not discounting! I see no reason to theorize in advance of my data!" John hoped Kusanagi's earlier guess was right, and the ship was occupied by Pegasus Galaxy humans who had stumbled on Ancient technology and figured out how to use it. The other option was aliens, and he really wasn't comfortable with that.

It wasn't that he didn't believe there were benign aliens. He had seen all the SGC reports and he knew about the Tok'ra and the Nox and all the assorted others, and he had met an Asgard in person, though he still thought Hermiod was a creepy little bastard. But his gut reaction wasn't ever going to change. In an argument where Rodney had called John a xenophobe, Rodney had pointed out that John's perception of aliens had been adversely affected because his first experience with one had involved being pinned to a dinner table by a life-sucking vampire that wanted to eat his entire species. John had replied, *yeah, so what?* and that was pretty much the end of rational discourse on that subject.

Of course, if it was humans in there, that certainly didn't mean they were out of the woods. Instead of sitting in there thinking *hey, other people with a spaceship, let's contact them*, it could be *hey, another spaceship, let's kill them all and steal it*.

But they could have done that with one burst of fire into the pit and they hadn't, and that was all John had to go on right now.

"Colonel! What's going on? What is the alien ship doing? What—" Rodney demanded.

"Nothing, yet." The ship was just looming silently on the sand, like a giant metal conch shell.

Forty yards now from the square dent in the sand that marked the jumper's position, John debated the relative merit of glaring suspiciously at the strange ship versus trying to pretend it wasn't there. Thirty yards and he was starting to think he was home free.

Then the dent in the purple hull made a metallic clunk and started to slide open. "Crap," John muttered, spinning to face it. He kept the P-90 aimed toward the growing opening, still backing toward the jumper.

"What? What is it?" Rodney said urgently. The others had gone quiet.

"The hatch is opening," John said through gritted teeth.

The hatch slid all the way up. The interior was too dark to see anything but a shallow airlock. Then a helmeted head peeked out.

John stumbled to a halt because he was having a *The Day the Earth Stood Still* moment. Except this figure was a lot smaller and more tentative than Gort. It was maybe a little over five feet tall, human-shaped from what he could tell; everything was concealed in the dark blue folds of a loose outfit that might be a pressure or environmental suit of some kind. The helmet was dark glass, opaque, and attached to a small purplish-gray unit strapped to its back. It was gripping one side of the hatch, braced as if to leap back into the ship, its whole stance conveying uncertainty and trepidation rather than hostility. John was still mostly expecting it to shoot at him, though its hands were empty.

They stared at each other for a very long moment. Then it lifted a gloved hand slowly, fingers spread in what had to be a greeting. *Five fingers,* John noticed. Slowly, he took one hand off his P-90 and waved back. He said, "Uh, hey there. I actually can't do this right now, because I'm running out of air, and I have to move my ship."

In his headset, he heard Rodney say, "What? Who are you talking to—Oh. Oh, God."

The figure hesitated, then a voice, light and a little tinny as it was filtered through whatever comm device the helmet used, said, "Oh." Then it added, "I—I'll wait here."

They stared at each other for a moment more, then John said, "Okay." He reached into his vest and triggered the remote. He heard the welcome hiss and thump as the jumper's ramp opened behind him, felt the cool breeze as the conditioned air flowed out. He backed up until his heel caught the end of the ramp and he barely managed not to fall on his ass. Fortunately the cloak extended far enough that the human-alien-person-whatever would have missed that part.

John bolted inside, hitting the switch to close the ramp. He went immediately to the cockpit, saying, "I'm in the jumper. You guys okay?"

"What? What happened?" Rodney shouted into his headset. "What was it? Human, alien, what?"

"We are fine," Teyla answered, sounding relieved. "What did you see?"

"The hatch opened, somebody stepped out." The jumper was already powering up as John dropped into the pilot's seat. The HUD flashed on, showing him the energy signatures and relative position of the alien ship. He saw with relief that as far as the jumper could tell, it was the only other ship in the area. And the sensors were only reading one life sign, but the handheld detector hadn't read anything, and this one might only be registering because the person-alien-whatever was standing in the hatch. Though something about the tentative way it had peeked out had suggested that it was alone. John wasn't

going to count on that, though. "He's wearing an EVA suit
and helmet; he mostly looked human, but I couldn't tell."
He hesitated, then dropped the cloak. The ship obviously
had instruments that could see through it, and he wanted
to try to keep this whole thing at the cordial level it had
started out on.

"You were communicating with it, you could have
asked if it was human," Rodney pointed out in exasperation.

"Well, yeah, but that seemed kind of rude. Get ready,
I'll be there in a minute."

He lifted the jumper up to a low hover, then took it
through a decorously slow turn and back toward the pit.
The sensors informed him the ground was stable, con-
firming that there was some kind of stone construction
buried under the dirt. He set her down close to the edge
of the steps and opened the ramp. It was going to take the
jumper some time to re-pressurize, so he rapidly changed
out his own air bottle, then loaded a pack with spares.
He carried it down to the shaft and lowered it with the
rope. And since there was no point in doing it the hard
way again, he got the collapsible chain-link ladder out,
secured it to the ramp, and dropped it down the shaft.

Teyla came up first, moving immediately to the edge
of the pit to keep watch. "He is still standing in the hatchway,
watching us," she reported quietly as John gave Rodney a
hand up out of the shaft.

"Good," Rodney said, heading toward Teyla and ducking to keep his head down. "If there's only one of them in
that thing, then no one is inside powering up weapons."

John had thought of that too, but they were still at their
most vulnerable right now. Leaning down to help Miko

over the edge of the shaft, John said, "Rodney, just get in the damn jumper."

Radek made it to the top, sweating and nervous, with an impassive Ronon right behind him. John sent Radek into the jumper after Miko, and he and Ronon hurriedly dragged the ladder up. Getting everybody into the jumper and closing the ramp didn't make him feel any more secure.

As the jumper re-pressurized the compartment, John dropped his pack and went forward to the cockpit. The others were already crowded inside, looking out the port at the other ship, Miko in the shotgun seat with Teyla and Zelenka standing behind her, craning to see. John moved Rodney out of the way so he could sit down in the pilot's seat, and Ronon ducked in, standing in the hatchway. They had a good view of the other ship, still sitting quietly in the sand near the jumper's previous position. The occupant had vanished.

"He went inside when you closed the ramp," Miko reported, flushed with excitement. She was holding one of the video cameras, aiming out the port. John was glad somebody had remembered to take DV of the ship.

The HUD was cycling through different sensor screens and Rodney shook his head, his mouth twisted. "We're not getting much data. I don't think it's an energy shield that's blocking us. It seems to be the material of the hull itself."

John nodded decisively. He could sympathize with the jumper; he had nothing at the moment either. "Right. So what are our options here?"

"Should we not go outside and try to speak to the pilot again?" Teyla said, studying the ship intently, her brows drawn together. "He does not seem hostile."

"Not yet," Ronon contributed grimly.

John wasn't exactly an optimist about this, but he couldn't side with Ronon on that one. "No, I don't think he's hostile. Unless he was faking...I think he was scared."

"We could run away," Radek offered. Everyone turned to look at him. He shrugged eloquently. "I just wanted to put it on the table, I'm not saying we should do it."

Rodney gave him a withering look. "You know, this is why I don't bring you along on these things—" He stopped suddenly and snapped his fingers. "Wait, we're being very stupid."

"'We?'" John asked him pointedly.

Rodney sat down in the other jump seat, opening the laptop and its interface into the jumper's systems. "Well, all right, you. He's probably trying to contact us right now, that's why he went back into his ship."

"Ah." Zelenka made an annoyed gesture. "You are right."

John frowned. "But the jumper should pick that up automatically."

Intent on the interface, Rodney huffed in exasperation. "No, because its comm system has been adjusted to scan our frequencies and the range the Wraith use. If he's broadcasting in a different range, which he probably is—" He went still, his face transfixed, one hand going to his headset. "It's there. This is... It's an Ancient frequency." He tapped the keypad hurriedly and the transmission filled the cockpit.

It was the light hesitant voice John had heard earlier, still tinny and now distorted by bursts of static. "...of the

Eidolon ship...hear me? Are you there?"

"Interference from the Mirror is causing the disruptions," Zelenka whispered.

"Did he say Eidolon?" John glanced back at Teyla and Ronon. "Anybody heard that before?"

"Never," Teyla said, frustrated. "And I could not tell if he is saying he is the Eidolon ship, or he thinks we are." Ronon shook his head, shrugging.

John chewed his lower lip, eyeing the controls. "Yeah, I didn't get that either."

Rodney was making frantic motions at John. "Will you answer him?"

"Okay, okay." John opened the channel, cleared his throat, and said, "We're here. Sorry about that. Uh, we... forgot that we didn't have the radio on."

Rodney glared and said furiously, "Excuse me! You're making us sound like idiots. What are you going to tell him next, that we startle easily because things try to eat us a lot—"

John glared back. "Do you want to do this? Then shut up."

"Dr. McKay, Colonel!" Miko pointed urgently at the comm readout. "He can hear us."

Crap, John thought, staring at the comm panel.

The voice corrected carefully, "I'm female."

"Oh." Miko bit her lip in embarrassment. "Sorry."

John mouthed the words, "Everybody, quiet. Especially Rodney." He said aloud, "Sorry about that, again. We're peaceful explorers, and, uh—" They weren't telling anyone that they were from Atlantis anymore, hoping to keep from spreading the information that the city hadn't self-destructed. Necessary, but it had made quite a hole in the standard "we come in peace, let's not try to kill each other" speech. Trying to get some idea whether he was talking to a human or not, he said, "We've never seen a ship like yours before. Is Eidolon the planet you come from?"

"No, I'm not from...here." There was a static-filled hesitation, then the voice blurted, "I came to this plane of existence through the Quantum Mirror."

There was a collective gasp from the others and Rodney pounded on the back of John's chair. "Okay," John said slowly, stalling. The first question that occurred to him was "was that really a good idea?" but he managed to keep that one to himself. He said, "Why?" Though if she was the scout for an invasion force, she probably wouldn't come out and say so.

"I was with my line studying the—" There was another burst of static and John thought he heard "...no alien races but I believe that...." more static, then "...common ancestor."

Rodney was now doing some kind of little dance behind him. John said carefully, "Say again? What was that last part?"

There was an edge of desperation in the voice. "I said, I believe we share a common ances- tor. We call them the Creators. They originated much of our technology, including many things we still do not understand fully, like the Mirror." *Holy crap,* John thought. *If that's true—*He was aware of Miko bouncing in her seat, Teyla lifting her brows in astonishment and Rodney and Radek having some sort of fervent sign language "I told you so" thing. The voice was continuing, "I didn't intend to come here. I was collecting data from the Mirror. There is a similar complex around it in my reality, a ruin of the Creators' civilization, and my research—" static fuzzed out a few words "—exploring it. The Mirror activated suddenly and my ship was pulled through. I tried to return, but the Mirror on this side seems to be more damaged, more unstable." There was another hesitation. "I am alone here and...I need help."

"Oh, yeah, apparently you have to watch that. Quantum Mirrors suck people in suddenly." John looked up to see even Teyla making urgent "get on with it" motions. "What kind of help do you need? Besides, obviously, you'd like to get back home."

"That, yes. And my ship is damaged. I know how to repair it, but I need materials. I was trying to scavenge supplies from the ruin and—It caused the security system to activate." She sounded deeply embarrassed. "I apologize for that. When the monitors came on, I saw you. I tried to turn it off, but I'd apparently removed a necessary component from that console. By the time I replaced it and regained control of the system, you were outside. I went to my ship and tried to call you on my communications system, then took the shuttle out to look for you. When I saw your ship, I was so relieved."

Rodney leaned over John's shoulder suddenly, cutting off the comm mic for the cockpit. He said, "That explains everything we found on the first level. Some of the doors must have been open, letting in the native plant and animal life. When she arrived, she must have activated the automatic systems, and the building sealed itself and pressurized. And that means—"

"She has the Ancient gene," John finished, lifting a

brow.

Rodney switched on the mic again, saying briskly, "Hello, Dr. Rodney McKay speaking. I'm a scientist with experience with this technology. Can you tell me what indication you saw that the Mirror wasn't forming a stable connection to your reality?"

"Yes." The voice sounded more certain. "Yes, my instruments show that the Mirror is experiencing periodic energy fluctuations, like the one that occurred just a little while ago. I've tried sending transmissions through, and then a probe with a recorded message, but I received no response, and from the energy discharge I believe the probe was destroyed."

"You realize the Mirror may not be set to the same destination," Rodney told her. "Finding your reality again could be problematic, to put it mildly."

"Oh, but in my reality, our research suggests that the instability was preventing the Mirror from switching destinations, even when it was shut down and reactivated. That's why I believe that if I could just activate it successfully, I could go home."

Rodney frowned, throwing a look back at Zelenka. Zelenka shrugged, mouthing the words, "It's a possibility."

"I know that," Rodney mouthed back, glaring irritably. He said aloud, "Right, yes. I'd have to take a look at your readings."

"Will you do that?" she asked anxiously. "Look at my data? My equipment is in my ship, which is in the open portion of the ruin, near the Mirror; this is only a shuttle unit." She hesitated, then said timidly, "Will you help me?"

CHAPTER FOUR

Everybody looked at John. He took a deep breath. *Well, here goes*, he thought. "What's your name?"

The answer came immediately, "I am Trishen, of the line of Frenya."

"Trishen, give us a couple of minutes to talk it over." John cut the channel.

Everybody started talking at once, which John had expected. Rodney out shouted them all with, "This is an incredible opportunity! We've taken far, far more stupid chances than this—" The environmental control display interrupted, informing them that the compartment had repressurized. John switched his breathing set off, pulling his mask down as the others followed suit. Rodney, by force of will and more practice, got his mask off faster and continued, "—and we can't pass this up because of your military paranoia—"

"Rodney!" John lifted his brows. "I didn't say I was against it."

"—and pointless suspicion in cases where—Oh." Rodney flung his hands in the air, deflating.

"Besides," Miko quickly added in the gap while Rodney was trying to switch gears, "If she shares her data with us, it will be much easier to discover how to shut down the Mirror." She looked around at their expressions, startled. She added hastily, "Oh, no, I meant after we help her to get back to her reality."

"Yes, we must find some way to help her, whatever

we do," Radek said, shaking his head. "It would be a terrible thing, trapped here and cut off from her companions. There are many days when I'm not happy to be here myself; I can't think what it would be like—" He made a vague gesture. "Alone."

"I agree," Teyla said, leaning forward in her chair, her face intent. "I can only think how we would feel if it was one of us trapped in their reality, and we had no means of retrieving her."

That one had crossed John's mind, too.

Rodney made an abrupt gesture. "This is what it comes down to. From what we found, it takes the Ancient gene to get into the upper control areas of the installation, and she's apparently been researching Ancient technology in her reality. She could even be more closely related to the Ancients than we are, and an exchange of data with her could give us the missing pieces to puzzles we've just barely begun to discover."

John leaned sideways to see Ronon, who was propped in the cabin hatch. "Ronon. What do you think?"

Ronon looked away, his mouth twisted, though he seemed more uneasy than cynical. "It sounds like a woman. It could be a trap, but..." He shrugged uncomfortably.

Teyla added, "But if she meant us harm, it would have made more sense to act when we were caught in the open."

Ronon nodded. John interpreted that as meaning that Ronon would like to be suspicious but just couldn't see his way clear to it. That pretty much summed up how John felt.

Rodney folded his arms. "Humanitarian considerations aside, if the Mirror is now too dangerously unstable to operate and she can't go back, that leaves us the opportunity to invite her back to Atlantis." He lifted his chin. "Her and her spaceship."

"I admit, that occurred to me also." Radek scratched his head ruefully. "It would be terrible thing for her, but not necessarily for us. And she has already been here for more than a day as measured by this moon's orbit. If there was a possibility she would experience entropic cascade failure, it would already have happened."

Ronon stirred, frowning. "What's that?"

Radek turned to him, explaining, "If more than one copy of the same person exists simultaneously in one reality, the newcomer experiences a quantum instability that causes massive cellular disruption throughout the entire body." He winced. "You become fuzzy, it's painful and terrible."

Ronon eyed him skeptically. "That doesn't make sense."

"Nothing involving Quantum Mirrors makes sense," Rodney said in annoyance. He looked at John and demanded, "Are we going to do this?"

"Yeah." John let out his breath. It was still a risk, but the fact remained that they didn't have a single reason to believe this woman wasn't exactly who and what she said she was. And Teyla had pegged it; he couldn't help thinking how he would feel if they lost someone through the Mirror, knowing he or she was right on the other side and unable to do a damn thing about it. And if they couldn't get Trishen back home, talking her into returning to Atlantis with them was a hell of a lot better option than leaving her sitting out here with no idea where the

nearest inhabited world was. "We're going to do this." He
glanced at his watch, and the HUD helpfully popped up
a diagram of the planetary system, with the current positions of the gas giant and the base moon. "The planet's
blocking a direct transmission back to base camp. We're
going to have to bounce a signal off one of those other
moons."

Rodney nodded sharply, his face caught between
relief, triumph, and trepidation. "I'll make a data packet
to update them on our situation. We should get an answer
in a few minutes."

"Right." John turned his chair back to the console, and
keyed on the comm channel. He said, "Trishen? We're
going to help you."

There was a little negotiation first.

According to Trishen, her ship and the little shuttle's
shielding had been specifically adjusted to deal with the
Mirror's discharges. Both had been specially designed
research vessels, developed after the other Eidolon ships
had suffered near misses similar to the one that had
almost taken out the jumper. She asked if they wanted
to move the jumper into the installation's inner ring, next
to her base ship. "That would be a big no," John told her.
Rodney was making emphatic boom gestures and mouthing the words "quantum instability." John added, "The
instability interferes too much with our ship's systems.
We need it to stay on this side of the installation." The reason he didn't give her was that while he didn't think she
was lying to them, he didn't see any reason to be stupid
about this, either. "Do you know if there's a direct passage
from the outside through to the Mirror?"

"Yes, it's on the far side of the structure. I found it when I was looking for anything I could scavenge for my repairs. It's a large doorway, perhaps meant to accommodate ground vehicles. There's a fairly direct passage through it to the Mirror platform, though that section of the installation seems more damaged, and isn't holding pressure." She hesitated, then offered, "If you would like to follow me in your ship, I can go back in that direction and show it to you."

"That would be fine," John told her.

He cut the comm channel, and Teyla frowned worriedly, saying, "I think she has realized we are somewhat distrustful."

Rodney leaned forward, watching as the conch shell-shaped shuttle lifted off in a cloud of swirling dust. "Yes, well, she should have picked up on that when our first reaction to seeing an alien spacecraft was to fling ourselves down a twenty-foot drop."

"You notice she didn't offer to give us a ride over there." John took the jumper out of standby, lifting it up to a low hover. "Not that we would have accepted, but we're both being careful here. That's not a bad thing." The HUD didn't read any signs of weapons powering up, but since it couldn't read life signs inside the other ship either, he had no idea how accurate it was. Trishen's shuttle moved slowly away, following the curve of the installation, and John guided the jumper after it.

"You think if she had...designs on us she would try harder to appear more trusting?" Radek asked, craning his neck to watch. The purple-shaded stern of the shuttle was centered in the viewport, the indigo wall of the installation looming over them both. "Haven't we said we would go to her ship anyway?"

"We're not all going," John told him. "Teyla, Rodney, and I will check it out first." The others were all looking at him, and he shrugged one shoulder. "I'd just rather not put all our eggs in one basket."

"Yes, that's a very comforting analogy, Colonel," Rodney said, preoccupied. "There's the door. She's right, it's probably a cargo entrance."

The shuttle slowed to a hover in front of a big square hatch, set deeper into the side of the building and at least three or four times the size of the other entrance. The sand drifts were higher on this side, washing up to the door's threshold, so it was impossible to tell if there was a road or ramp leading up to it. John clicked on the comm channel again to say, "We've got it. We'll see you on the other side."

There was a brief acknowledgement from Trishen, then the shuttle lifted up, vanishing over the top of the building.

While Rodney was busy downloading diagnostic programs and data he thought he might need from the jumper's systems, and Zelenka and Teyla were recharging the air tanks, John took Miko aside. Or as aside as he could get in a rear cabin only slightly larger than a Winnebago. He said, "Look, I don't want to scare you, but..." It was hard to say this when she was looking up at him with big worried eyes, magnified even more by her glasses. "If worse comes to worst, not that I think it will, but—"

Miko blinked. "You want to know if I can fly the jumper back to the base moon if I had to."

"Uh, yeah."

She pushed her glasses up, considering the question with a grave expression. "I think so. The navigation is relatively simple, and the guidance system assists with re-entry. With Dr. Zelenka's extensive knowledge of all the systems, I don't think I would have any trouble." She winced. "As long as nothing is shooting at me."

"Right." John folded his arms, chewing his lower lip. Her training had included the basics of how to avoid an incoming hiveship. Which wouldn't do her much good against an alien ship of unknown capabilities that had demonstrated an ability to see through the cloak. "Just fly really fast."

Miko went to help with the air tanks, and Ronon took her place, looking down at John with a stony expression. He said, "Why aren't you taking me?"

"Because Teyla is good at first contact. Your idea of first contact is stunning people unconscious and tying them up," John told him. He was long over any pique caused by their initial encounter with Ronon, but he wanted to make his point. "And I need you here to protect Radek and Miko. And no matter what happens, you stay with them, and you do what they say." He added with emphasis, "That's an order."

Ronon flicked a look toward the front of the jumper. Rodney was in the cockpit, disconnecting his laptop from the jumper's systems, practically bouncing with nervous excitement. Miko and Teyla crouched on the floor, getting the tanks reattached to the field packs, and Zelenka was earnestly explaining something to Teyla about the interfaces. Ronon turned back to John, and actually looked sheepish for an instant, as if he had forgotten there were other considerations besides whether John trusted him to go fight aliens or not. "I won't leave them."

John held his gaze, and believed him. "Good."

As they were ready to leave, the jumper received a reply from base camp, which had relayed their transmission through the 'gate to Atlantis. It was just an acknowledgement that the report had been received and a brief formal message from Elizabeth which translated to "Be careful and don't get killed."

The others went into the cockpit and sealed the cabin door, and John, Rodney, and Teyla got their breathing sets attached and switched on. John opened the ramp to a view of the empty plain stretching out to the mountains, the gas giant hanging heavily above them. The light was a little dimmer since the moon had entered its night phase, though like the night on the base moon, it would never get much darker than this. This moon's eclipse was still a couple of hours off. John's ears popped as the rear cabin's air flowed out, and he said, "There's got to be an easier way to do this."

"Ask Zelenka," Rodney grumbled, adjusting his pack and squinting against the dust as they started down the ramp. "I've been telling him to work on converting the cloak to a shield, to make a temporary barrier to hold in the air while the rear cabin hatch is open, but he's baffled by the elementary principles of—"

"I can hear you, Rodney," Zelenka said in their headsets.

"I know you can hear me, otherwise why bother?" Rodney demanded.

John interrupted with, "We're clear. Lock it up tight and don't open the door to strangers. And I want radio silence until I tell you otherwise."

"Yes, Colonel," Zelenka replied. "Take care."

John waited until the ramp sealed and the jumper vanished under its cloak, then led the way to the installation.

The heavy metal door was set into a deep recess, the sill covered with drifts of the red sand, the whole more than big enough to fly something the size of the jumper through. With his pocket flashlight, Rodney found the wall console buried in the side of the recess. He said, "Ready? Here we go," hit the console, and backed hurriedly out of the way.

John and Teyla covered the door as it groaned and the metal split diagonally into two triangles, one section sliding down and the other up. It revealed a cavernous passage, poorly lit, leading deep into the structure. It looked damaged, with broken lights and shattered stone and metal debris scattered on the dusty floor. If there had been any kind of airlock arrangement, it was long gone. "Okay." John lowered the P-90 a little and stepped inside. "I say we leave this door open."

"I'm reading one life sign," Rodney reported, "On the other side of the structure. She must be waiting for us at the far end of this corridor."

They started down the passage. It ran straight for a little distance, then took an angle to the left, then back, but Trishen was right, it was obviously heading through to the inner side of the building and the Mirror platform. There were blocky pillars along the walls, but only a few of the white lights set into them were lit, and there was a constant whistle of escaping air. "Looks like the Wraith came through here," John said, shining his light up into some twisted metal girders. Smaller passages led off into other parts of the building, some open and dark, others closed off by blast doors.

"Or the Mirror itself," Rodney said, eyeing the damage thoughtfully. "A severe discharge could have caused those impacts that look like energy weapon scars."

Teyla frowned. "I just realized. Trishen did not mention the Wraith." She threw a pensive look at John. "Perhaps there are none in her reality."

John shrugged a little dubiously. "Maybe. You'd think she would have asked about it otherwise." If John was trapped in another reality, he thought that would have been pretty high on his list of questions.

"We may be looking at the best possible scenario, that the Ancients were able to discover a reality with an uninhabited Pegasus," Rodney reminded them, sounding testy. "I did say that was a possibility."

"Yeah, but then why aren't they still there?" John felt compelled to point out. "She said we were descended from a common ancestor that had left freaky advanced technology scattered everywhere. That sounds just like here."

"Not being psychic, I won't know until I ask her," Rodney retorted. "The Ancients could have been wiped out by the same plague that hit the Milky Way. Or only a small group may have managed to go through the Mirror in the first place." He waved the life signs detector. "Obviously, they planned this installation to accommodate a massive evacuation, but if they were cut off by the Wraith advance, only the people working here and anyone left on the base moon may have managed to make it through."

"To succeed, only to die anyway," Teyla said quietly. "It is a bleak fate."

Rodney tapped the detector against his hand, his eyes on the intriguing gaps in the wall where machinery had been attached. "True, but they did manage to seed the human race in the new reality. That was obviously very important to them, considering how often they spread their genetic wealth around." He checked the life signs detector again, and his voice betrayed a little nervousness. "We're nearly there."

"Yes, there is light ahead," Teyla added, her eyes on the end of the corridor.

Ahead, as the passage angled again, John saw dim natural light, and a moment later he could see the large square doorway opening out into the Mirror platform. Trishen, still in her EVA suit, stood just inside it. Behind her John could see the stone platform stretching out to the big silvery wall of the Mirror's frame. "She's holding something," he said, low-voiced. She had a round dark object in her arms.

"We're holding things," Rodney said, tense and impatient.

"Yes, and a lot of the things we're holding are guns," John told him, exasperated.

"It does not look like a weapon," Teyla pointed out softly. Then she admitted, "Unless it is an explosive of some kind. But that seems unlikely."

John thought it was unlikely too, unless Trishen was a suicide bomber, but it still made him uneasy. He signaled the others to halt about ten long paces from her. Even at this distance, her helmet didn't reveal much. The faceplate wasn't as reflective here in the dimmer light, and he could almost see the outline of her forehead and eyes, though the lower part was still opaque. The thing she was holding looked like a black metal soccer ball, except the bottom seemed to be flattened slightly. He lifted a hand in greeting, and said, amiably, "Hi. What you got there?"

Trishen juggled the thing a little, caught between returning the greeting and answering the question. "It's a data display device. I thought I could show you some of the readings from the anomalies that occurred when I tried to send the probe through." She sat down awkwardly, placing the thing on the dusty metal floor. She made a vague gesture. "We can go out onto the platform for a closer look at the Mirror if you like, but if we're out here for any length of time we should stay inside the structure, for the shielding." She touched the device and something slid open in the top. Suddenly a glittering haze of color burst out of it.

John and Teyla both flinched backward, jerking up their weapons. Then John saw it was actually a holographic display, showing the three-dimensional figures that were the Ancient equivalents of charts and graphs. Teyla threw him an abashed look; John didn't exactly feel like an expert intergalactic explorer at the moment either. Trishen was staring up at them, startled at their recoil. She said hurriedly, "It is only a three-dimensional display—"

Rodney stepped forward, giving John and Teyla an exasperated look. "Yes, they have actually seen a hologram before, they're just—Never mind. I'm Dr. Rodney McKay, she's Teyla Emmagan, he's Colonel Sheppard." He eased forward, staring intently at the glittering column and digging a camera out of his vest. "You use the Ancient system for numbers and symbols?"

"Yes." Trishen looked uncertainly from John and Teyla

to Rodney, then evidently decided to talk to the rational person. "For this type of data, it's the best method. You use them as well?"

"To a certain extent." Rodney moved closer, crouching to get a better look. "This is just a recording device." He showed her the camera, then nodded toward the figures suspended in the display. "This one is the progression of energy signatures? That was directly after you deployed the probe? Can you bring up the sequence that you took when your ship was drawn through the Mirror? You did record that, right?"

"Oh, oh, yes, this is my initial reading." Sounding relieved, Trishen leaned forward, placing her gloved hands on the surface of the device. John motioned for Teyla to stay in position where she could cover them and moved up beside Rodney. Trishen was manipulating the device in some way John couldn't quite see, and more figures blossomed in the display. She said, "And as you can see the variation with the singularity's later signatures is pronounced."

"Yes, the instability is starting to grow and extend across the lower right quadrant," Rodney muttered, shifting a little closer. He set the camera aside to get his tablet out, and rapidly brought up a series of files. "What were your figures for the accretion surface?"

After that it got a little over John's head. Rodney and Trishen talked numbers and quantum singularities in perfect accord long enough that John signaled Teyla to relax. She lowered the P-90 and came to stand next to him.

Then Rodney said, "Hold it, hold it, I need to check something." He sat back, keying his radio. "Zelenka. Zelenka. Radek, answer the damn—" He looked up at

John in sudden anxiety. "Why aren't they answering?"

John lifted a brow. "What does radio silence mean, Rodney?"

Rodney glared. "Oh, for the—Tell him he can talk, then!"

John said, "Go ahead, Dr. Zelenka." He had had his radio open the entire time so the others could listen in.

"I am here, Rodney," Zelenka said in their headsets, sounding perfectly composed. "You need to reference the data the jumper managed to gather before the disruption?"

Rodney pushed to his feet with a grimace and walked away a few paces, presumably to berate Zelenka in relative privacy.

Trishen looked from John to Teyla, as if not quite sure which one of them to talk to, and asked uncertainly, "Do you live in this system, or did you come here to research the Mirror, as we did in my reality? I didn't think there was anyone else on this moon. I listened for communications traffic and flew around the circumference in my shuttle, but I saw nothing except these ruins."

Teyla answered, "No, we live far away. We only discovered this place a short time ago." She hesitated, flicking a look at John as she gauged how much to say. "We have explored many ruins of the Ancestors, but we have never before found a device such as this Mirror."

John thought this was a good time to ask, "You didn't send any distress calls or anything like that, did you? Because there's some things out here whose attention you really don't want to attract."

Trishen made a little gesture, turning her palms up. "No. My ship has an automatic beacon, but I turned it off.

I admit, I was afraid." She did something on the device that caused the hologram display to freeze, and twisted around to face them. "We had long speculated that the Creators came to our galaxy fleeing a terrible force."

John looked away, out toward the platform and the looming frame of the Mirror. He hated giving the bad news. "It's true. The Ancients were wiped out in this galaxy."

Teyla added, "The enemy you speak of is called the Wraith. They use humans for food, and have destroyed many worlds." She tilted her head, watching Trishen carefully. "There are no Wraith in your reality?"

"Food," Trishen repeated nervously. She laughed a little weakly. "I was hoping that part wasn't true." She looked up. "No, my people have never been attacked by anything." She hesitated again, then added tentatively, "I have never seen people like you before."

John exchanged a baffled look with Teyla. *The hell?* He said, "Uh, okay."

Teyla began, "I am not certain I understand what—"

"That's it," Rodney interrupted, cutting off his radio with a sharp gesture. "Our data confirms it. The problem is definitely with the accretion disk itself; it's size is causing the singularity to react to any energy fluctuation with these instabilities. The Ancients must have had some sort of tuning process to get it to work in the first place." He turned to Trishen. "I need to see the whole range of data before the Mirror activated and pulled your ship in, everything your research group collected. Do you have that with you?"

Trishen nodded anxiously. "Yes, but this device doesn't have enough storage space to contain it. Can you come to my ship to view it on the system there?"

"Of course, I—" Rodney stopped, flustered, obviously recalling their situation. He looked at John, brows lifted. "Ah, can we do that?"

John had been thinking about their next step, and had been ready to say yes. It was what they had agreed to do, and he wanted a look at the inside of that ship as bad as Rodney did. But that last comment of Trishen's had thrown him a little and he couldn't exactly pinpoint why. "People like you" coming from somebody from another planet, let alone another reality, could mean anything, from his and Teyla's relative heights to their skin or hair color to their obvious hair-trigger wariness. Or the way she had heard them bitching at each other over the comm system. Whatever it was, though, she seemed okay with it. He said, "Yeah, we can do that."

Trishen gathered her equipment hurriedly, and she and Rodney stopped in the big doorway out onto the platform, both taking readings. "If the Mirror discharges while we're out on the platform, the concussion wave would slam us into the walls with possibly lethal force," Rodney explained, studying the detector intently.

"Great." John was looking at the ship, sitting on the platform about a hundred yards away. The oddly organic shading of blue and purple on the hull didn't fade into the darker stone of the installation as much from this angle, so it was easy to see the round shape of the hatch and a small ramp leading up to it at the base. The conch-shell shuttle seemed to fit neatly into the top of the tulip, not easy to recognize as a separate craft unless you knew to look for it.

Rodney admitted that the readings suggested that for

the moment the Mirror was not inclined to kill them, and they started across the platform toward the ship. They were moving quickly, Rodney and Trishen a few steps ahead. Trishen said, "I'm beginning to wonder if my ship's energy signature itself is causing the increase in the Mirror's instabilities. If it's affecting the accretion disk, even from a distance—"

Rodney launched into a theory of his own, and Teyla took the opportunity to say, low-voiced, to John, "She said 'people like us.' What could she mean?"

"I don't know. Unless she's got fur or scales or something under that suit." Teyla looked up sharply, her brow furrowed in worry, and John said, "That was supposed to be a joke."

"She said we shared the Creators as a common ancestor. She must be very close to human." Teyla shook her head helplessly. "She sounds entirely human. And I think she is harmless to us."

"Yeah, probably," John found himself reluctant to admit it. They had just gotten burned too many times in the past. "But we don't know what the rest of her people are like."

"I should ask more questions," Trishen was saying. "When I return, our historians will be very angry with me if I have no answers for them." She made a vague gesture back toward John and Teyla. "I don't even understand how your hierarchy is organized."

Rodney began, "Yes, of course. I'm head of the expedition's science team, and our—" John cleared his throat pointedly. It was mission policy not to go into detail about their organizational structure on short acquaintance, and he wasn't ready to relax the restriction on that yet.

Rodney threw John a glare, not happy to be reminded, and finished, "But if you could tell me more about the collection method you used for your energy readings—"

As they reached the ship, Zelenka's voice in John's headset said, "Colonel, I'm hoping it is still okay to talk, but your transmissions are breaking up very badly. If you remain close to the Mirror, we will not be able to hear you."

John said, "Copy that," and clicked an acknowledgement.

Trishen touched a control on the black data device, and the round hatch started to rotate, spiraling open instead of sliding up in one piece. John caught Rodney's eye, telling him with a slight jerk of his head to hang back. Rodney huffed impatiently but fell back a little, obviously torn between eagerness to see the inside of the ship and the paranoid caution they had all had beaten into them by life in the Pegasus Galaxy.

The open hatch revealed what a seemed to be a standard airlock, except the walls were dark-colored, almost matte black. Following Trishen's lead, John stepped in, seeing it was big enough for all of them without crowding, which was a relief. He signaled Rodney and Teyla to come in, noticing the controls were recessed into the wall surface, barely visible.

The outer hatch shut and the lock cycled quickly, and John's ears popped again. Rodney was bouncing with impatience. As the inner hatch dilated open and Trishen moved inside, John took hold of the handy strap on the back of Rodney's tac vest, making certain he remembered to let John go first.

The interior was poorly lit, the light purple-tinted, and

if John hadn't been already used to the relative dimness outside he would have been temporarily blind. The funny smell struck him next, even filtered as it was through the SCBA's breathing mask. It was peaty and rich, like walking into the organic fertilizer storage bay in the Botany lab. Not unpleasant, just different and not what he had been expecting. As Rodney and Teyla stepped in behind him, John looked around, squinting, still wary, seeing that the walls were a dark purplish rubbery substance. Teyla was looking around too, frowning uncertainly. There was a scatter of weird-looking tools and equipment near a wall cubbie, as if someone had been making a repair. Trishen was fussing with her suit, gesturing around a little anxiously with the air of someone hoping her guests would excuse the mess. She said, "The atmosphere in here should be breathable for you, since we can both tolerate the air inside the pressurized portion of the installation. I've been lucky that none of my environmental systems were damaged." She laughed a little nervously. "Though I didn't know what I would do if I was trapped here long enough to run out of provisions."

Deeply preoccupied, Rodney said, "We have plenty of food in the jumper." He was standing near the center of the space and looking upward. John stepped up beside him and saw a shaft that ran straight up through the ship, with arching struts and supports that gave it the look of a gothic cathedral. Turning back to Trishen, Rodney continued, "And if we're compatible enough to tolerate the same oxygen mix, then we should be able to—" Rodney's voice climbed an octave and the sentence ended on a gasp.

That made John whip around, jerking the P-90 up,

made Teyla turn automatically and lift her weapon.

Trishen was taking off her helmet, silver hair spilling out in a long braid as the back plate opened. Teyla gasped with astonishment and horror, and John saw what Rodney had seen, the dead-white paleness of Trishen's skin, glowing even in this bad light. He whispered incredulously, "Son of a bitch." In the next instant she had lifted off the helmet and he saw her face clearly, the gill-like slits to either side of her nose, the glimpse of malformed teeth past her pale lips. John snapped, "Don't move," and stepped in front of Rodney, backing them both up until he was even with Teyla, Rodney behind them.

Trishen stared blankly at the guns pointed at her. There was surprise in the yellow slit-pupilled eyes, and that just pissed John off all the more. She said, "I don't understand." Her voice was hushed, but without the distortion of the helmet's comm unit, it was obviously a Wraith's voice.

Behind John, Rodney choked out, "This can't—This can't—" He burst out, "Tell me we're not this stupid!"

"We are this stupid," John said through gritted teeth. "Look, Trish, sorry we can't stay, but unlock the hatch or I'll blow your damn head off." He didn't know why he hadn't already killed her. He told himself it was a bad idea to fire enough rounds to kill a Wraith in the small confines of this cabin. But he knew it was because she was small and female and unarmed, and staring at him with this look of fear and betrayal, and he just couldn't make himself pull the trigger.

Trishen whispered, "It isn't locked. Just touch the control pad beside it." She stood frozen, still holding the helmet. "I don't understand—"

John didn't want to hear it. He said, tightly, "Rodney."

Rodney unfroze and ducked back to the hatch, and a moment later John heard the airlock start to cycle. He felt the tightness in his chest ease a little; he had been certain she had done something to seal them in here. Now all they had to worry about was more Wraith dropping out of that shaft leading into the upper levels of the ship.

Sounding sick, Teyla said, "Colonel, this is not possible."

"I wish, Teyla, but it really is." Teyla should have been able to tell Trishen was a Wraith, and the fact that she hadn't was just one more kick in the ass. John heard the hatch open behind them and Teyla pivoted to cover it. "Rodney, can you fix it so she can't trap us in there?"

"On it," Rodney muttered, and John heard thumps and a weird tearing noise.

Trishen shook her head a little, still pretending incomprehension. "I wouldn't do that. Why would I—"

"Sorry, but you're just going to have to do without these provisions," John said with acid emphasis.

"Got it," Rodney said, his voice tight. "I can only override the outer door's safety for a few seconds, so hurry. On my mark...Go!"

John felt the rush of air pouring out as the outer hatch spiraled open. Still covering Trishen, he took two long steps back as Teyla and Rodney ducked out, then turned at the last second and leapt through the closing hatch.

Out on the Mirror platform, under the dim light of the gas giant, John backed rapidly away from the ship. He and Teyla kept their weapons aimed, but nothing lunged out after them. Breathing hard, Rodney flung up a hand in frustration, saying, "That ship, that was hybrid Wraith-

Ancient technology, I should have seen it!" There was rage and disappointment in his voice, both of which John got completely. Their cool alien contact had turned into just a frigging Wraith trap. Though at the moment John was still in the rage end of the spectrum. "That textured wall material is an organic, the same thing they use on the interiors of the hiveships and cruisers! I can't believe—hybrid Wraith and Ancient tech!" Rodney finished miserably, "We could be very, very dead, and by we I mean all of humanity."

"It's got to be new," John said. Past the adrenaline rush of rage, he was starting to realize just how bad this was. This ship could see through the jumper's cloak. *Rodney's right, we are so screwed.* As they moved further away from the ship, John tapped his radio. "Zelenka, can you read me?"

The answer came readily, though so thick with static John could barely understand him. "Yes, yes, Colonel, what is wrong?"

"It was a trap, she's a goddamn Wraith," John told him. "Move the jumper, now, just get it out of there. Send a message to base camp when you can. I'll contact you when we're clear."

Zelenka sounded flabbergasted. "Yes, we'll move it. But—But how can this be?"

"When you figure it out, let us know!" Rodney snapped.

"But I did not sense Wraith, even when I was looking right at her," Teyla protested, almost anguished. "How is that possible?"

John shook his head. Teyla should have known Trishen was a Wraith the first time the shuttle appeared. *Oh yeah, screwed.* "She has to have something that blocks your Wraith-sensing thing, like the shielding on her ship."

"Hello, that doesn't make sense!" Rodney protested.

John wasn't in the mood for an argument about semantics. "Whatever, Rodney, you know what I mean!"

Rodney began, "But—" Then a tremor traveled through the pavement under their feet and John heard a low rumble, like distant thunder. Rodney snarled in frustration, "Oh fine, now the Mirror's discharging!"

"Run," John ordered and they bolted. They made it through the cargo door before the tremor started to escalate, but the open corridor didn't provide any protection.

Over the growing rumble, Rodney yelled, "Keep going, find the nearest side corridor!"

John had noted the last branching passage that wasn't sealed off. He found it just past the first angle in the main corridor, an empty doorway with a shattered blast door, leading into darkness. John flicked on the P-90's light to see it was filled with broken crystal and stone debris. They could get trapped down here if the end was blocked, but from Rodney's increasingly urgent gestures, there wasn't time for another choice. They managed to get about twenty yards down it when the rumble turned into a dull roar and the floor shook hard enough to knock Teyla off her feet. Rodney caught her, and John caught him, and they dropped into a huddle against the base of the wall. The shaking intensified, sending dust and chips of loosened stone down on their heads. John pushed them both down and huddled over them, covering his head with his arm, hoping the whole building didn't come down on top of them.

But the shaking died away, the sound fading into

silence, except for the pounding echo in John's head. He pushed himself up off Rodney and Teyla, pulling the P-90 up to flash the light across the ceiling. There was a network of cracks, still leaking a fine haze of debris, but no sign of imminent collapse. "You guys okay?" he asked. The breath mask had mostly kept the dust out of his mouth and nose, but his eyes burned with it, and the violent shaking made him feel like he had been pummeled by something.

Rodney sat up and sneezed, shifting his mask awkwardly. "You kneed me in the back and Teyla's P-90 hit me in the eye," he reported, "But other than that—"

"We are fine," Teyla finished, wincing as she held a hand to her head. "I—"

She took a sharp breath, and John looked at her worriedly. "What is it?" He didn't think any of the dislodged stone had been big enough to cause a serious injury, but—

She rolled her eyes and said wearily, "Now I sense Wraith."

Rodney swore. "Well, better late than never."

John nodded grimly. Whatever Trishen had that could block Teyla's ability must be shut down now. And that was weird, that she had even given herself a name; none of the Wraith they had run into that had condescended to speak to their cattle had ever done that. He tried his radio. "Zelenka, do you copy?" No answer but static.

"That last discharge is still disrupting the atmosphere," Rodney said, wiping dust off his forehead. "We're not going to be able to reach them for a while."

More good news. John grimaced. "Come on, we need to get out of here."

They all climbed to their feet, wincing, and Rodney said, "Yes, having failed to die in the moonquake caused by the Mirror's periodic bursts of quantum instability, we can now get back to running from the Wraith."

"I do not understand why a female Wraith would come here alone," Teyla said, sounding bitter. She checked her P-90, adjusting the tangled strap. "We have always believed they were few, and never left the hiveships."

"We couldn't read life signs inside her ship," John reminded her, starting back down the passage. "She could have had a dozen males and drones in there waiting for her to walk in with dinner."

Rodney gestured in annoyance. "None of this makes sense. That ship, this elaborate story she told us. She couldn't have faked that data—She came through the Mirror." Rodney froze for an instant. "Oh, no. She came through the Mirror. She said we had a common ancestor—"

Startled, Teyla added, "She told us she had never seen people like us—"

"She meant people who were this easy to catch," John said sourly.

CHAPTER FIVE

Carson Beckett folded his arms, looking over Dr. Chandar's shoulder at the monitor. "I don't suppose you can tell what's happening up there from that thing." He was down in the Ancient monitoring room, watching the tech team work. The underground ruin wasn't exactly a pleasant place to be, with air that was stale and too warm, and inadequate light from the battery lamps, and he really should have returned to Atlantis by now. But he was anxious for word of Rodney and Sheppard and the others, and of the woman they had contacted, and at least here he could get the news first hand. The other teams still on the base moon were continuing their research for the moment, though the general feeling was that the sole purpose for this city's existence was as a support center for the Mirror installation on the other moon.

Dr. Chandar, taking the question in a far less irritable manner than Rodney would have, sat back with a preoccupied frown. "Not exactly, no, but now that we know that this device is monitoring a Quantum Mirror, it's possible to interpret its readings more accurately."

Carson frowned at the innocuous device. In the past day, it had begun to flash much more frequently, and he was finding it worrisome. "So just how unstable is the Mirror?" From Sheppard's last report, they knew the people in the other reality hadn't meant to use the damn thing, that their efforts to study it had probably caused the Mirror in this reality to activate. It all sounded very dangerous and uncertain.

Chandar shook his head, his expression worried. "There is some odd variance in the readings. It's almost as if the Mirror's singularity is becoming increasingly unstable—"

Carson flinched at a burst of static from his headset, the military channel suddenly alive with chatter. Major Lorne's tense voice overrode the others with, "All personnel, all personnel, we are evacuating immediately. We have incoming Wraith darts on sensors." He added sharply, "Move it, people, now!"

"Bloody hell," Carson gasped.

Chandar looked up, wide-eyed. "But—This system is uninhabited, the Wraith shouldn't have any interest in—"

"It's the Mirror, lad, they're after it." It was just as Rodney had said in the first transmission. The reactivated Mirror's bursts of energy must have drawn the attention of a hiveship, and the Wraith had come to investigate. Carson pulled Chandar out of his chair and shut the laptop. The techs were already scrambling to gather their equipment, moving with sternly controlled terror. "Now get your things and move!"

Just as they finished breaking down the temporary lab, two Marines arrived to lead them to the jumpers. Burdened with a couple of bulky equipment cases, Carson followed the Marines through the narrow streets with Chandar and the others, fighting the urge to hunch his shoulders and duck. They were all sweating even in the cool air and one of the older techs, O'Keefe, was getting a bit red-faced with exertion and stress. Carson had been walking these streets for the past few days, and they had never seemed so claustrophobic and confining. He uneasily remembered his recent near miss, when Laura Cadman had pushed him out of the path of a culling beam, and she and Rodney had been caught in it. That had all turned out badly enough, though in the end they had both survived. He didn't think they would be that lucky again.

He heard the tense acknowledgements on the headset as Lorne ordered Jumper Three, already loaded, to leave. Carson didn't see it pass overhead, but he heard the 'gate activate. One of the techs recently arrived on the *Daedalus* said nervously, "They won't leave us, will they?"

Audley, one of the Marines, flicked a disgusted look back at him, obviously not appreciating this sentiment. Carson didn't particularly appreciate it either, knowing just how far the military contingent was willing to go to protect the science team. O'Keefe, another Atlantis veteran, answered the man, gasping derisively, "Bloody unlikely."

"They might dock Major Lorne's pay," Audley said, with acid sarcasm.

The other Marine, Ramirez, just grinned and added, "Yeah, after the Colonel shot him."

More Marines met them at the last turn, hurrying them out onto the plaza. Corrigan and Rousseau from the archeology team were still outside, tossing a last few cases into the already-cloaked jumper. As Carson's group started across the pavement, he heard the distinctive whine of a dart. Marines shouted, "Move it, move it!" and they dashed for the jumper.

Everyone tumbled up the ramp, stumbling over

the loose equipment, pushing forward to make room. Sergeant Benson shouted, "That's everybody, Major!" and the ramp started to lift upward. Carson sat down hard on the bench and Rousseau fell into his lap. She said breathlessly, "*Pardon,* Carson."

"Quite all right, love." He helped her stand, then stepped over a couple of people to reach the cockpit.

Lorne was in the pilot's seat, studying the HUD with a worried frown. "Major," Carson said, watching him anxiously. "What about Sheppard's team? Can you get a message to them?"

Lorne glanced back at him. "I already tried. We'd just picked up a transmission packet from them when the darts showed up on longrange. I sent them a warning, but I don't know if they got it." He jerked his chin up at the HUD. "We've got lots of company here."

Carson focused on the HUD. It was the life signs screen, and there were lights appearing on it, all around their position. Wraith, beaming down from the darts. "Good lord," he muttered. "They must suspect we're here." He hesitated, a cold sensation growing in his stomach. "You don't think they found the others..."

"I hope not, Doc," Lorne said, but his expression was grim. More life signs appeared on the screen, close to the jumper, and Lorne swore. He looked back at the rear cabin, at the scientists and techs under his charge, and grimaced. "Dammit. I hate to do this, but we can't hang around."

The jumper lifted smoothly off the pavement, heading for the Stargate.

"So this whole thing was a Wraith trap?" Colonel

Caldwell said, his voice coming in over Atlantis' comm system, a little too loud in Elizabeth's currently crowded office.

Elizabeth sat at her desk, still studying her copy of the last transmission from John's team. In the puddlejumper bay above the gateroom, the teams from the moon base camp were still unloading their equipment. As soon as Major Lorne had brought her the transmission, she had called Caldwell, wanting to get the *Daedalus* on its way as quickly as possible. The ship had only arrived this morning, and hadn't finished offloading the supplies it had brought yet. Lorne and Carson Beckett were sitting across from her, and Chuck, Laroque, and several other members of the operations staff were clustered in the doorway. She really should have sent everyone back to work, but she knew they were as anxious as she was.

"I don't know, Colonel," she answered Caldwell. From what Zelenka had said in the last transmission, John and the others had assumed the contact from the Wraith calling itself "Trishen" was a trap. But that didn't feel right, somehow. "The Mirror itself is genuine, obviously. And making them believe they were being contacted by an alien ship... That seems a bit imaginative for the Wraith. We've never seen them do anything quite so elaborate."

"Unless they suspected your team was from Atlantis, and wanted to try to get some information out of them," Caldwell said.

"That's a possibility," she admitted. As far as they knew, the Wraith still believed Atlantis had been destroyed, but they would certainly still be looking for survivors who had escaped with Ancient technology. "This makes it all the more imperative that the *Daedalus* reach the system as soon as possible."

"No need to convince me, Doctor, I understand that you have personnel in danger. And we can't allow the Wraith to get their hands on that Mirror, not to mention sensor technology that can see through the Ancient cloak. I'll be breaking orbit immediately." Caldwell sounded somewhat sourly resigned, and Elizabeth winced in equal parts chagrin and annoyance.

She hadn't meant to imply that she thought Caldwell would resist the idea of a rescue mission, or that he wouldn't understand the implications of what the team had found. But their working relationship had gotten off to a rocky start when she had had to squash his attempt to replace John, and things hadn't exactly been going smoothly since. She felt it would work out eventually; she and John had had clashes and arguments at first, too. But then John, for all his quirks, was far less prickly than Caldwell and had always been much easier to get along with. And at this point the original expedition members had all been through too much together to let disagreements get in the way of friendship.

Frustrated, Elizabeth frowned at her laptop screen and didn't apologize to Caldwell. She wondered if he understood that some of her closest friends were on that lost jumper. She just said, "Thank you, Colonel."

Major Lorne sat forward, his expression urgent, and Carson waved frantically at her. She added, "I believe Major Lorne and Dr. Beckett would like to accompany you."

Caldwell sounded slightly more resigned. "Then tell them to get ready to be beamed up."

He signed off, and there were murmurs of relief from

the people waiting outside. Major Lorne pushed to his feet, looking relieved. "Thanks, Dr. Weir. We'll bring them back."

Elizabeth nodded firmly. "I know you will, Major." And she thought privately, *I hope you will*. She kept the worry off her face, but she had the bad feeling that this was going to be more complicated than just a Wraith trap.

CHAPTER SIX

Ronon hated waiting. He could stand the stillness and silence required for hunting and stalking, but this was different.

Pacing the rear cabin was the only outlet for his frustration. Sheppard had ordered them to move, and Kusanagi had been trying to take the puddlejumper toward the hills to the south, but the Mirror's last abrupt discharge had forced them down in the grassy plain not far from their original position. Now Ronon couldn't even help Kusanagi and Zelenka by volunteering to stare at a screen; the interference had turned all the sensors to glittering multi-colored static. They had sent the transmission to the camp on the other moon, but now the comm wasn't working either, and they had no idea if there had been a reply.

And the whole thing had been a trick, a Wraith trap. He should have seen past it, even if the others hadn't. That was the whole reason he was here. But he had never heard a Wraith speak like that before. Speak to people as if they were equals, not just prey. The voice on the comm had sounded as much like a human woman as Teyla or Kusanagi, and he had been deceived by it as easily as the less wary Atlanteans.

"Still nothing. I can't get through this interference." In the jump seat, Zelenka typed on one of the little portable computers, glancing worriedly at the hazy cloud hovering in the air where the HUD was normally displayed.

"Surely they weren't hurt. They were moving away from the Mirror or they would not have been able to get that last transmission through."

In the pilot's chair, Kusanagi tapped the control board impatiently. The holographic display just responded with more fuzzy bursts. She said, "I don't understand how Trishen could be a Wraith. The data that Dr. McKay described—"

"Yes, I don't see how Wraith could fake those readings, not well enough to fool Rodney," Zelenka said. They shared an uneasy look. "Perhaps Wraith from some other reality have come through the Quantum Mirror."

Ronon felt his jaw tighten. "That's all we need."

"Perhaps they'll fight with the Wraith here and kill each other." Zelenka saw the expression on Ronon's face and shrugged philosophically. "Well, we can hope. Wait, wait—" Looking back to his small screen, he waved a hand excitedly. "I'm receiving sensor data—" He touched his headset. "Colonel Sheppard, are you there? Can you hear me, anyone? Rodney, Teyla?"

Kusanagi's hands moved competently over the board. Her face intent, she said, "The HUD is coming back online. The life signs detector should show us—" But when the HUD screen popped up, she gasped. "Dr. Zelenka—"

Zelenka flung his arms up in frustration. "I can't get through to the others! *Do prdele!* There is still too much interference!" He turned his chair, looking at the HUD, then froze. "Oh, no."

Ronon stepped forward, leaning on the back of Kusanagi's chair. He couldn't read the language scrolling along the sides and bottom of the image, but he knew that glowing dot in the center was a ship. "Wraith." He felt his lip curl into a silent snarl. This was just getting worse. "A hiveship?"

Zelenka shook his head, going pale as he studied the screen. He said faintly, "Too small. It's a scout ship, already in orbit. The interference from the Mirror must have concealed its approach." He touched his radio headset again, his voice tight with urgency. "Perhaps they did not detect—"Another screen popped up in the HUD, displacing the longrange sensors, flashing with urgency.

Ronon knew this one, too. It was the jumper's life signs detector, blinking dots superimposed over a grid. It was picking up three signs close together, moving through the lower level of the giant building behind them. And five more signs moving toward those. Ronon's hands tightened into fists. "They're heading right for them."

John led the way back down the passage, glancing warily at the ceiling, checking for signs of imminent collapse. The dust was a thick haze in the air, glittering in their lights.

His voice tight, Rodney whispered suddenly, "Wait, wait, I'm getting life signs." John looked back to see him studying the detector, his face set in a grim expression. "Five, out in the main corridor. We were right, she must have had company."

John fell back a step to look at the detector's screen. It was still fuzzy from the Mirror's interference, but he could see the five signs were moving fast down the corridor from the direction of the Mirror platform, blocking the clear path to the outside. "Crap. Come on." He turned back the other way, deeper into the building, hoping this passage wasn't blocked.

Teyla kept an eye on their six, saying sourly, "At least I can sense them now that they are not in Trishen's ship."

"It's still only an assumption that they came from her ship," Rodney corrected her sharply. "If they have some kind of advanced shielding now that our sensors can't penetrate, they could have been concealed anywhere——" He stared at John, appalled. "They could have already found the jumper. That ship has sensors that can penetrate the jumper's cloak——"

Still trying his radio and getting nothing but static, John shook his head. "They had time to get away." He didn't want to say anymore, because it was all too frigging possible the Wraith had found the others.

His eyes on the detector again, Rodney reported, "They're turning down this passage." His voice was urgent. "We need to——"

"Yeah." John increased his pace to a fast jog.

A short distance up ahead the corridor took an abrupt turn, ending in a triangular hatch. John stepped back to the corner to cover the passage behind them, while Rodney hurriedly wrenched off the wall console and Teyla watched the door. Rodney said in frustration, "And how the hell do they know we came this way? As far as we know, they don't have bio-sensors this exact and they can't use the Ancient devices——"

"The corridor floor was covered with sand," Teyla pointed out, her voice grim as she kept a wary eye on the door. "Our tracks led them to us."

John flicked off the P-90's light before he risked

a look back down the passage. He could hear a faint scraping that might be footsteps. "Now would be good, Rodney," he whispered harshly.

"No, really?" Rodney snapped, "I thought we'd just stand around here and wait for — Got it," and the doors were sliding open, releasing a rush of air.

In another moment they were through the hatch, with the doors sealed safely behind them. Rodney pulled two of the crystals from the wall console on this side and tucked them into a vest pocket. "That should hold them for...a minute or so, anyway."

"That's all we need," John said, flashing his light around. It glinted off cool blue stone and embossed metal. They were in a large foyer, with three open corridors heading off in different directions. Teyla shone her light across the floor. No sand, so they wouldn't leave tracks. This section was pressurized and the seals must have kept out the dust and dirt. The Wraith would be expecting them to head for the outer edge of the installation, toward the jumper's last position, so John picked the corridor leading back toward the inner ring and Mirror platform. "This way."

They started down the new corridor, and not far along they were rewarded with another set of branching passages. His eyes on the life signs detector, Rodney said in relief, "We're good. They picked the wrong corridor." As if in response, a low vibration trembled through the floor; the Mirror was still dangerously active. "They might be doing something that's setting off that interference," Rodney added with a grimace. "If they have darts or another ship close enough to affect the Mirror's nimbus, it could be causing those energy bursts."

Teyla said reluctantly, "There may have already been another Wraith ship in position to attack the jumper. Once we entered Trishen's ship, the trap would have been sprung."

"Yes, but the problem is that the trap wasn't sprung," Rodney bit the words out. "Why didn't she lock the hatch before she showed us what she was? It doesn't make sense! If she had just left her helmet on, she could have kept us there, out of radio contact, with no chance to warn the jumper until the attack was over." He waved his free hand, warming to his point. "Trust me on this one, if Miko was in a dogfight with darts or Ronon was manfully wrestling drones in the rear cabin, Radek would have mentioned it!"

"I don't know," John said, teeth gritted. The radio was still picking up nothing but static. "You said that data wasn't fake. If these Wraith got that ship and that shielding technology from some place they went to through the Mirror—"

"Maybe." Rodney shook his head, frustrated. "I still think we could actually be dealing with Wraith from another reality."

"I believe you are right," Teyla told him. "She did seem different. And it is strange that she gave us a name. I did not believe they had names, even among themselves."

"But it doesn't matter which reality they came from." Rodney's face was grim, his mouth a hard line. "We have to shut this Mirror down permanently, now. Even if it destroys this entire installation in the process."

John exchanged a look with Teyla, just in time to see a flicker of hope in her eyes. If this new technology spread to all the other Wraith... That wasn't an option. They couldn't let it be an option. "What do you need?"

"I don't know yet..." His expression intent, Rodney dug into one of the pockets of his tac vest, pulling out the camera he had used to record Trishen's data display. "But this might tell me."

Rodney needed a place to concentrate with a little less threat of imminent painful life-sucking death. He would have preferred his main lab at Atlantis, but that not being available, he settled for following Sheppard and Teyla further up into this section of the installation.

A short distance down the passage they found a stairwell and went up a couple of levels, further away from the area the Wraith were searching. The power was fluctuating all through this section, lights blinking out at random, doors wedged partly open, drafts where bursts of recycled air came out of broken vents. Now that Rodney knew that Trishen might be monitoring the security system, he set his equipment to scan for the video signals. But fortunately the system didn't seem to be active here.

Sheppard found an empty lab where most of the vents were working, providing enough air to let them turn off their SCBAs and save the tanks. Rodney sat down on a broken stone plinth and said, "Don't talk to me." He ignored Sheppard's eye roll, got the camera out, and started reviewing the playback and the data downloaded to his tablet. Sheppard and Teyla took up guard positions on the door, and Sheppard tried to raise the jumper again.

The static on the radio seemed to be dying down, but Sheppard still couldn't get any response. Rodney swal-

lowed in a dry throat, put that out of his mind, and tried
to concentrate.

At one point, Sheppard showed the life signs detector
screen to Teyla, telling her, "The interference keeps messing with the signal, but it looks like the Wraith are leaving
this section, heading in toward the Mirror platform."

She frowned. "Perhaps they are going to Trishen's
ship. But I wonder why."

"Maybe they're having a meeting," Sheppard said.
He sounded sarcastic, but then everything Sheppard
said sounded sarcastic, even things like "pass the salt,"
and Rodney had always put it down as an unintentional
byproduct resulting from the combination of his uniden-
tifiable accent and his slacker attitude. Sheppard seemed
completely unaware of it, though it probably explained
the recurring problems with his military career. And of
course, the damn Mirror could pick now to have one of
its catastrophic discharges and wipe out the Wraith on the
platform, but Rodney knew their luck didn't run that way,
and if the Mirror was going to kill anybody that way it
would be them.

Then his headset crackled and Rodney heard a babble
of familiar voices. Startled, he looked up as Sheppard
hurriedly keyed his radio, saying, "Jumper One, please
respond. This is Sheppard."

Over the rush of static, Rodney heard Zelenka saying,
"Colonel! Such a relief to hear your voice!"

Rodney felt the tightness in his chest unclench just a
little. The Wraith hadn't found the jumper. So far, despite
the Mirror, the Wraith, and what was apparently a group
inclination for suicidal behavior, they had all managed
not to get killed. He went back to verifying the direc-

tional indicator on that elusive power signature that kept reappearing in the data. "You too," Sheppard replied to Zelenka, exchanging a look of relief with Teyla. "What's your situation?"

Zelenka began, "We thought—" In the static-obscured background, Miko said something urgently and Sheppard's pet caveman growled. Zelenka finished, "Yes, yes, I'm telling him! Colonel, there are Wraith everywhere."

Rodney rolled his eyes and spared a moment to contribute, "You don't say."

"Zelenka, I need you to define 'everywhere,'" Sheppard persisted. "Is it a hiveship?"

"No, not yet," Zelenka replied hurriedly. "The jumper has detected a small ship in polar orbit, matching our data on the energy signatures for a Wraith scout ship."

Teyla's brow furrowed. "We must assume a hiveship is on the way."

Ah ha. Here we go. "Got it." Rodney pushed to his feet. He stepped over to Sheppard and Teyla, tapping the tablet's display. "I was certain I saw this but I wanted to verify the location. Trishen's equipment registered an energy pulse coming from along the top of the installation." He pointed up for emphasis. "If I'm correct, that pulse is designed to generate a containment field just above the Mirror's accretion surface, to stabilize the singularity's event horizon. Without it, the singularity keeps trying to expand, pushing at the naquadah frame, the structure of the installation, the bedrock beneath it. Like the rest of the installation, the pulse generator is drawing power from the Mirror's subspace conduit, but something is causing it to only function erratically at the moment, which is why the discharges are occurring. And the energy signatures of the jumper and any Wraith darts may be disrupting the pulse itself whenever they come within range, causing the discharges to occur more frequently." Rodney tucked the tablet under his arm. "The Mirror is already dangerously unstable. The key to rendering it unusable is going to be in destabilizing it further—"

"So you want to blow up the thing that's generating the pulse?" Sheppard said.

Watching Rodney intently, Teyla asked, "Can we use the jumper's weapons?"

"The shielding!" Zelenka was saying in the headset. "The shielding may prevent—!"

Rodney waved at them all to shut up, even though Zelenka couldn't see him. "Yes, and no. We need to disable the pulse generator, but taking the jumper up into a firing position above the roof may just trigger another violent discharge; we could be smashed into the building before we have a chance to fire. And the shielding on the installation's inner ring and the roof must be designed to deflect the full force of the energy spikes that the Mirror can generate; the jumper's energy drones may not be able to penetrate it." He rubbed his hands together in anticipation. "But the good news is, the pulse array stretches along the entire circumference of the roof, and we should be able to disrupt it at any point."

Sheppard was watching Rodney as if he didn't have a clue what Rodney was saying, as if he wasn't even sure Rodney was speaking English, but Rodney had learned long ago that was just as deceptive as the involuntary sarcasm. Proving it, Sheppard said, "So we need to get up there and disable one section so the whole thing will shut down. And the Mirror will do what?"

"The Mirror is going to—" Rodney hesitated uneasily, thinking it over. The singularity would take time to collapse, but the discharges would become more violent immediately. "We're going to have to get back inside the installation as quickly as possible. The instability should cause the singularity to begin a collapse, but it'll take some time. Hours, probably days. After the initial reaction, we should be able to lift off in the jumper and get away." Remembering all his practical experience was with a Quantum Mirror the size of a bathtub rather than an Olympic stadium, he added, "Theoretically."

"Right." Sheppard looked at Teyla and got a grim nod in response. In Rodney's headset he could hear Zelenka and Kusanagi unhelpfully debating the possibility of the collapsing singularity punching a hole straight through the moon and taking all matter in the area with it. Sheppard asked, "What about the jumper? Are they going to be safe out there during this?"

"In a word, no." Rodney touched his headset. "Radek, does your life signs screen show the Wraith anywhere near that big freight corridor?"

Zelenka answered, "No, they are not there. We can not see their positions exactly—there is still much interference—but we saw them move into the center section."

Rodney nodded briskly. "Good. I need you to move the jumper, still cloaked, into that passage. That's what it was designed for; there's plenty of room. Look for a stable bay along the side and take the jumper into it. That should shield you from the initial reaction discharge and cut down the chances of the Wraith stumbling into you if they come back down that way."

Teyla lifted her brows doubtfully and looked at Sheppard. Sheppard got that expression he always got when someone other than him wanted to do something crazy with a puddlejumper. There was a static-laden silence from the radio. Then Zelenka said, "Ah... Colonel, is that good idea?"

Rodney mentally rewrote Zelenka's next performance evaluation to include the term "mutinous."

But Sheppard just said, "Affirmative, Zelenka, take the jumper inside."

The comm was chiming for attention, but Trishen hesitated, leaning on her control console. Unlike her drive, her sensors had survived the abrupt unplanned trip through the Quantum Mirror, and her holo display showed the newly arrived ship in orbit. She had seen the energy signatures when it had used a transport beam to send a landing party to the installation, and the effect that had had on the dangerously unstable Mirror.

She should answer the comm. Except...*something's wrong,* she told herself, grimly eyeing the screen. She hadn't been able to sense the humans' presence. But these newcomers were not humans, and she could taste the matrix of their minds, just on the edge of her awareness.

It felt wrong. There was nothing she could articulate, no one element that seemed to warn of danger. But deep inside her, a buried instinct said, *fear this.*

The humans had spoken of Wraith, of the danger of revealing her presence in this place. *Of course, then they went mad and threatened to kill you,* she told herself ruefully.

Their fear she had been able to understand; she was too

different from them, perhaps they had never seen an alien being before. It was the hate that baffled her.

When she had first glimpsed them on the security camera she hadn't known what she was looking at. They were so alien, so unlike Eidolon, all different sizes and colors. Then one had looked directly at the camera, and she had had a sudden clear view of his face. It had been like looking at one of the ancient holo recordings of the Creators.

She had gripped the cold metal of the console, staring in shock. If the Creators were alive in this reality... *This is incredible; all our questions could be answered!* But surely Creators would know how to override their own security measures. She had turned the damn system on accidentally when trying to power up the complex and it had taken her hours to figure out how to keep it from locking her in constantly. If she hadn't had the Creators' gene, it would have been impossible.

That was when she had realized that they must be humans. The Eidolon knew that the first human colonies had died out even before the Creators, the first victims of the plague that had eventually destroyed the Creators' civilization. She had been desperate to speak to them, and not only for the value to Eidolon science. She wasn't accustomed to being alone, to being separated from her own kind; she was desperate to speak to anyone.

The comm chimed again and she grimaced at it. The humans could have been lying about the danger... *Why? They weren't afraid until they saw your face, until they saw you weren't one of them.* Before that, she thought they had honestly meant to help her. She knotted her fists. She still needed that help. *You should be able to deal with this. You're not a child, you're an adult, skilled in your*

calling, an expert in the Creators' lost technology. She
was also alone, trapped away from her world, away from
the protection of her mother and her male lineage, and it
frightened her in a way that struck her to the core.

She had to find out who was on that newly arrived ship.
She took a deep breath and closed her eyes. She carefully
stretched out toward that tenuous mental connection,
toward the alien ship in orbit.

It came almost immediately.

*Hunger. They had traveled far from the hive, chasing
the elusive energy traces that might indicate Lantian technology, and there had been little to feed on along their
route. There were tantalizing hints from other hives that
a new feeding ground existed, rich beyond measure, that
Lantian technology might lead to it.*

Trishen retreated, startled. She didn't think they were
aware of her; there was something primitive about most
of the minds in the matrix, and she could tell there was no
female onboard. *That can't be a good sign.* She pushed
harder, slipping past the higher levels of awareness,
choosing an individual mind at random.

She saw with his eyes.

He was walking through the ship. It was primitive too,
at least this section of it. She caught sight of another crew
member, and was baffled by the heavy mask of what
looked like bone concealing his—its?—face. Another
passed by, but this one looked like an Eidolon male. *That
doesn't make sense.* The humans had acted as if they had
never seen an Eidolon before. Trishen opened her senses
further, trying to understand. Then she gagged, her throat
nearly closing at the stench of death; the sweetness of rotting flesh was thick in the air. *There's been an accident,*

she thought, bewildered, *a hull breach*. But she could see the crew, Eidolon and the masked beings, passing in the corridor as if nothing was wrong. And the stink; had they just left the bodies where they lay? And there was web everywhere, thick bundles of it. *What in the name of the Creators are they doing?* she wondered incredulously.

Then the being she was riding stopped in front of a small chamber, in front of a mass of web, and she saw a body trapped in it. A human female, naked except for a few rags, slumped over with only the web holding her upright. Dead, surely she was dead. He reached toward her, his hand on her chest, and Trishen's thoughts dissolved in horror. *No. It can't be. This can't be.*

The human jerked and screamed.

Trishen fled, snatching her awareness away. Back in her own body she shoved away from the console, staggered blindly to the wall. Bile rose in her throat as her body tried to revolt. *Wraith. Not Eidolon. Wraith.* The species that had destroyed the Creators.

This...explained a great deal.

Ignoring the chiming of the comm unit, she leaned on the wall, breathing in the clean air of her own ship. Squeezing her eyes shut didn't help; the human female's horrific death was burned into her brain. *Now you know why the humans ran from you*, she told herself.

Now she understood the hate, too.

They found the roof access on the uppermost level, a lift platform that took them up into a circular structure with one section open to the outside. The elevator doors opened and John stepped out cautiously, Teyla beside him, warily surveying the scene. The flat roof stretched away, an empty expanse of dust-streaked blue stone, under a sky that was starting to dim as the moon's orbit took it into eclipse again. John said, "This the right place?"

"No, the elevator took us to another dimension." Rodney was already checking his various screens.

John exchanged a startled look with Teyla, then he rolled his eyes in annoyance and they both glared at Rodney. "McKay."

"What?" Rodney demanded, not looking up.

Brows lowered and sounding distinctly testy, Teyla began, "Considering where we are—"

John finished in a flat voice, "That wasn't funny."

On the headset, John heard Zelenka confide in an undertone to either Kusanagi or Ronon, "Rodney thinks he is hilarious."

"I can hear you, Zelenka, and all right, fine, yes, this is the right part of the roof." Rodney checked his tablet again. "The array is straight ahead, on the inside edge."

John waited while Rodney did a last check through of all his equipment. Mirror: probably not about to discharge and kill them. Life signs: currently clear except for the three of them. Wraith darts: none close enough to detect. Scout ship: at the far end of its polar orbit, out of range for at least the next half hour. Then John stepped out into the open, trying to ignore the sensation of being fully exposed to the view of every Wraith in the entire system.

As they started across the open expanse of the roof, Radek reported that they had reached the freight entrance and that Miko was maneuvering the cloaked jumper down the corridor. A moment later John heard a yelp and a faint metallic crunch. Miko snapped, "*Shimatta!*"

STARGATE ATLANTIS: ENTANGLEMENT   135

John winced in genuine pain. It was his favorite jumper. "What happened?"

"Nothing," Radek replied hurriedly. "It's a small scratch, I'll fix it when we get home."

Rodney snorted in exasperation. "It's 'The Bobbsey Twins Try to Park a Puddlejumper.'"

"Just be careful," John told Radek.

As they neared the edge of the roof, John saw a wide square trench, close to thirty feet across and about five feet deep, apparently running the full circumference of the building, just as Rodney had predicted. The far side curved up into a blue-green metallic housing that he hoped was for the pulse generator, forming a square block that extended out over the edge of the installation like a porch roof. *Okay, this is what I saw from the window bubble in that monitoring room.* There were a scatter of low stone platforms of different heights along the trench, probably bases for equipment that had been long removed.

John jumped down into the trench and Rodney and Teyla used the little set of steps. After a little searching, they found the nearly invisible seams of a large square access port. Rodney set his tablet down and unslung his pack, taking out his toolkit. He tapped his radio. "Radek, we've found it. Pull up the database on Ancient conductivity and energy control—"

"I have it, Rodney," Radek replied. "And we have found a nice bay to sit in."

Studying the sky uneasily, John asked, "How long is this going to take?"

Still holding the toolkit, Rodney rolled his eyes. "A long long time, if someone interrupts me every ten seconds to ask—"

Then Teyla shouted, "Colonel!"

John turned, saw the white flash. Wraith were beaming down on the inside edge of the trench, between them and the lift platform. He yelled, "Wraith!"

He opened fire with Teyla as the Wraith materialized. A high-flying dart must have picked them up on its sensors, beamed down this search group. There were at least seven of them, males and drones, and that was too many. One drone dropped, then another. The others were lifting stunners. In his peripheral vision, John saw Rodney turn, aim his pistol at his tablet where it sat on the pavement, squeeze off two shots. *Good,* John thought, right before the stun blast hit him in the chest.

John saw the ground rushing toward him, and slammed into it.

Dazed, Rodney opened his eyes when something tugged at his SCBA. *No, no, what the hell? I need that.* He fumbled for the chest strap with numb fingers, trying to hold on to it. The next tug was violent, ripping the mask away, taking the tank and his tac vest with it. It yanked him around so that he was sprawled on his side; Rodney choked on a breath, the thin air laden with dust, and stared upward.

There was a Wraith drone standing over him, faceless in the bone mask it wore. He choked on an outcry, his throat closing. He tried to scramble away but his muscles were limp, his body like an unstrung puppet.

The drone stepped back and Rodney saw Sheppard lying on his side a few feet away. His jacket, vest, and SCBA had been pulled off and tossed aside. Teyla lay in a crumpled heap not far beyond Sheppard, another drone just now dragging off her vest and breathing unit, ignoring her startled outcry and her weak attempt to punch it. Rodney gasped, "No, we need those," the words came out in a weak wheeze and Rodney felt the first pressure on his lungs. The Wraith had taken their weapons, the headsets. And their air.

Hypoxia. Ten or twelve percent oxygen, just enough to die slowly. It meant gasping for breath, muddled thinking and inability to make decisions, fatigue, and other things that weren't going to matter because they were going to be fed on, they were going to die, very, very painfully and very, very soon.

He saw Sheppard shove at the pavement, trying to push himself up and falling back helplessly. He looked feral and desperate and furious, like a trapped predator. He met Rodney's gaze, and for a moment there was nothing there but wide-eyed despair, before Sheppard looked away. *It's not fair*, Rodney thought, feeling the odd detachment of incipient hysteria. It should have been quick, an explosion; Rodney had been mentally prepared for them all to die in an explosion, eventually. Not this, they didn't deserve this.

At least he had destroyed his tablet, with its information on the Mirror. *Small consolation,* he told himself bitterly.

A male Wraith stepped into Rodney's view, its long white hair and dead pale skin almost glowing against the dark stone. It had at least a dozen bullet holes in the dull silver armor on its chest, but it must have fully regenerated already. It wore something around its neck, a gray bulbous device with nodes clamped over the slits on its face. *Some sort of breather unit,* Rodney thought. It nudged the shattered tablet with a foot and hissed with displeasure. Then it paced toward them, standing over them, barring its teeth in a sneer. It said, "How did you get to this moon?"

Right, there's no Stargate here. Rodney groaned under his breath. There was just no good answer to that question.

Teyla tried to push herself up, shaking the hair out of her eyes, her face set in a snarl nearly as intimidating as the Wraith's. Sheppard looked up at it with narrowed eyes, sneering back. "We walked."

The Wraith hissed and leaned down toward him, lifting a hand. Rodney choked out, "No! Stop, God——" But the Wraith only slapped Sheppard, the open-handed blow slamming him back into the pavement. Rodney winced away.

Teyla made a strangled noise of rage, nearly shoving herself upright. Rodney didn't see the drone, not until it stepped in, swinging the butt of its stunner, striking her across the face. It knocked her flat; she twitched once and lay unmoving. Rodney shouted, "Dammit, we're stunned already, you didn't have to——" He ran out of air at that point and slumped, gasping.

Ignoring him, the male Wraith grabbed Sheppard by the shirt, dragging him up as if he weighed no more than a rag doll. It turned, slamming him down on his back on the nearest platform. Sheppard was moving slowly, dazed and weak, but he clawed at its hand, tried to kick it in the chest. "There is no Stargate on this moon," the Wraith said, apparently thinking that it had to spell out the problem. "You came here in a Lantian ship."

"What ship?" Sheppard managed to wheeze. The Wraith hit him again, snapping his head back against the stone.

It's going to kill him, Rodney thought, sick with the certainty. *It's going to kill all of us.* He found himself saying, "We were brought here——" He had to pause to gasp in another breath, wheezing out, "By Wraith. Other Wraith, not you, of course—We escaped, we were trapped here—"

The Wraith let go of Sheppard and he rolled off the platform, collapsing into a limp heap on the dusty stone. It stalked toward Rodney, saying, "You have Lantian devices. How did you get them?"

"We stole them. When we escaped." It was an incredibly ludicrous lie. Rodney didn't know if he was stalling, trying to put off the inevitable, or just trying to get the Wraith to take him first so he wouldn't have to watch it happen to Sheppard and Teyla. He wheezed, "I suppose they're holding out on you, maybe you'd better check into that."

The Wraith canted its head to stare down at him, as if it was seriously considering this. "The alien ship is Lantian. Where did it come from?"

Rodney said, "What alien ship?" In retrospect, not the best response.

It snarled, drew its hand stunner, and before Rodney could even flinch it shot him again.

Rodney fell back against the pavement, his body suddenly an inert slab of meat. *Bastard,* Rodney thought in outrage, barely managing to drag in another breath. *Wait, what just happened? By alien ship, it must have meant Trishen's ship.* Then these Wraith hadn't known about it before they arrived here, they weren't allied with her. And...that wasn't going to help because they were going to kill them all anyway.

The Wraith turned away, then froze, staring upward. A shadow fell over the roof, and Rodney heard a rushing blast of wind.

Then everything dissolved into white light.

Rodney hit a soft rubbery floor, unable to even tense at the impact. His ears popped from the sudden transition to a pressurized environment, and he gasped in a real breath. He was in a room with dark walls, dimly lit. He lay sprawled next to Sheppard, who was half-twisted on his side; Teyla was a few feet away, a fall of red-brown hair partially obscuring her face. *Alive, still alive.* For now.

Rodney tried desperately to move and couldn't even twitch; the second stun had completely immobilized him. *Where the hell are we?* he thought, sick terror settling in his stomach. He knew they had been picked up by a transport beam, but a Wraith culling beam should have left him completely unconscious. He couldn't see Teyla's face, but Sheppard's eyes were closed, his brow furrowed in pain. If he was out, it was probably from that last punch.

Then a figure moved into his narrow field of vision. White hair, a Wraith... Trishen.

This...doesn't make sense, Rodney thought, startled and incredulous. That noise he had heard right before the transport beam must have been her shuttle. *She stole us from the other Wraith?* That was more support for his theory that she was from a different reality, not working with these Wraith at all.

She hesitated, then slowly moved toward them. His heart pounding, Rodney concentrated on keeping his eyes slitted and his breathing even. They had always suspected that much of the pleasure Wraith took in feeding came from the terror of their victims, from attempts at resistance. He didn't think she would want to feed on them when she didn't believe they were conscious. *This would be a very, very bad time to discover we're wrong about that.*

Then she knelt next to Sheppard. Rodney went cold. He tried to make his throat work, tried to say something, to argue, distract her, stall, but the second stun blast had frozen his vocal cords. She reached out tentatively, cautiously, and lightly touched Sheppard's hair.

If she had been human, Rodney would have said her expression was caught between curiosity and wariness. She touched Sheppard's face, just above his right brow, then put the back of her hand against his cheek. She looked like someone daring to touch a sleeping tiger; frightened and aware this probably wasn't the best idea, but too overcome by curiosity to resist the opportunity.

Rodney felt a pain between his eyes that he was certain was an aneurism, then he remembered to take a shallow breath. She must have heard him because she started, jerking her hand back, looking around nervously. Then she pushed to her feet and hurriedly backed away.

Rodney shuddered inwardly with relief. He saw her glance around, lean down to pick something up. Then he realized some of their equipment had been beamed up with them. *Oh fine, that's handy*, he thought bitterly. Squinting, he could see the pile of their tac vests and SCBAs, at least one of the P-90s. She was gathering all of it, carrying it away. He heard a few thumps and bumping noises, then finally a low power hum.

He waited, tense and hyperaware of every sound, but she didn't come near them again. *She said she had never seen a human before*. If she was telling the truth, if her species really had been created by a band of refugee Ancients from this reality... *We'd be like living artifacts, relics of an almost mythical past*.

He just hoped she meant to keep them alive.

CHAPTER SEVEN

Ronon knew the others were dead when he heard Sheppard shout, "Wraith!"

The radio went to static and Zelenka slammed his hand on the console, shouting, "Rodney! Colonel, Teyla!" Kusanagi gasped in horror.

They stared at the useless screens while time crawled. Then the three life signs winked out like candles.

Kusanagi made a noise in her throat, pressing her hands over her face. Zelenka pushed out of his seat and stumbled out of the cockpit into the rear cabin; Ronon heard him retching.

Ronon just turned away. He stared blindly at the jumper's curved wall, his fists knotting. He should be used to this. He had seen so many people taken by the Wraith that it had all blurred into a haze of rage and pain and loss. He shouldn't feel it like this anymore. He didn't want to feel it like this anymore.

Zelenka stepped back into the cockpit, wiping his face with a cloth. "We must do something." He steadied himself on the back of the co-pilot's seat, dropping into it and studying the screens again. He said hesitantly, "Did it sound like... Did they have the chance to damage pulse generator, do you think?"

Kusanagi shook her head. "I don't think Dr. McKay would have had time—" She pressed her hand over her mouth and shuddered, then took a sharp breath.

She managed to finish, "Time to get into the device. And there has been no discharge. It must still be operating."

"I can do it," Ronon said. Zelenka and Kusanagi turned to stare up at him blankly, and he explained, "Go up to the roof, see how far they got. You can tell me what to do to it over the radio."

Startled, Zelenka frowned at him, then looked at Kusanagi. She said softly, "It may be the only way." Ronon saw she had tears running down her cheeks, though she seemed unaware of them. "We can't leave the Mirror to the Wraith. If they can use it to get this superior technology—"

"Yes. Yes, we have to do this." Zelenka looked up uncertainly. "Perhaps I should go with you—"

"No." Ronon shook his head. He could see the little man was terrified of the prospect. And he had sworn to Sheppard that he would protect these two. He had also sworn that he wouldn't leave them, but he thought this was more important. "I'll move faster alone."

Zelenka hesitated, then nodded, his mouth set in a rueful line. Kusanagi turned back to the control board, awkwardly wiping the tears off her face. "You'll have to wait until they leave the area." She frowned at the life signs screen. The lighted dots were still moving around that section of the roof. Ronon allowed himself a grim smile. The Wraith were searching, trying to figure out what the three humans had been up to. That meant nobody had broken. Kusanagi said, "If the Wraith realize we were trying to sabotage the pulse generator—"

Zelenka studied the screen worriedly. "Surely they

won't leave it unguarded."

Ronon bared his teeth. He was looking forward to the chance to deliver some payback. "Good."

John's first conscious thought was relief that he could draw a full breath. His second thought was that his face hurt. A lot. And his head. And pretty much his entire body. He heard Rodney say worriedly, "Shake him again. Careful, he might have brain damage."

John blinked, wincing. "How will that help if I have—" It hurt to talk. "Ow."

He managed to get his eyes open all the way when someone touched his shoulder. It was Teyla looking anxiously down at him, her hair in a disordered tumble and a darkening bruise on her cheek. "Are you all right?" she asked.

"Yeah, are you okay? What—" *Wraith*, John remembered. Gritting his teeth, he shoved himself upright. Rodney lay a short distance away, one arm flung over his eyes. He looked like he felt like hell, but otherwise he seemed unhurt. John looked down at himself; his shirt was torn where the Wraith had grabbed him, but there was no feeding mark. *What do you know about that?* They were all three alive and they hadn't been fed on, and John really hadn't been expecting that.

Their prison was an empty cabin, the walls and floor the same dark rubbery substance they had seen in Trishen's base ship. This place had the same smell too, earthy and a little acrid. There was an oval hatchway looking out into another compartment, but John could see the faint shimmer in the air of a force shield blocking it. He said, "We're in Trishen's ship?"

"We believe so." Teyla looked around the room, her expression grim. "Apparently she beamed us up, away from the other Wraith."

"Who stunned me twice, and yes, I have a migraine, thank you for asking," Rodney added, his voice tight. "We're in her shuttle, but I think it's docked with the base ship now."

"Great." John spotted something on the floor, a round blue thing, a foot or so inside the hatchway. He squinted at it suspiciously. "What's that?"

Teyla's lips thinned. "It contains water, and some items that may be packaged rations."

John grimaced in disgust. The caretaker on the first hiveship they had encountered had liked to feed her human prey before she fed on them; Trishen must have the same taste. John rolled to his knees, and Teyla grabbed his arm to steady him. After a moment of dizziness, he managed to shove himself to his feet. Glancing up, he froze. "What the hell?"

The ceiling arched up into a circular dome, and in the center was a bulbous mottled purple thing, covered by a chased silver metal web. It looked organic and alien and possibly about to do something to them. Teyla looked up with a worried wince. "I do not know."

From the floor, Rodney said, "It's not a death ray, it's the rematerialization mechanism for the beaming device." He lowered his arm to peer suspiciously at it, and amended, "It's probably not a death ray."

"Okay." *Probably not a death ray* was likely as good as the situation was going to get. John looked around the cabin again, as Teyla stepped away to make a circuit of the walls. John didn't see anything that looked like an obvious surveillance camera, but the ship was too alien to really tell. And the beaming device thing worried him. He said, "So she could beam us out of here any time she wants." Into the thin atmosphere, with no breathing units. "Or beam something in here with us."

Rodney pulled his arm down again to give John an acid glare. "Yes, please continue to come up with as many horrible death scenarios as possible; really, it's helping my headache."

"You seem to enjoy it when you do it." John made it to the force-shielded hatchway, peering out into the next compartment.

"Yes, but when I—" Rodney gave in grudgingly. "All right, fine."

From what John could see, the outer compartment wasn't much larger than this cabin, empty except for open storage units set into the walls. The only visible exit was in the opposite wall, another oval doorway, with a sealed hatch. He stretched out a cautious hand, flinching back when the field zapped him. Wincing, he tucked his hand under his arm.

Teyla had crouched down, testing the field to make sure it went all the way to the floor. "I do not see any way we can get through this."

John nodded, looking down at her. "No equipment, no breathing gear, no weapons..." He lifted his brows.

She flicked him a rueful look and tapped her ankle, the gesture telling him that the Wraith hadn't found the knife she kept strapped to her calf. *Right.* It was better than nothing. He looked at the outer compartment again, and said, "Maybe she wasn't lying about wanting to fix the Mirror. Or maybe she just wants dinner."

Still on the floor nursing his headache, Rodney said, "The fact that this is the Pegasus Galaxy and the worst-case scenario is always a statistically likely probability notwithstanding, I don't think she's allied with the Wraith that arrived in the scout ship. They tried to question me about her ship, called it 'alien,' as if finding it here was as big a surprise to them as it was to us. And I don't think she's like the Wraith of our reality."

Teyla pushed to her feet, turning to watch him dubiously. "What do you mean?"

"She was acting," John said, poking sourly at the force shield.

"Since when do Wraith act?" Rodney started to struggle into a sitting position, and Teyla moved to help him. "I don't think she was lying about never having seen a human before."

Frowning, John stepped over to him and leaned down, offering Rodney a hand up. "Why?"

Rodney gripped John's hand and groaned as John hauled him to his feet. Rodney eyed him a moment, then made an erratic gesture. "Some of our equipment was beamed up with us. She came in here to get it while you and Teyla were unconscious. It just didn't look like...she had seen a human before."

"Whatever. If they don't eat humans, they eat somebody else." John looked around again, frustrated. He hated being locked up. "You want to check these walls, see if there's any way to—"

"Wait." Teyla was staring intently toward the door. "Someone is coming."

John turned, stepping sideways so he could see into the outer compartment. The hatch was sliding up. *Yeah, here we go,* he thought.

Trishen stepped through the hatch into the outer compartment, stopping just inside it as if she was afraid, as if they weren't across the room and trapped behind this force shield. Instead of the concealing environmental suit, she was wearing a dress, purple-gray in the tinted light, with a utility belt around her waist holding various tools and pouches. She also had a silver wristband with control pads on it, like the others John had seen Wraith wear, but more compact.

"Long time no see," John said easily.

Trishen didn't come any closer. She pressed her hands together; if she had been human, John would have said she looked nervous but resolved. And he wished like hell she would stop doing that, stop acting like a person, because it was pissing him off. She said stiffly, "What were you trying to do to the Mirror?"

Rodney lifted his chin and folded his arms. "Why should we tell you?"

She blinked at him. "I know what you think I am now, I know why you were afraid. But I am not one of them. My species may appear similar, but we do not...use sentient beings for sustenance. I won't harm you."

John exchanged a look with Teyla, whose expression of grim skepticism said she wasn't buying this either. John said, "Okay. Then drop the force shield and let us out of here."

Trishen had the audacity to sound pissed. "I can't. I know you would kill me."

Teyla lifted her brows, her expression dry. "We would be fools to believe you when you can offer us no proof."

Trishen shook her head in apparent frustration. "I'm

not lying! There are no humans in my reality. We know that the Creators tried to seed a human race at the same time they created us, but their early colonies died out from some sort of plague."

Rodney snorted with annoyance, giving them all a sour look. "Do you people have all day to stand here and argue this point? Because I don't." He turned to Trishen, waving a hand dismissively. "Let's stipulate for the moment that I believe you're telling the truth. If you don't intend to feed on us, what exactly do you want?"

She took a step forward, her fists knotting. "There's an array on the roof that has an effect on the Mirror's accretion surface. Were you trying to destabilize it?"

Rodney gave her a withering look. "Of course we were. And again, why do you ask?"

John shot him a glare and Rodney glared back. *Okay fine, if she knows what the pulse generator is for, then she probably already realizes what we were doing there,* John thought. But Rodney needed to be a little more reticent with the information, here.

She took a sharp breath. "If you help me stabilize the Mirror, I will let you go. I'll take you back to your ship—"

"No." Rodney's mouth twisted. "Next question."

Trishen shook her head, frustrated and angry. "I just want to get back to my own reality—"

Rodney's voice was acid. "Yes, well, I'm sorry we can't make your welfare a priority, since we're a little more concerned at the moment with saving the lives of our entire species."

It was her turn to glare at Rodney. "The Mirror is not a weapon. I thought you understood that."

Rodney gave her the little "you're so stupid" laugh, the one guaranteed to send his science team colleagues into paroxysms of fury. "Please, not counting any stray Ascendants, I'm the Pegasus Galaxy's foremost expert on Quantum Mirrors, and yes, it's not a weapon." His expression hardened. "But your ship is."

Teyla shifted uncertainly, throwing a look at John. Yeah, he really didn't want to put those cards on the table. He said, "Rodney."

Trishen made a sharp gesture, apparently genuinely exasperated. "This ship has no offensive weapons! You're the ones with weapons—"

Rodney set his jaw. "Our weapons are woefully inadequate against the Wraith, and most of the humans here have no weapons, they've been bombed back into a pre-industrial level of technology—"

John stared at him incredulously. "Rodney!"

Rodney raised his voice, out-shouting John to finish with, "—so the Wraith, your nearest genetic relatives in this reality, can keep them like cattle and feed on them at their leisure!" He shot a look at John and said, low-voiced, "I know what I'm doing."

John hoped like hell Rodney knew what he was doing, that he hadn't just issued an invitation to a whole different set of Wraith from another reality to invade Pegasus and feed on its nearly helpless inhabitants. He just said, "You'd better."

Ignoring him, watching Trishen narrowly, Rodney said, "The Wraith destroyed the Ancients, drove the last of them out of this galaxy by sheer force of numbers, but they never defeated their technology. The weapons, the sensors, and the cloaking device on our ship are the only way that we can put up any effective resistance whatsoever. Do you see where I'm going with this?'"

Trishen stared at him, and it was hard to read the expression in those alien eyes. "My sensors. They use technology left behind by the Creators—your Ancients. That's why I could see your ship through its cloaking device." She shook her head. "If you think I will give it to the Wraith—I have no reason to do that! I just want to go home."

"I don't think you'll give it to them." Rodney stepped forward, his face grim as he hammered his point home. "I think they'll take it. And if they know there's more in your reality, I think they'll go through the Mirror to get it."

Teyla was watching Trishen with clinical detachment. She added, "And if you believe your resemblance to them makes you safe, you are wrong. They will feed on their own kind when no humans are available. And there are far too many of them awake now; for the past year they have been in search of a new feeding ground."

John added, "So if you're not going to eat us, let us go."

Trishen stood there, staring at them, breathing hard. "I can't—I have to think about this." She turned in a whirl of skirts and vanished back through the hatch, the door sliding shut after her.

John let his breath out, pacing a few steps away and rubbing his eyes. His jaw hurt, they were stuck here, and he wasn't seeing much hope of keeping this ship and its technology away from the Wraith. He wasn't seeing much hope of keeping them away from the Wraith, either. "I see where you're trying to go with this, Rodney, but we could have tried to string her along a little."

"We don't have time for that." Rodney turned to him impatiently. "A hiveship is probably on the way here right now."

"Do we have time for this?" Teyla asked him pointedly. "You really think she will see reason and release us to destroy the Mirror?"

Rodney's jaw set in stubborn certainty. "She's a scientist. Yes, I think she'll see reason."

"She is a Wraith, whatever she calls herself." Teyla's voice was hard. "She will have no concern for anything except feeding and her own hive."

Rodney waved an arm, frustrated. "Then why isn't she making a deal with these Wraith?"

John shook his head in exasperation, glaring up at the death ray/beaming thing in the ceiling. "We don't know that she isn't."

Teyla paced away from the door, frowning. "And I still cannot believe that she is what she claims to be, even if it is true that she came here through the Mirror. Why would the Ancestors who escaped to her reality deliberately re-create the Wraith? It makes no sense."

Rodney said impatiently, "It does, if you consider the plague; she said her people thought the 'Creators' and the other race they tried to seed were wiped out by it. If it was at all similar to the plague that destroyed the Ancients in the Milky Way, we know how virulent it was, that they never discovered a cure." Rodney paced, warming to his theory. "If these Ancients thought the only way to pass along their DNA was to use the Iratus bug mutation, which they already knew could be combined with human DNA—" He stopped, facing them, pointing toward the sealed hatch. "If they controlled its development, bred out the need to feed off sentient beings, made it as human as they could without allowing it to be susceptible to the plague, they could have produced something like Trishen. A Wraith-like being with pronounced human behavioral characteristics who has the Ancient gene."

Teyla shook her head, looking away. "I hope you are right," she said quietly.

"And she didn't say her species couldn't feed on sentient beings, Rodney," John pointed out. "She said they didn't." He lifted his brows. "That's a big difference."

The Wraith were taking their time searching the roof, so Ronon went into the jumper's rear cabin, sitting on the bench to check his gun and sharpen his knives. Much as he would like to take on the whole group, he knew destroying the Mirror was more important.

Sheppard, Teyla Emmagan, and McKay had died for it.

Finally Zelenka ducked into the rear cabin, saying anxiously, "They are leaving the roof. There are only two left near the place where the others—Two, that's good?"

Ronon's mouth twisted in grim amusement. "That's good." He pushed to his feet, sliding his long knife back into the scabbard.

From the cockpit, Kusanagi said, "I can lift the jumper further up the shaft." Ronon looked through the hatchway to see the HUD pop up a skeletal outline of the space directly above the jumper, showing the straight shaft and then what looked like a large doorway, maybe two levels up. The image was fuzzy on the edges, the Mirror still interfering with the ship's scanning abilities. Kusanagi pointed. "There. That opening, maybe it would give you a quicker route to the roof."

Ronon nodded. "Try it."

While Kusanagi slowly guided the jumper up the shaft, Ronon let Zelenka fuss around checking his radio and making sure his air tanks were topped off. The odd thing was that Ronon thought Zelenka was doing it because he really wanted Ronon to come back alive, not because he was afraid of being left with no one to guard him. "You have enough guns?" Zelenka asked him finally, waving a hand around at the supplies and weapons stored in the overhead racks. "There are extras."

"I've got enough," Ronon said, but he took a few of the small explosives meant for throwing, the ones called "grenades."

Kusanagi found the opening, a shattered hatchway leading into a space that might be for unloading freight, and rotated the jumper so the ramp was facing it. Ronon took a last look at the life signs screen, committing the Wraith's current positions to memory. The hand-held detector wouldn't work unless somebody with the Ancestors' blood, like Sheppard or McKay or Kusanagi, was close enough to touch it. But Kusanagi and Zelenka could follow his progress with the jumper's screens, and warn him if the Wraith were about to cross his path. Ronon had survived a long time without that kind of help, but he wasn't fool enough to turn it down when it was freely offered.

He waited in the rear cabin while Kusanagi sealed the cockpit door to keep the air in, then opened the ramp. All that was left of the hatchway into the freight bay was jagged metal and broken stone, leading into a dark dusty passage. Ronon didn't wait for the ramp to open all the way; he caught the edge of the hatch and swung across, landing on the platform. The metal creaked under his boots, but didn't give, and a moment later he was moving fast down the passage. He heard the ramp closing behind him, and Kusanagi's soft voice on the radio, whispering, "Be careful."

"Will you two sit down?" Rodney asked in exasperation.

"In a minute." John wasn't pacing because he was stir-crazy, he was pacing because he was trying to keep sore and strained muscles from stiffening up. If they had a chance to do anything, he wanted to be able to move. Rodney was sitting on the floor, leaning back against the wall, and Teyla, who did look stir-crazy, was pacing on the opposite side of the room from John.

They had poked all around the cabin, looking for a way to disarm the force shield. Rodney had used Teyla's knife on the rubbery wall-covering near the doorway, cutting through it to get to the controls to open and close the hatch. But those controls didn't affect the force shield, which was apparently generated by a separate unit somewhere on the other side of the wall. John figured that was why Trishen had used it to make their little prison; she had seen Rodney finesse the control panel for the ship's outer lock and had to know an inside hatchway wouldn't hold him long.

Rodney let his breath out, rubbing his face. "I don't suppose it's a good idea to try the rations she left. Or the water."

"It could be drugged." Teyla eyed the box with disapproval. "If she truly does not mean to feed on us, then she may have other designs."

Rodney frowned at her. "Drugged how?"

"It could turn us into zombies," John told him, picking a fate worse than death at random. His throat was painfully dry too, but he didn't think it was worth taking the chance.

Rodney contemplated the ceiling of the cabin in mock despair. "Yes, I'd worry about brain damage from the oxygen deprivation and the head injury, if I didn't know you were always like this."

John was watching Teyla. She had stopped pacing, and was rubbing her temple, her expression strained. She said abruptly, "I have been sensing Wraith, which is to be expected. But they seem...closer now, than they did before. Very close."

"How close is very?" John asked. The cabin suddenly felt a lot smaller and even more cage-like. If Trishen had cut a deal with the other Wraith... "Inside the ship?"

"Wait, maybe you're sensing Trishen." Rodney shoved to his feet, steadying himself on the wall with a wince. "She could be in a cabin next to this one—"

"It is not her." Teyla shook her head, her lips pressed together. "I have never been able to sense her presence, even when she was standing in front of me." She looked at John, lifting a brow. "These Wraith are close, and angry."

John heard something outside and stepped to where he could see the sealed hatch in the outer compartment. A moment later it slid open and Trishen stepped in. John stood on his toes and craned his neck, trying to see if there were any more Wraith lurking in the passage behind her.

Trishen moved nearly to the force-shielded doorway.

It was still hard for John to read her expression, but her body radiated tension. She looked at Teyla. "Were you telling the truth about the Wraith searching for new sentients to feed on?"

Folding her arms, Teyla eyed her deliberately. "To the best of my knowledge. There are not enough humans to support the number of hives, and on some worlds they have already culled entire populations. We know they grow increasingly desperate."

Trishen looked away, taking a sharp breath. "They're at the outer lock, trying to break into the ship." She pressed her hands together, as if steeling herself. "I don't have any weapons to stop them, and I can't repair the shields on the base ship, or the drive."

John shook his head with a grimace. *Crap. I knew this was going to happen.* Teyla's face hardened and she threw a grim look at John. Rodney threw his arms in the air in exasperation, saying, "Well, that limits your options, doesn't it? I told you they would want this ship, and they're going to want to know where you got it. Believe me, you won't like the way they ask the questions!" He added with bitter emphasis, "And if you don't let us go now, you might as well kill us yourself."

John snorted derisively to himself, thinking there wasn't a chance in hell of that. So it caught him completely by surprise when Trishen said, "I'll let you go, but listen to me first." She hesitated, shook her head a little. "I could take this shuttle, leave this system, but it isn't meant for long-range trips, and I know I have nowhere to go." She looked at Rodney, intent and desperate. "You told me you thought you could make the Mirror functional. If you agree to do that, or at least to try, I'll agree to destroy my base ship, so there is no possibility the Wraith will get its technology. If the Mirror can be activated, I'll take this shuttle back to my reality, and then you'll be free to do what you like to the Mirror."

Teyla lifted her brows, startled. Rodney stared at Trishen, so taken aback it was obvious he hadn't really expected her to give in either. He said, "Wait, that... sounds reasonable. That would work for us." He looked at John. "Right?"

John just really hoped this wasn't a trick, because otherwise he didn't see what the hell they were going to do. He asked Trishen, "What if he can't fix it?"

"Oh, fine!" Rodney objected, turning to John in outrage. "Let's cast doubt on my abilities right now! That'll help!"

Trishen shook her head impatiently. "I understand it may be impossible to make it operate again. I won't try to stop you from destabilizing it, if it comes to that. I'm trusting you to just give me a chance." She hesitated nervously. "I'm also trusting you not to kill me."

"Yeah, we're trusting you about that, too," John felt he had to point out. If the only thing she really wanted was to get back to her home reality, then this had half a chance of working. He threw a look at Teyla, got a sharp nod in reply. Rodney was making *get on with it* gestures. John said, "You've got a deal."

Trishen nodded tightly, and touched a control on her wristband. John saw the force shield shimmer. He moved forward, waved a hand to make sure it was really gone, then stepped through. Trishen backed away hastily, all the way to the far wall, which was fine with him. He said, "Where's our weapons?"

"In that cabinet." She pointed and he headed for it. The door was dark metal, thin and pleated into tiny ridges, almost like fabric. She began, "I have to unlock—" But when John touched it, the door slid open. She laughed a little, sounding startled rather than amused. "You really are descended from the Creators."

John didn't bother to reply, hauling out the P-90 that lay atop the pile and taking rapid inventory of the rest. Only one pistol, still holstered in Teyla's gun belt, but all three of their tac vests were there, Rodney's pack, and the SCBAs.

Rodney said, "It was set to respond only to the Ancient gene? Colonel Sheppard is a natural carrier, I have it artificially." He added, "What?" when John shoved his pack at him with a meaningful glare.

"We don't have time to chat." John handed Teyla her gun belt and tac vest and rapidly checked the P-90, making sure it hadn't been damaged or tampered with. So they had a temporary deal; he didn't want to give Trishen any more intel on them than they absolutely had to.

"We have no other weapons?" Teyla asked, buckling on her gun belt as she kept one eye on Trishen.

"That's it. At least we've got plenty of ammo." John pulled on his vest, clipping the P-90 to it, thinking, *so far so good*. He found a stray headset caught in the velcro on the vest and hooked it over his ear, switching the base unit on. He winced at the roar of static he got in response. He looked at Trishen, who was still watching them nervously. "We'll have to use your comm system to call our ship."

Rodney had torn open his pack, muttering a quick inventory of the contents. "Yes, I'm going to need Radek

and Miko to work on this too, but first things first."
He turned to Trishen. "Does the base ship have a self-
destruct?"

She shook her head. "No, it's a research vessel, there
was no need for one. I was going to overload the drive.
Should we—"

Rodney held up a finger. "First, I'll need to con-
vert your shields to a cloak. The Wraith scout ship
won't detect the shuttle's lift off, and when the base
ship is destroyed, they'll assume everything went with
it. Hopefully any Wraith on the ground close enough to
notice the shuttle's sudden disappearance won't survive
the explosion."

Trishen nodded, starting out of the compartment. "Yes,
that's an excellent strategy."

Following her, Rodney's mouth twisted in grim
amusement. "We've had some success with it in the
past."

She led the way down the passage, past two other
small compartments. The shuttle was filled with weird
semi-organic devices, in colors from black to purple to
pink. John had to admit, disturbing as the organic part
was, it didn't look like a Wraith ship. But then the lack
of webbing and skeletons and cocooned captives made a
big impact.

Trishen stepped into a semi-circular cabin filled with
the organic control consoles. Several round holographic
displays floated in the air, most of them data readouts. She
pointed to one of the consoles. "These are the controls for
the shields. Can you—"

"Yes." Rodney studied the rapidly shifting display
floating above it, and touched a few of the colored pads.

"It's extremely similar to At—" Rodney turned the word into a cough, and finished hurriedly, "To shield consoles I've seen before. It should only take a few minutes."

Teyla kept her expression perfectly neutral and John rubbed the bridge of his nose, thinking *that was close.* Trishen's version of the Pegasus Galaxy wasn't likely to have an Atlantis, unless the Ancients had built one there, but the name might have appeared in their history some-where. Even if the Mirror was destroyed, John just didn't want to send Trishen home with the idea that there was anything in this reality worth having.

But she hadn't appeared to notice Rodney's near-mis-step. She nodded, saying, "Good. I've already set the drive to build up power, but I have to manually disengage the failsafes because—"

Rodney nodded, absorbed in the controls and readouts. "Because the drive is specifically designed not to do what you're trying to make it do, right. Get to it."

She hesitated. "I need to use the main console in the base ship..."

John got it. She didn't want to leave them up here alone, since Rodney was obviously capable of operat-ing the shuttle without her help. He said, "I'll come with you."

She nodded, relieved, and started back into the pas-sage. John followed her, Teyla with him. The passage led into a lock that apparently connected it to the base ship. It was open, but John stopped, lifting a brow.

The shuttle apparently fit into the base ship in such a way that its deck was at a right angle to the base ship's deck. The hatch was looking down the base ship's open central core; straight down, so it appeared as if they should be falling down it already. "Just step through," Trishen said, noticing his hesitation. "The artificial gravity adjusts automatically."

"Okay," John said, figuring he had a fifty-fifty chance of breaking his neck. He stepped through and suddenly found himself standing on the small stair platform, clinging to the railing.

Teyla lifted her brows. "That is clever."

"Yeah." John grimaced, waited until Trishen had stepped through, and gave Teyla a signal to guard the hatch area. She nodded and he followed Trishen down the stairs that spiraled around the core area.

Compartments opened off the platforms on each level, much like the shuttle, only on a slightly larger scale. John realized he could hear a high-pitched buzz from below. Trishen had said the other Wraith were trying to break in. "Is that from the outer hatch?"

She said, "Yes, I think they're using some sort of cutting tool to get into the control panel, but that should take them some time." On the next to lowest level, she stopped at another control area, bigger than the shuttle's cockpit, with more of the floating displays. She started hitting control pads, and said, "Main console to shuttle. I've turned on the internal comm throughout the ship, so you can—"

Rodney's voice on a loudspeaker interrupted, "Notify you when I'm ready, yes, yes, get to work."

John left her to it, going down half a level until he had a view of the hatch for the main airlock. The buzzing noise from outside the hatch didn't get any louder, but it was still making John's nerves twitch. He listened to Rodney and Trishen talking back and forth on the comm, mostly incomprehensible techno-babble. It sounded like Rodney had finished converting the shields to a cloaking device and they were just waiting on the drive build-up.

Then Rodney's voice said abruptly, "Wait, what the hell is that?" John tensed, pushing to his feet and stepping back onto the platform. Before he could ask what the hell was what, Rodney said, "Trishen, do you have a view of the outer hatch?"

Alarmed, Trishen hit a control. One of the display bubbles expanded to a view of the outside of the ship. The vantage point looked like it was up on the shuttle, and the image was blue-gray, as if it was from a nightvision scope; the daily eclipse must have started.

There was a cluster of drones and a few male Wraith around the ship. Three of the drones had strange tools about the size of an AT-4 Rocket Launcher, and were just pointing them at the outer hatch. The beams came on, so intense the glare washed out the image. Sounding appalled, Trishen said, "They're cutting the hatch out!"

Rodney's voice was sour. "They must have heard the drive build-up and decided not to bother trying to take the ship intact. That's typical."

John ducked back to the steps to look at the outer lock from this side. Even from here, he could see a hot blue glow growing in the center of the hatch. *Oh, hell.* "Hurry it up, guys, they're burning through the inner hatch!"

He heard Rodney ask Trishen, "Can you seal off that section? Oh, at what point does that make sense!" John guessed the answer had been "no." Rodney added urgently, "Then keep going, overload everything—"

The blue glow was getting larger. The hatch was steaming, giving off a sharp odor far too close to burning flesh for John's comfort. He moved back up a few steps, crouching to keep the P-90 aimed at the outer hatch. The metal of the whole central core was starting to tremble and over the whine from the cutting tools he could hear a muted reverberation that had to be the overloaded drive. Trishen pushed away from the controls, saying, "It's done! We have to get away——"

John saw the blue glow of the cutting beams suddenly expand, the black hatch material turning white with heat. He yelled, "Go, now!" The hatch exploded inward, and John fired down at the first of the drones that slammed through the white-hot remnants. The first two drones collapsed in the lock; they would regenerate in a couple of minutes but right now they were dead weight, slowing the others down, forcing them to clamber over the temporarily inert bodies.

Trishen bolted out onto the platform, then started up the steps.

John fired at the hatch again, then pushed to his feet and darted up the stairs after her. At the next platform, he turned to fire down, catching a male Wraith just as it stuck its head out into the central well to look upward. It fell back and John charged up the stairs.

From above, Teyla fired her 9mm down the central well. John reached the shuttle connection platform and backed toward the hatch, firing to cover Teyla as she drew back from the railing. Then something hit him, sending him staggering. The right side of his body went instantly numb, and he sagged, barely clinging to the railing; he must have been clipped with the edge of a stun blast. Teyla shouted in alarm, firing down the stairs, and John knew the Wraith were almost on them. "Teyla, get out of here!"

Then Rodney ducked out of the hatch and grabbed John's numb arm, hauling him across the platform.

Teyla emptied her second clip as John and Rodney reached the shuttle's hatch. Turning, she shoved both of them through. The gravity field grabbed them and John slammed into the shuttle's deck, Rodney landing half on top of him. John managed to turn his head in time to see Teyla land on her feet beside him. A Wraith snarled up at them from the platform directly below, just lifting its stunner to fire. John awkwardly scrabbled for the P-90 with his good arm, but Rodney and Teyla were yelling, "Now, now!"

The hatch slid shut.

John let his head drop back. "Yeah, that was close," he gasped. "Thanks, Rodney, Teyla."

"Close?" Rodney shouted incredulously. "Shut up! And you're welcome!"

Teyla let her breath out in relief, sliding down the wall to sit on the deck. She looked at the sleeve of her jacket, where there was now a hand-shaped rip in the gray material. "Very close," she said with a rueful grimace.

Too close, John thought. A little less momentum, and that thing would have had her. He heard muted banging on the lock, and tried to shove himself upright. "We need to get out of here—" He felt a thump through the deck that sounded a lot like a docking clamp releasing, then a gentle push as the shuttle lifted away from the base ship.

Trishen's voice called from a nearby compartment, "We're away!"

"That's nice." Rodney shoved himself into a sitting position, planting an elbow in John's numb side in the process. He called back to her, "Are we cloaked?"

"Yes, it seems to be working!"

Rodney rolled his eyes. "Seems to. Oh, that's fine. We'll know for certain when the scout ship starts shooting at us." He yelled, "Is the base ship blowing up?" He added in a lower voice, "Please, please blow up."

Somewhere below the hatch, muted by distance, thin air, and the shuttle's shielding, John heard an explosion.

Rodney slumped in relief. "Thank you."

CHAPTER EIGHT

The sky was a deep purple when Ronon made it up to the roof, the big planet that filled the sky almost blocking all but the last light of the sun. He paused in the doorway of the little dome that sheltered the lift platform; it was too dark to see more than the outlines of the various lumps and projections on the roof, but he couldn't hear any movement.

"Ronon, they are still heading away from you," Zelenka whispered in his headset. "Five hundred yards, a little further. They are moving fairly slowly, crossing back and forth in a search pattern. I think they are looking for the puddlejumper."

He heard Kusanagi add, "Perhaps they think the others landed on the roof, that the ship is still there, cloaked. They must suspect we are from Atlantis."

"Suspecting is fine," Zelenka told her. "As long as they don't know for certain. And even the possibility of a jumper doesn't tell them the city is still there. It would be unreasonable for them to believe that none of us escaped through the Stargate before the destruction."

Using the low platforms as cover, Ronon headed for the roof's edge. There was still just enough light for him to see the darker shadow of the trench. He took out the little battery lightstick and crouched low, cupping his hand over it to shield the beam, and flashed it over the floor of the trench. He moved along the edge until the light found disturbed dust, the marks of tracks and scuffling. Then the light caught the glint of the metal shells cast off by the Atlantean weapons. *It happened here,* he thought.

He jumped down into the trench, landing lightly, and paced down it. After a few moments' search, he frowned. This was the right place, but something important was missing. He touched his headset. "They aren't here."

"The Wraith?" Zelenka asked, a little startled. "The detector shows they are still searching—"

"No. The others." Ronon had thought he would find their bodies. The Wraith discarded human corpses like trash, leaving them where they fell; they would never have bothered to move the bodies after a feeding. Something else caught the light and he crouched, running his fingers through a scatter of plastic and metal debris. The remains of one of McKay's computers. He allowed himself a grim smile; the destruction was thorough, nothing left to give the Wraith any information, any hint that Atlantis still lived.

"Oh, you mean...no bodies?" Zelenka hesitated. "But then perhaps they are alive? If the Wraith beamed them up, their life signs would disappear from screen—"

"Maybe. That doesn't mean they're alive now." Ronon stood, moving to the metal housing that shielded the device they needed to destroy. He felt along it, looking for an access panel. If the others were alive... They would be aboard that Wraith scout ship.

The jumper couldn't take on a Wraith ship that size. Ronon would have to figure out a way to get onboard. And then get off again, if he found them alive. And he couldn't believe he was planning something this mad, but then the Atlanteans seemed to encourage this kind of thinking. *Sheppard would do it,* he thought. *So would*

Emmagan.

He shook his head. *This first,* he told himself. Ronon's fingers found an indentation in the metal; an access panel. "I found—"

The sudden explosion sent him to the ground, crouching low. A moment later he realized it couldn't be the Mirror; the blast hadn't even made the building tremble. "Zelenka, what was that?"

Zelenka was cursing in his own language again. "We heard it, but whatever it was was too close to Mirror platform for our sensors to detect the source. Wraith scout ship is still in orbit, we're detecting no darts—"

The Wraith had no reason to blow things up near the Mirror. And explosions made Ronon think of Sheppard and McKay. He stood, feeling for purchase on the housing, and found a spot to plant his boot; he pushed himself up. Craning his neck, he could just see over the top.

It was too dark to see much, but near the far side of the Mirror's frame there was a large scatter of debris that was sparking with energy. It was right about where the strange Wraith ship had been. "It's been blown up," Ronon reported. "The Wraith female's ship."

Then his headset crackled with static and he heard, "This is Sheppard. Ronon, is that you?"

"Sheppard?" Ronon grinned, jumping down from the housing. That explained the explosion.

On the headset, Zelenka demanded incredulously, "What? Colonel? Colonel, you are all alive? Rodney and Teyla?"

Sheppard's voice answered, "We're all fine. Zelenka, what's your position?"

"The same one we had before," Zelenka said, sounding deeply relieved. Ronon could hear Kusanagi laughing and clapping with joy in the background.

Sheppard said, "Good. Just stay there for now and wait for instructions."

Ronon broke in, "Sheppard, I'm on the roof, near the pulse generator."

"There are Wraith up there with him," Zelenka added hastily. "Well, not with him, but they have turned and are heading back in his direction. I think they are only heading back toward the explosion, but—"

Ronon heard McKay in the background this time, then Sheppard said, "Ronon, we're going to beam you off the roof, back outside the installation, near where the jumper is."

"Uh, okay." Ronon studied the dark sky uneasily. *Beam?* "Where are you?"

"That's a long story." From Sheppard's tone, Ronon didn't think he was going to like this story. "I'll tell you once we get you out of there."

Nobody had liked John's brief summation of their plan: John could practically hear Ronon's expression of deep cynicism over the radio, Radek had muttered in Czech, and even Miko had said doubtfully, "Dr. McKay thinks this is a good idea?"

"Yes, yes he does," Rodney had inserted into the conversation. "Now just shut up and do it."

The jumper rendezvoused with the shuttle, and with both ships cloaked, they headed toward the mountains. They were looking for a spot where they could land and regroup; they needed the breathing room, and Rodney needed the jumper's equipment to come up with a way to fix the Mirror.

The flight away from the installation would only take a few minutes, but John could tell it was going to be an awkward few minutes. He and Teyla were standing back in the main compartment area, watching Trishen in the cockpit while Rodney worked at pulling more data out of the terminals. Trishen was flying the shuttle using only the instruments and a couple of bubble displays; there wasn't anything like a viewport, and that was making John's nerves jump. He was used to flying by instrument, but no windows at all just felt all kinds of wrong. And Trishen didn't trust them, and they didn't trust her. Even Rodney, who had pushed the "let's work together" solution, was jumpy and uncomfortable in the confined space of the compartment and passages.

At least they had intel on the Wraith's movements. The shuttle was still receiving data from sensor buoys Trishen had placed around the Mirror when she had first arrived. She had set one of the holographic bubbles in the compartment to display the video feed, and they had a good view of the Mirror platform.

The eclipse was waning, the light getting steadily brighter. They could see the base ship's glowing debris field, and the Wraith climbing around the Mirror's frame. John asked Teyla, "You think they know what it's for yet?"

Teyla studied the little figures moving in the display, her brows drawn together. "It is hard to tell. As the shuttle was lifting off, I could sense their frustration, their anger at being thwarted, that was all. There was no feeling that they had made a great discovery." She shook her head. "But they must realize the Mirror is a portal to somewhere."

"They probably think it's just a giant Stargate, like
we did at first," John said, then snorted at himself. *Just
a giant Stargate, like that's something to sneeze at.* The
Wraith might think it went to some hidden refuge of the
Ancients, some nice new feeding ground for them. *Well,
it could, if we don't get the damn thing shut down.* He
stretched, rolling his shoulders, wincing as sore muscles
and bruises protested the motion. From the cockpit,
Trishen glanced up, saw he and Teyla watching her, and
quickly looked down at her terminal again. John let his
breath out. He really hated this. There was just too much
about her they didn't know. He lowered his voice and
said, "If she can do that mental communication thing...
she could tell them where we are without even touching
a radio."

Teyla didn't look happy either, but she said, "But she
released us, destroyed her ship. She seems as if she truly
wishes to escape them, and this reality."

John shrugged, resigned. "Yeah, I know. I'm just...
paranoid. Every time we trust somebody new they turn
around and stab us in the ass." And he couldn't help
thinking that her description of the Eidolon or whatever
they called themselves was too good to be true. "And if
the Wraith in her reality don't feed on humans or any
other kind of people-like alien, what do they feed on?"

"She does have water and some sort of rations in this
ship." Teyla's lips twisted and her brows indicated skepticism. "Though I find it hard to believe that her kind
are entirely human in that respect. Perhaps, unlike the
Wraith here, they are able to feed on the life force of
animals."

John nodded to himself. "Well, we're never going to find out, and I'm okay with that."

They reached the foothills a short time later, and found a low plateau for a landing site. It was stony and bare of the tall red grass that would betray the presence of two cloaked ships, and sheltered by high bluffs and rocky overhangs.

The shuttle was bigger but John had made it clear that they were doing any joint research in the jumper. It was awkward, as they would need to keep the ramp down and everyone would have to wear SCBAs the whole time, but he didn't want any unpleasant surprises. Rodney agreed with an impatient grimace. "Yes, let's skip the possibility of an intruder control system that leaves us all helpless now that we've introduced her to the other members of our little group," he muttered, watching Trishen as she was absorbed in her instruments. She was carefully guiding the shuttle into a landing on the stone shelf. "I thought she'd at least try to keep one of us as a hostage, and that we'd waste an hour threatening each other and arguing about it."

"Yeah." John had thought so too, and he wasn't sure if the fact that she hadn't gone that route made him less suspicious or more so. "Maybe she realized just how badly that would go over." Who knew, it could be common sense. Controlling a hostage was harder than it looked, and Trishen had been working on the Mirror for a while now without success; she knew she needed their help, or specifically Rodney's help. And that she wasn't likely to get it if they thought she was a danger to them.

Once the shuttle was down, John got on the headset

and talked Miko through landing the jumper. The jumper's sensors couldn't pick up the cloaked shuttle, though the cloaked jumper appeared as a ghostly outline on the shuttle's display. John figured the two ships crashing into each other at some point would be the perfect cap to this day, but the jumper set down safely on the stony ground about thirty yards away.

They got their SCBAs on, and went out to meet the others. Ronon came down the ramp first, eyeing Trishen warily. She was standing back near her shuttle's open hatch, holding the black sphere that was her portable terminal. She was wearing the helmet part of her environmental outfit, but hadn't bothered with the rest of the concealing suit. With the dead-white skin of her hands visible, it was a lot more obvious what she was. Ronon began, "How do you know—"

John cut him off, "We don't know anything. We just know that this is the deal we made, and so far she's keeping up her end of it."

"Seriously, we've gone over it all already," Rodney told him wearily. "Several times."

Zelenka stopped in the hatchway, peering around Ronon. "*Proboha!*" He looked at Rodney, his eyes wide above the SCBA mask. "She's a Wraith."

Rodney glared at him in irritation. "What, did you think it was a cruel joke?"

Zelenka gestured in annoyance. "Of course not! But you said she was not like the Wraith of our reality. I was hoping there wouldn't be so much...with the hands, and everything."

John took Zelenka's arm, turning him so they weren't facing toward Trishen. "Listen, we've got a temporary deal with her, but don't let down your guard, don't let her get you alone." He gave Rodney a meaningful look, including him in the admonition. "Don't forget what she is."

Rodney just nodded tightly. With an aghast expression, Zelenka said, "I don't think that will be a problem."

Rodney rolled his eyes. "On that note, let's get to work." He waved imperatively to Trishen, calling her over.

Under Ronon's highly suspicious gaze, they got two laptops set up at the end of the rear cabin, and Trishen put her portable terminal on the ramp. It was a little reassuring that she still seemed just as nervous of them as they were of her.

Miko was using the station tied into the jumper's systems in the cockpit, so she could keep an eye on the HUD. John ended up in the jumper's cockpit with her, Rodney, and Teyla, not so much for a secret meeting out of Trishen's hearing, but because the cockpit was pressurized and they could take off the SCBAs long enough to eat and drink something.

As they stood around knocking back water and power bars, Miko looked up from her laptop to tell them, "We were so afraid! And you all look—"

Rodney interrupted her with, "Work now, sympathy later." He crumpled a wrapper. "I want this over with as soon as possible."

John could get behind that attitude.

Rodney and Teyla went back outside, but the HUD showed that the interference from the Mirror had calmed down enough to send another databurst back to base camp, so John stayed to record a brief report. He just hit

the highlights: Wraith, more Wraith, what they were planning to do. Miko added compressed files with copies of
Rodney's data on the Mirror, and sent it. It worried him
that they hadn't gotten a reply back from the last transmission Zelenka had made. But if it had come during the
Mirror's last big discharge, the jumper's comm might not
have been able to receive it.

John went back outside, where Teyla and Ronon were
standing out in the open space between the two ships.
This spot was shadowed by the cliffs, which were striped
with red and yellow mineral deposits. The sky was reassuringly empty of anything but the gas giant, growing
brighter as the moon moved further out of the eclipse.

Trishen was working on her terminal while Rodney
and Radek pointed at different laptop and tablet screens
and argued. Ronon stood with one hand not-so-casually
on his energy gun. "Everything okay?" John asked.

Ronon shrugged one shoulder. "So far."

Rodney and Radek had to go back and forth into the
shuttle a few times, to take special readings or copy over
something else from her stored data. John made sure they
were never alone with Trishen, while Teyla and Ronon
kept an eye on their perimeter. The active cloaks on the
ships made things a little awkward, since neither the
shuttle nor the jumper were visible unless you were
standing in them, and people occasionally got lost moving from one ship to the other and had to be directed back
on course.

Then Miko's voice came over their headsets, shouting,
"There are Wraith! There are two darts! I mean, incoming!"

"Everybody inside." John turned, scanning the sky.

There was nothing visible yet, but the HUD would have picked them up long before they were in visible range.

"Me too?" Trishen asked uncertainly, standing up and clutching her terminal. Zelenka had already shifted his equipment away from the hatch, further back into the rear cabin. Rodney was standing, his eyes on the handheld life signs detector.

They couldn't chance sending Trishen across the open area to the shuttle. "Yeah, you too," John said, trying not to sound too grudging about it.

Trishen edged up the ramp a little, still staying as far away from them as possible.

Miko came out of the cockpit, stepping up beside John, uneasily peering up at the sky. "They should be—Yes, right there."

She pointed and John made out the shape of the darts, nearly lost against the colors of the gas giant. Ronon stepped past Miko, stationing himself between her and the hatch opening; he was watching Trishen rather than the darts.

After an endless moment, John could tell the darts' course was taking them off to the west. He said, "Rodney?"

Rodney shook his head, his eyes on the life signs detector. "There's nothing on the ground." He looked up, squinting to follow the dart's progress. "They didn't beam down."

He and John exchanged a look of weary relief. Yeah, John had had more than enough Wraith for today, too. The darts zigzagged back and forth a few times, then finally turned, heading east. Considering it, John said, "Funny how with this whole moon to search, they're pay-ing so much attention to these mountains."

Rodney's brow furrowed suspiciously as he glanced up at the retreating darts. "I'll check again for signal leakage, but if they knew where we were, they'd attack."

Trishen looked at them, at Zelenka clutching his laptop and nervously studying the sky, at Miko still squeezed in between John and Ronon, at Rodney intently watching the life signs detector. Trishen asked, "This is how you live?"

John just looked at her, having no idea what to say to that. They were so much safer, so much better off, than most of the other human inhabitants of Pegasus, that the question was impossible to answer. Ronon looked away, his face set in a sardonic grimace. Teyla said, coldly, "Yes. But we have weapons, and the Ancestors' cloaking devices. Others do not." Canting her head thoughtfully, she added, "They have come this way because they sense your presence, have they not?"

Trishen hesitated, and John swore under his breath. He had had the feeling there was another shoe about to drop, but he had hoped to put it off for a while longer. Trishen made a frustrated gesture, saying, "I didn't think they would be able to. Their minds are so...different. But they only have a vague awareness of my existence. Obviously they can't pinpoint my location."

"What?" Rodney stared at her. "Hello, were you not standing right there when I explained the plan to make it look like we were all dead, so the Wraith would stop looking for us?"

Ronon grunted in a way that clearly meant *I told you so.*

John ignored both of them, pointing out to Trishen,

"You could have mentioned this earlier."

"I didn't know," she insisted. "I've kept myself closed off from their minds, I thought that would be enough." John's expression must have conveyed what he thought of that excuse. Sounding urgent, she added, "But you can use it to your advantage. I can distract them away from you."

Rodney clapped a hand over his eyes in exasperation. John just said, "I hope you're right about that."

The work was interrupted twice more by searching darts, but Trishen was right in that they didn't seem able to pinpoint her. And the base moon hadn't responded to John's transmission yet, giving him something else to worry about. He knew it was all too possible for the Wraith to have followed the signal traces the Mirror was sending to the monitoring station in the ruined city. *Lorne would've gotten them out of there,* he told himself. *Lorne better have gotten them out of there.*

Rodney finally said, "All right, we've got it." He motioned everyone to gather around the ramp, and turned the laptop, which was displaying a partial schematic of the top half of the installation. "As I suspected all along, the key is in the pulse generator that stabilizes the Mirror's accretion surface. Since it was first constructed, factors that affected the required degree of stabilization have changed. Now these factors could be anything from the decreasing levels of oxygen in the atmosphere, changes in the ozone layer caused by the Mirror itself, orbital drift, and so on. There was apparently no compensation mechanism for this because the Mirror was meant to be abandoned—" He glared at John, who was making "get on with it" gestures. "Fine. The instability has kept the Mirror active since Trishen's ship came through, and it's still connected to the correct destination; we just have to make that connection stable enough for transport by adjusting the pulse. We've done the calculations, but the corrections are going to have to be made directly to the consoles that control the array."

"Okay." John thought it sounded deceptively easy. "Do we have a clue where that is?"

"Yes, yes, I'm getting to it." Rodney hit a few keys to change the schematic, bringing up another section. "From the exploration that Trishen managed to do before we arrived, we suspect it's here, on the roof, above the section of the installation where the environmental and security system controls are located." He indicated a highlighted spot on the roof, not too far from the observation area they had found when they had first managed to get into the building.

"You suspect?" Teyla said, before John could. "What if you are wrong?"

Rodney gave them all a sour grimace. "I'm not wrong. According to everything we've discovered about this place so far, and the exploration Trishen did before we arrived, the controls we need have to be in this section."

Zelenka shifted forward. "The good news is, once the shuttle has passed through the Mirror—which should take only seconds—we can shut the entire pulse generator down from that location. It's much more effective method of destabilizing the Mirror than just destroying a section of the array itself, as we originally planned. Instead of dramatic discharge, the singularity is likely to just collapse inward and disappear." He shrugged. "And we will probably not be killed."

"And the Wraith can't find these controls and turn it back on?" John said, wanting to be absolutely certain.

Rodney signed in annoyance and folded his arms. "That would be a yes, since it's the entire point of this insane exercise."

"It would do no good to turn it back on." Zelenka made motions indicating something big getting suddenly very small, and then waved his hands rapidly. "Some of the physical structure of the Mirror may remain, but the quantum components will no longer exist in this reality."

"Thank you, Dr. Zelenka, that was the answer I was hoping for." John smiled engagingly at Rodney. "I assume you've got some way for us to land on the roof without triggering another discharge from the Mirror?"

Rodney appeared to take a lot of pleasure in saying, "For once, you assume correctly. Trishen's shuttle emits a field which keeps it from disrupting the pulse array, and we're going to temporarily adjust the jumper's cloak signatures to mimic that field. That should allow us to fly above the Mirror platform and land on the roof without triggering another discharge."

"Which would cause us to crash and die," Zelenka added helpfully.

Rodney checked his watch. "We'll have to time our arrival for the moment that the Wraith scout ship's orbit takes it out of scanning range. It'll be out of range for only forty-five minutes, so we'll need to move quickly. Not that the scout ship wasn't out of range the last time we tried the roof, but it gives us a slight advantage." With a wince, he added, "Very slight."

"This is where I can help," Trishen said, sitting forward. "I can draw the darts away from the area with my shuttle."

Rodney eyed her, as if reluctant to let her participate. "Not too far away. Even once we enter the corrections, the Mirror won't be stable for long. We'll need you to be ready to go through as soon as we make the adjustments." He looked at John impatiently. "Well?"

John nodded. It sounded like a plan. It also sounded like their only option. "Let's do it."

"Looks pretty quiet," John said, studying the jumper's screens as he guided it in a smooth arc above the installation's roof. The adjustments Zelenka had made to the jumper's cloak must be working; the Mirror hadn't made so much as a grumble. "Good job, Radek."

"Thank you, Colonel," Zelenka said from the right hand jump seat. "It's nice not to crash." Rodney was in the co-pilot's seat, comparing a tablet to the energy signatures the jumper was displaying on the HUD. Teyla was sitting behind John, with Kusanagi and Ronon watching from the rear cabin. Trishen's shuttle should be paralleling their course, though it was invisible to both instruments and visual contact. Relying on Trishen not to crash into him wasn't exactly John's favorite part of this trip.

"I do not see any Wraith on the platform," Teyla said from behind him.

"Yeah, they're probably inside." The life signs screen wasn't showing any Wraith in the open at all; they were probably busy ransacking the building, looking for more intel on the Mirror. Most of the darts were out of the immediate area, searching the mountains and the surrounding area. "Rodney?"

"Will you slow down? Hold it—" Rodney sat forward,

pointing out the viewport. "Here we go. Right there."

John slowed, bringing the jumper in a little lower. Rodney was pointing at a small dome on top of the roof, not far from the trench that bordered the curved housing of the pulse array. It was the same dark stone as the rest of the building, and from the air it looked like one of the round elevator-access kiosks. The HUD popped up a terrain sensor screen, comparing this dome to the other structures on the roof, and John could see it was somewhat larger. He hit the comm channel. "Jumper One to Trishen. We're about to set down. If you can proceed to the south side of the complex and circle around, we'd appreciate that."

"Yes, yes, I'll do that," she replied. She sounded a little nervous. It caused John to recalculate all the ways she might possibly be planning to screw them over; except he couldn't think of that many ways. If she really didn't want to feed on them, then the only thing they had that she wanted was her way home, and they were giving her that.

John put the jumper down gently near the dome as the others were adjusting their SCBAs, getting their masks on, and grabbing their equipment. They lowered the ramp and John went out first with Ronon and Teyla. The stirred dust settled slowly in the thin air, and he could see the dome had a triangular doorway, sheltered by a low porch roof extending out from the structure. "We're clear. Teyla, you're with Miko and the jumper. Ronon, find a good vantage point and keep an eye out for company."

Teyla nodded, telling them, "Good luck." Ronon jogged off toward one of the platforms that offered a good view of this section of the roof.

John went to the dome with Rodney and Zelenka. The door slid open to reveal a round chamber with a circular bank of consoles on stone pedestals in the center. It wasn't pressurized, though it had the round silver vents in the walls. But the lights that were set into the dark blue ceiling and along the top of the pillars glowed gently as they stepped inside. "Well, this makes sense," Rodney said, acidly thoughtful. "Recognize it?"

"No. Should I?" John circled warily around the room, P-90 aimed, making certain there weren't any lurking surprises.

"It's laid out like the inexplicable chamber of tantalizing energy signatures back in the ruin on the Stargate moon." Rodney frowned as he selected a console, hitting a couple of touchpads. A holographic display blinked into life above it.

"Oh, good," Zelenka said wearily, sitting down on the floor and opening his laptop. "Because we had such good luck with that room."

"Great," John said, and went out to watch the jumper, the life signs detector, and the sky.

Then things started to go wrong.

First the Mirror started to rumble again, a long low sustained groan, as if mammoth granite blocks were grinding against each other under the installation. Vibrations traveled through the roof, just strong enough for John to feel through the soles of his boots. He ducked into the control room to see Rodney frantically checking his tablet. "It's not building up for a discharge," Rodney said, before John could ask. "Signatures are still normal, pulse generator is erratic but working. We should be fine," he finished briskly, lifting his chin.

John pointed back over his shoulder. "Okay, because it sounds really—"

Rodney glared. "I know! Believe me, I know! But it's fine!"

John went out to the observation porch again. The pulse array at the roof's edge blocked the view from here. He keyed his radio and said, "Ronon, this is Sheppard. Can you see the Mirror from your position?"

Ronon's answer came a moment later. "Yes."

John thought, *note to self: teach Ronon to use proper radio protocol*. "Is it doing anything?"

"Like what?"

John saw Teyla suddenly appear out of nowhere as she stepped out of the cloaked jumper, her expression caught between annoyance and amusement. John said, "Oh, glowing, turning colors, transporting an armada of alien spaceships into the galaxy—"

Ronon sounded thoughtful. "No, it looks the same."

"Thank you, Ronon. Sheppard out."

Teyla shook her head and turned back to the jumper, disappearing as she stepped onto the ramp.

John waited, and paced. The low rumble from the Mirror didn't seem to increase, as far as he could tell. Then Teyla reported via headset, "Colonel, Miko says the screens show that the darts are returning." Her voice was tight with tension. "They are all moving to the south, toward the shuttle."

John grimaced. "Trishen, you copy that?"

"Yes." Her voice in his headset sounded human, young, and very tense. "What should I do?"

Teyla stepped out of the jumper again, her eyes worried. John made his voice even, telling Trishen, "You want to widen your flight path and vary your pattern. They couldn't pinpoint you in the mountains, so they can't do it here. Just stay out of their way."

"Oh yes, I see." She sounded a little calmer.

"Okay. Just call if you have any problems." John exchanged a look with Teyla, who shook her head and winced. Trishen had suggested this part of the plan herself, and he had just assumed she could handle it. *Yeah, there's one of those assumptions again.* And they couldn't even see the damn shuttle on the jumper's sensors and follow her progress.

They had been here half an hour already for what Rodney had described as a five minute job, darts were circling the plain to the south and the Mirror was keeping up its steady grumbling threat. John stepped back into the doorway of the lab. "Rodney—"

"Busy!" Rodney snarled. He was standing at the center console, hitting touchpads and glaring at the results. Radek was still on the floor with the laptop and the tablet, apparently comparing one screen to the other while making little abortive gestures suggesting it was an effort not to tear his hair out.

"Rodney, this is going to be tight. I need an ETA," John persisted.

"I don't know," Rodney said through gritted teeth.

And everything's been going so well up to now, John thought. "What's wrong? I thought you had this all worked out."

"So did I." Rodney pressed the heel of his hand to his forehead. He looked frustrated and desperate. "It should work, but it won't. The system isn't accepting our corrections."

"What does that mean?" John demanded.

"It means our corrections are so far from being right that the system is refusing to implement them because it would cause the entire installation to disappear in a massive naquadah explosion!" Rodney rubbed his face, then slammed his hands down on the console. "That's what it means."

"Figures cannot be right!" Zelenka shook his head furiously, hair flying. "There must be an error in our calculations, somewhere—"

Miko's voice in the headset said impatiently, "I've just run it again, Dr. Zelenka, it isn't—"

"We've run it over and over again, it's not an error, we don't have time for this!" Rodney snapped. He knotted his fists, as if it was an effort not to punch the console. "We're missing something."

"Right, right. We took account of orbital drift—" Zelenka began to tick the various points off on his fingers. "—of increased ionization in atmosphere, of degradation of singularity field—"

On the other channel, John could hear Miko muttering darkly to herself in Japanese. He stepped back out onto the porch and resisted the urge to beat his head against the wall. In his headset, Ronon's voice rumbled, "Sheppard. What's going on?"

John told him, "Something's wrong with their...something. What's your situation?"

"The same. This area's clear."

"Copy that." John was going to have to put a stop to this, they just didn't have the time to make the damn Mirror work. But he found himself reluctant to doom Trishen. She had held up her end of the bargain so far, and if they couldn't send her back to her own reality, he didn't know what the hell they were going to do with her. Even if she didn't need to feed on humans, they couldn't chance the Wraith finding her. *It'll have to be Atlantis,* he told himself reluctantly. And once she had seen it, they couldn't let her leave. Not unless the SGC had some sort of settlement program for displaced aliens in the Milky Way. And that was only if they could prove she was safe around people. "Ronon, Teyla—"

From inside the room, Zelenka was saying, "The field phase adjustment—"

Rodney snapped his fingers. "Wait."

John knew that tone. He stepped back into the control room.

Rodney fumbled at his headset, saying urgently. "You, Trishen! When did you say that data was recorded?"

John heard Trishen's voice on the radio channel. "As my ship was pulled into the Mirror. That's why I was so close to it, to collect the data from the buoys—"

"Yes, yes, on the other side of the Mirror!" Rodney crouched down, shouldering Zelenka aside to get to the laptop keyboard, typing frantically. "The phase is—"

"Inverted!" Zelenka clapped a hand to his forehead. "Ah, we are fools!"

"Yes, exactly!" Rodney nodded urgently, still typing. "Well, not me, but you, yes. We've never had a chance for data collection during an active Quantum Mirror activation. Obviously, as the accretion surface prepares for the transition, it inverts the phase. Kusanagi, are you getting this?"

Sounding relieved, Miko's voice replied, "Yes, Dr. McKay, I'm running my figures again now!"

John prompted, "Rodney, still need an ETA."

Rodney pushed to his feet, giving John a harried grimace as he turned to the console. "We've got it. Just let me—Radek, dammit—"

"Enter the numbers, here, here!" Radek stood up, holding the laptop so Rodney could see the screen.

"Colonel," Teyla said in John's headset. "The Wraith scout ship is within range again and the darts are coming back in this direction."

"Crap," John muttered. The Wraith had to be wondering why the Mirror was being so damn active, and they must suspect that someone was messing with it. The darts were coming back to sweep the open areas for any signs of activity. He said, "Copy that, Teyla. Ronon, fall back to the jumper. Zelenka, you too, get out of here."

Zelenka hesitated, and Rodney waved him off. "I've got it, go on!"

Zelenka nodded tensely, jammed the tablet under his arm and grabbed his laptop. He headed for the door and John followed him, watching until he reached Teyla at the jumper's ramp. They both disappeared as they stepped through the cloak and John went back to the control room. "Rodney, now would be good—"

Rodney shook his head, the reflected blue glow of the consoles' screens giving his face an unhealthy cast. "The system's accepting my commands now, I have to make these last adjustments." He touched his headset again, saying, "Trishen, your sensors should detect the change in the accretion surface when the Mirror becomes safe to activate. When that happens—"

Sounding more confident, Trishen's voice replied, "Yes, I lower the shuttle over the surface. I'm ready."

Rodney cut the channel. "Oh, that's good. I'm glad everyone's ready to go," he muttered, still hitting touch-pads. "Unfortunately the giant Quantum Mirror decided not to follow our schedule—"

John debated just dragging him away from the console. "Rodney, there's no time now, we can come back when the scout ship's out of range—"

"We can't wait, the hiveship could get here any moment—"

"Then we forget this and blow up the pulse array!"

"That's not helping!" Rodney shouted. He gave John a look that combined impatience and desperation. "Two minutes, that's all, just two minutes! Look, just go, I'll pull the crystals out of the door, they're not going to know I'm here—"

"Rodney, I'm not leaving you here alone!" John yelled, then he realized the reason they were shouting at each other was that the dull roar from the Mirror had gradually grown louder. It was resonating through the stone now, like the building was one giant soundboard. "Are you doing that?" he asked.

"No!" Rodney stared at the console. The Ancient display was flashing symbols that John knew meant "danger." Data, graphs, and images were scrolling through it too rapidly to read. "That has to be a discharge but it's not registering—The system can't even recognize what's happening. It's as if something else is controlling it." Rodney backed away from the console, swallowing nervously. "I think we need to get out of here."

"Oh, you think?" John said incredulously, and they both turned to run.

As they reached the door, the roar of sound escalated

suddenly into an ear-piercing blast and the stone under-foot rippled, sending them both staggering sideways. John caught himself on the wall, then caught Rodney, keeping them both upright. It felt like the entire giant structure of stone and metal had turned into jelly. Rodney knotted a fist in John's shirt and pointed. John looked up and saw a silvery haze filling the air above the Mirror platform, extending upward until it vanished from sight high in the upper atmosphere. He could see two darts caught in it, tumbling helplessly in slow motion, as if the air was solidifying around them. *Crap,* John thought, staring, *I think we broke the giant Quantum Mirror.* He pushed away from the wall, hauling Rodney with him, and ran toward the invisible jumper.

The stone jolting underfoot made it hard to move in a straight line. Just as John was thinking that now would be a really bad time to overshoot the ramp, Ronon appeared so suddenly in front of them that John slammed into his chest.

Ronon grabbed them both and fell backward. John tumbled through the cloak, landing heavily on the ramp between Rodney and Ronon as the jumper snapped into visibility around them. Teyla and Zelenka stood over them, both looking horrified, and Teyla dodged forward to hit the control to raise the ramp. Everyone was trying to talk but the noise was still so intense John could barely hear anything over it. He scrambled up, staggering to his feet and lunging for the cockpit.

Miko pushed out of the pilot's chair, gesturing help-lessly to the HUD. The screens were flashing random diagnostics, distorted readings, static. John dropped into the chair, checking the board. Comm was dead, sensors were going crazy. The building was shaking so hard he could feel the jumper starting to bounce. If Trishen's shuttle was still in the air, it was caught in that field, whatever it was. *Oh yeah, this is not good.*

John knew the instant the ramp shut because the shielding dropped the sound to a bearable level. Rodney stumbled up beside him, catching hold of the co-pilot's seat to steady himself. He stared out the port in horror. "Can we lift off?"

"Good question." John could feel the jumper's resistance through the control yoke. The only thing that did seem to work was the terrain sensors, and they were showing a pressure build-up on the outside of the hull; the shaking had to be climbing the Richter scale to an apocalyptic level. *Stay on the ground and be crushed, lift off and break apart,* John thought. *Six of one, half dozen of the other.* If the building collapsed under them... He would rather be in the air. His radio was dead so he raised his voice to yell, "Don't take off your breathing units! Find a seat and strap in!"

"Oh God," Rodney said thickly, dropping into the co-pilot's seat and hastily buckling the straps. John looked back to see the others taking seats on the rear cabin benches, reaching for the safety straps.

The next instant the jumper lurched forward as if something had snatched it off the roof. John slammed back in the seat, the force a solid punch right to his chest. The Mirror platform filled the port as the jumper was sucked down toward it.

The next slam was forward into the port, and the world went silver, then black.

CHAPTER NINE

Carson found Major Lorne in the *Daedalus'* mess. The long compartment was mostly empty, with only a few off-duty crew members having coffee or early dinners. Carson took a seat across the table from Lorne, admitting, "I keep wanting to ask you if there's been any word, but that's not likely in hyperspace, is it?"

Lorne shook his head, and didn't have to check his watch. He had the air of a man who had been watching the clock for so long he had an intimate awareness of the passage of minutes and seconds. "Not for another half hour or so. That's still our projected arrival time."

Carson tasted his coffee and winced. It was terrible, but unfortunately, the tea was worse. He had been clock-watching himself, in between reading the reports about the previous Quantum Mirror incidents. He had a better understanding now of just what Rodney and the others might have gotten themselves into. He was still hoping that in the time the *Daedalus* had been underway, Sheppard's team would have found their way back through the Stargate on the base moon. *Colonel Caldwell might not be happy about the wasted trip, but then Colonel Caldwell can lump it*, he thought.

Some of the old guard tended to be a little resentful of Caldwell, wanting to close ranks against an outside authority, against someone who hadn't spent the last year isolated and under the constant threat of the Wraith. Carson didn't think it was a fair or logical attitude, but he didn't know Caldwell very well, and the man was hard to read. *That might be part of the problem. We've all been living in a close-knit little community for so long, we're too used to each others' ways.* An outsider, especially someone who was seen as a potential rival to Elizabeth's and Sheppard's authority, was bound to have a hard row to hoe.

And there was a rumor that Carson kept hearing, that Caldwell had suggested Sheppard had killed Colonel Sumner unnecessarily, that Sheppard could have rescued him if he bothered. If the rumor was true, it would explain a great deal of the tension. *The man should review the report on poor Colonel Everett*, Carson thought uncharitably. Or stop by the medlab the next time Carson and Biro were autopsying a Wraith victim. Carson shook off that unpleasant image. He told Lorne, "Perhaps when we come out of hyper there'll be a message from home, saying they arrived safely sometime after we left."

He saw Lorne smile wryly. He supposed he had been sounding a bit like a Pollyanna again. Carson sighed. "I know, I know, I'm something of an optimist. It helps balance out Rodney."

"I wish I was an optimist," Lorne admitted. "I should have—" He cut himself off with grimace, and put more sugar in his coffee.

Carson watched him a moment, then said firmly, "You didn't abandon your post, lad. You had to get the others out, and that needed both jumpers. What were you going to do, hide out there alone? That wouldn't have done anybody any good."

"I know, Doc, there wasn't a choice." Lorne still didn't say it like he believed it. He shook his head. "If we don't find them—"

Then Carson felt the low steady thrum of the ship's engines change in pitch. After all these long hours en route, he hadn't been aware of the engine noise at all, but the slight change made him sit up straight. The *Daedalus* was coming out of hyperspace. Startled, Lorne set his mug down with a thump and checked his watch, saying, "We're early."

"Thank God for that." By the time Carson shoved out of his chair, Lorne had already raced down the corridor. Carson caught up with him at the lift and they made it onto the bridge together. Heart pounding, Carson followed Lorne through the maze of consoles and suspended screens to the forward area. Colonel Caldwell was on his feet, watching one of the console screens over the operator's shoulder.

The view out the big port didn't tell Carson much. He could see the moon, presumably the correct moon, hanging red and full in the lower quarter of the port.

Caldwell glanced up at their arrival. "We've got a little problem, gentlemen."

"Colonel?" Lorne asked warily. Carson swallowed frustration, supposing that if the sensors had picked up puddlejumper wreckage and human bodies, the man wouldn't use quite those words to announce it.

Caldwell folded his arms, frowning at the screen. "We've found the Quantum Mirror, exactly as described. But there's no sign of the jumper."

Major Meyers at the right hand control board touched some buttons, studying her screen carefully. "Sir, I'm still not picking up any life signs, and there are no ships in the area."

"Not even Wraith?" Beckett asked, feeling his heart sink.

"We've identified some orbital debris that looks like it might be from darts, several of them." Caldwell saw Carson's expression. He added, "The Mirror is interfering with our sensors, Doctor, and we just got here. At the moment, all it means is that we've got a lot of searching to do."

Carson swallowed in a dry throat, and nodded. It didn't mean they had all been captured—taken—by Wraith. It just meant that they had had to go to ground somewhere, to hide in some other part of the system.

One of the airmen said, "Sir, we've got a sensor scan of the structure."

Caldwell stepped over to the man's station. "Let's see it."

The image that formed on the screen could have been a weather satellite's view of a massive hurricane. It seemed to cover half the moon's surface, the sensors rendering the detected energy into angry swirls of color, spiraling outward. It looked like the images the jumpers had collected of the killer storm that had nearly destroyed Atlantis, like a powerful malevolent entity. Baffled, Carson said, "What the bloody hell is that?"

Lorne shook his head a little, staring incredulously. "That's not the—"

Caldwell's expression was grim. "That's the Mirror."

"Colonel, answer me! Are you all right? Colonel!"

John pried his eyes open. Rodney was leaning over him, pale and wide-eyed with anxiety. "Yeah. What?" Groggy and finding it difficult to think, John couldn't figure out why his perspective was so skewed. He was lying on his side, on a painfully knobby surface, but he could see part of the cockpit's ceiling past Rodney's head, and he didn't think he had ever seen it from this angle before. It was like an Escher print or a *Twilight Zone* episode. And Rodney was clinging to the pilot's seat like he needed it to keep himself upright, and his breathing mask was down around his neck. John didn't seem to be wearing his anymore either, though he could feel the tank jammed into his back. He asked vaguely, "You okay?"

"No, no, I'm not, actually." Rodney laughed a little, with just a touch of hysteria. "But back to my original question—No, never mind. First things first. You need to get off the console."

"The what?" John's head hurt and his ears were ringing, but he could hear Teyla and Miko in the rear cabin. Miko sounded frightened and shaky, and there was a note of urgency in Teyla's voice that worried him a lot. He tried to sit up, and that was when he realized the thing his knee was jammed against was the jumper's DHD, and it suddenly dawned on him why everything looked so strange. He was on top of the control console, wedged between it and the port. And the jumper was sitting at an odd angle, tilted slightly forward. *Oh crap, we crashed. No, something—the Mirror?—grabbed us off the roof.* He looked over his shoulder, out the port. It was dark outside, but the cockpit's emergency lighting fell on a dart smashed up against the jumper's nose. A Wraith arm, unmoving, was sticking up out of the wreckage, the hand clenched as if grasping for something. John blinked. "Uh oh."

"Yes, that's a brief but accurate summation." Rodney

took John's arm, trying to pull him upright. "We're on the Mirror platform, and the deck has a couple of feet of incline, so I suspect there's another dart underneath us. The inertial dampeners must have held on until the last possible instant or we'd all be smashed to bloody pulp, you especially. Next time you tell us to strap in, you should actually do it too."

"Rodney, is he all right?" Teyla called from the rear cabin.

"Not really, no," Rodney called back.

"I'm fine." John shoved away from the port, then gasped as little knives stabbed his back, ribs, and right knee all at once. He gritted his teeth against the pain and said, "Anybody hurt?"

Still trying to pull John off the panel, Rodney winced. "Radek and Ronon didn't finish strapping in either. Radek's still unconscious but Ronon's coming around." Rodney braced a foot on the base of the DHD, grabbed John by the tac vest and hauled him up. "Oof, you're heavy when you're half-conscious," he gasped. "And trust me, this is not a good time for my back to go out. Did I mention there are Wraith everywhere? There are life signs and dart energy signatures all around us."

We could be seriously screwed here, John thought, grabbing the pilot's seat and dragging himself upright and off the console. The blood rushed from his head and he squeezed his eyes shut, holding onto Rodney, riding out the wave of dizziness. His side hurt in one particular spot when he took more than a shallow breath, and he knew he must have a couple of cracked ribs. "Do we have the cloak, weapons, radio?"

"No, we have nothing, we're down to emergency

power." Rodney's voice was hard, edgy with fear. "The Mirror's field may have overloaded the crystals in the main bus. I have to check under the console. Please don't throw up on me."

"I'm not going to throw up." John got his eyes open. The emergency lighting was on, but all the other screens in the cockpit were dead. His heart was pounding, the adrenaline helping clear his head. They couldn't stay in the jumper without power for weapons or the cloak, the Wraith could cut their way in, jimmy the hatch controls from outside, or just blow them up. They had to get to a place they could defend. "If we can't fix the jumper, we need to make for the building." He pushed away from the pilot's seat and managed to stagger past Rodney, who immediately crouched down and started to rip open the panel under the console.

Teyla was just inside the rear cabin hatch, stuffing ammo into her vest pockets, two extra P-90s slung over one shoulder. She met John's eyes, her face tense and desperate. Yeah, John didn't know how they were going to get out of this one either. Past her he saw Zelenka lying on the deck unconscious, the front of his blue uniform shirt spattered with blood; Miko was just fixing a bandage to a gash on his forehead. Ronon sat on the bench, mostly upright but listing to one side and holding his head. Everybody looked bruised, scraped, battered. Teyla handed John a P-90 and said, "I can sense the Wraith. They are confused, angry. Hungry." She took a sharp breath and added, "If they have been away from their hive for some time, and have not run across any inhabited worlds to cull, the drones may not have been allowed to feed."

"Great." That was about all they needed. John got the P-90 clipped to his vest.

Rodney pushed out of the cockpit, and from his desperate expression, the news wasn't good. "The main power crystals are dead. If it's what I think—" He stepped across to the rack with the emergency supplies, pulled out a padded case, and tore it open. His mouth twisted in despair. "Yes, it's what I think. The field drained all of them, even these spares that weren't connected into the system. Unless we want to live out the rest of our very short lives in this jumper, we have to go."

John hadn't thought it would be anything else. The jumper just felt...dead. "Right. Everybody, check your breathing units. Miko, you're on the life signs detector. Rodney get a P-90. Ronon, can you carry Radek?" John hoped like hell Ronon could carry Radek, because he wasn't leaving anybody behind.

Ronon spat blood out onto the deck and shoved unsteadily to his feet. He was well on the way to developing two perfect black eyes. "Yeah. Let's go."

It took time they didn't have to scramble for extra ammo, and to get their breathing gear back on, and John made sure they were stocked up on grenades. They had smoke, flash-bangs, and fragmentation, and that might give them just enough of an extra edge. Miko grabbed the medical kit and Rodney stuffed the tablets and laptops into a couple of supply packs. John checked Miko's sidearm, making sure it was loaded and that she had extra clips in her vest. He knew she was checked out on it on the firing range, but he didn't think she had had to use it in earnest before.

Once Ronon had Zelenka slung over one shoulder

and his energy gun in his free hand, John said, "Are we clear?"

"Closest life sign is one hundred yards," Miko reported, her eyes wide and bruised in the dim light. "But they are all around us."

Right, John thought. "Stay together," he reminded them, and nodded to Rodney.

"Oh here we go." Rodney, his face set in bleak misery, hit the emergency release for the ramp. "Nice working with you all."

As the ramp started to drop, John saw that the sky was dark, the gas giant eclipsing the sun again. The jumper's hatch was facing the Mirror's frame, the flat dull silver wall of it looming over them, but it was dimly lit by a muted white glow. The light was coming from above, from the Mirror, which was a little freaky. And he hadn't thought enough time had passed for another eclipse but whatever, it would help cover their retreat. "Keep your lights off," he said, and swung down to the pavement, wincing as his weight came down on his right leg.

Teyla jumped out behind him, P-90 ready. As the others climbed out, John looked cautiously around the side of the jumper. A cold wind moved over the vast stretch of the Mirror platform, stirring dust, cutting right through the material of his shirt. In the ghostly light from the Mirror, he could see a scatter of wrecked darts, some nearly intact and some crumpled smoking wrecks. The jumper was nosed into the dart he had seen through the port, and the long outline of a second dart was sticking out from under this side. *Score two for us.* There was no movement nearby, and he stepped out to get his bearings on the nearest entrance to the installation.

And he stopped, staring. "Uh."

Teyla moved up beside him, then halted in shock. "Colonel, what—How—"

John's eyes couldn't make sense of it. He stared, but it wasn't an optical illusion or a head injury. The installation was different.

There were towers evenly spaced along the flat roof, caught in the reflected light from the glowing Mirror. Tall narrow ones, with gracefully angular spires, like the ones on Atlantis.

John had a really bad feeling about this.

The others gathered behind him, and Miko said in astonishment, "Dr. McKay, I'm reading a breathable atmosphere now, twenty-one percent oxygen." She added, "Oh, I think we are—I think we must have—This is—"

Rodney dragged his mask down, took a deep breath. He groaned. "Yes, this is...bad. Very, very bad."

John pulled his mask down too. The air was cold, full of ozone and the acrid scent of the charred darts, but there was plenty of it. As the others pulled their masks off, he asked, "Rodney, where the hell are we?" But he had the sinking feeling that he already knew.

"The Mirror." Rodney sounded sick. "Something must have activated it before I finished adjusting the pulse array. The accretion disk was still unstable and it created a gravity well and pulled us in. And the darts, everything in range."

Teyla shook her head uncertainly. "But then we are...in the other reality? Trishen's reality, where there are nothing but Wraith?"

There was a moment of horrified silence. John bit his

lip, searching for a reaction that didn't involve a hysterical scream.

His voice flat, Ronon said, "You're joking."

"Yes, yes, I'm kidding, hah hah, it's a hilarious joke!" Rodney snarled. "Face it, we're in another reality. With the Wraith or Eidolon or whatever they call themselves."

John swallowed down panic and managed to say evenly, "Rodney, is the Mirror still connected to our reality? If we can get up over the frame, can we just jump into it? Or would it—"

Rodney blinked. "Dissolve us instantly in the crushing gravitational forces the unstable accretion surface may be generating?"

John eyed him worriedly. "Yeah, that."

"I have no idea," Rodney admitted, sounding bleak. "But I suspect this Mirror was specifically designed only to be used by spaceships or other vehicles with heavy energy shielding. An unprotected human body wouldn't survive the transition. And if it doesn't activate, that would be worse. I'll have to find a monitoring console."

Zelenka, slung over Ronon's shoulder, muttered, "*My všichni zemřeme.*"

Rodney snapped automatically, "Will you stop with the profanity you think we can't understand? Tone and context make it perfectly obvious what you're—Wait, are you conscious?"

"I wish I was not." Zelenka sounded sorrowful.

Miko looked up from the life signs detector, saying anxiously, "Colonel, the Wraith are moving. I see signs—"

Teyla jerked her chin. "Over there."

John turned and saw three male Wraith, about a hun-

dred and fifty yards away, standing near one of the crumpled darts. The Mirror's light reflected silver off their
clothes and hair, and they seemed to be looking around
in angry confusion. He didn't think that confusion would
last long.

There were dark triangular shapes along the wall of the
installation that looked like hatches or passages leading
inside, and they had to get under cover. "Come on." As
they started away, John pressed the button on the jumper
remote, hoping there was just enough emergency power
left. The ramp responded sluggishly, moving upward to
close, and that was a relief. John wasn't sure why it mat-
tered, why keeping the Wraith out of the empty jumper
for a little while longer meant something, but it did. John
looked back in time to see the ramp seal itself, and the
emergency lights in the jumper's nose flicker and die.

Teyla dropped back to cover their six, with Ronon,
still burdened with Zelenka, and Miko and Rodney close
behind John. Rodney, holding his P-90 tightly and watching the nearest darts, said, "Yes, I understand being pro-
active and getting off the platform and away from these
Wraith, but what about the Wraith that live here?"

"If you have any suggestions, Rodney, feel free," John
hissed. He was trying to maintain a quick jog, but all he
could manage was a quick limping hobble, and it wasn't
improving his outlook on life at the moment.

"What, do I have to think of everything?" Rodney
demanded. He threw a glance back and stopped abruptly.
"Oh, you have got to be kidding me!" he said in outrage.

"Rodney, keep moving!" Then John looked back.

Across the giant length of the Mirror, a big dark shape
was lifting off the platform. The shadowy outline was just

rising high enough for the Mirror's light to bathe it, and John could see the rough brown hull, the flattened saucer shape that was still weirdly organic, like a giant fungus. "Son of a bitch," John said. *This just keeps getting better.* It was about half the size of the *Daedalus*, and there was no telling how many Wraith were aboard.

Teyla gasped. "That is the Wraith scout ship. How could—It was pulled through the Mirror as well?"

"Pulled out of orbit?" Miko said, horrified.

Rodney waved a hand wearily. "Apparently so. Trishen's ship was a completely different conformation and design. That's definitely from our reality. And its shields must have protected it from the power drain that destroyed the jumper's crystals." He rubbed his eyes. "How much worse can this get?"

Light flashed from the lower part of the ship, the distinctive blue-white ripple of the culling beam. John said, "And I think that answers your question." The ship had just beamed something onto the platform, probably drones. "Come on, keep moving." Because it was that or die out here in the next five minutes.

From Ronon's shoulder, Zelenka moaned, "Oh, God."

They were only about sixty yards from the installation when Teyla shouted, "They have seen us!" and opened fire.

John yelled, "Ronon, take point!" and dropped back to her side. Several Wraith were running toward them from the north side of the platform, a dozen or so others from the south, and stunner fire flashed in the dark. John pitched a couple of smoke grenades across the platform, then opened fire.

More Wraith converged on them, but the chemical

haze confused their aim just enough, and Ronon turning to pick them off with single shots made them wary. John kept the group moving as fast as he could, and he really hoped the door they were heading toward would open. Rodney was beside him, firing, shouting, "I have the feeling they think we're responsible for this!"

"I don't think that's going to matter, Rodney!" John shouted back.

Then lights flashed in the sky and John looked up to see another ship. At first he thought it was Trishen's shuttle, but realized this conch-shell shape was different, more convoluted, and it was half again as large. It flashed a spotlight over the Mirror platform, picking out the wrecked darts and the moving Wraith. The Wraith stopped, snarling as the light crossed over them, firing up at the ship.

"Hold your fire," John said, and the others stopped shooting. The Wraith were distracted and he wanted that to last as long as possible. "Now run."

With one last sprint, they reached the wall of the installation and one of the big triangular hatchways, set deep into the stone. John said, "Rodney, get the door," as he, Teyla, and Ronon took up guard positions.

"No life signs inside," Miko reported tensely, "But the shielding may be interfering."

"Please open," Rodney was muttering as he pried off the console. "If things could just go well, just this once, I'd really appreciate—"

"Put me down, put me down," Zelenka said with a groan. "I can walk."

Taking the opportunity to reload, John gave Ronon a nod. Zelenka still sounded woozy, but they would be better off if Ronon had both hands free.

Ronon bent down, setting him on his feet. Zelenka staggered but stayed upright and Ronon gave him a careful push, steering him over to Miko and Rodney.

More Wraith were firing up at the Eidolon ship. "Why won't they shoot back?" Ronon said, his voice a frustrated growl.

"Yeah, that would come in handy." John squinted up at the strange ship, gleaming pink and purple in the Mirror's light. "But they're probably talking on the comm." If the Eidolon made some kind of deal with the Wraith... John didn't think they could get more screwed than they already were, but that wouldn't help.

"Perhaps Trishen was not lying about their ships being unarmed," Teyla said, watching the scene uncertainly. "Perhaps—"

Then the Wraith scout ship drifted upward, the whine of its drive adding to the din of the Wraith's weapons and the rushing sound of the Eidolon ship. The scout ship rotated, light pulsed along its sides and John yelled, "Get down!"

He ducked with Teyla and Ronon, and Rodney grabbed Zelenka, pulling him down beside Miko in the slight shelter of the hatch. The blast impact rattled the ground, a flare of heat and light washing over the platform. John looked up to see debris raining down; the Eidolon ship had vanished in the blast.

"What the hell was that?" Rodney said, looking up in horror. "I thought you said they were probably talking!"

"Yeah, well, they didn't like what they heard." John's ears were ringing again, and the Wraith weren't distracted anymore. "Just get the door open!"

"Oh, yes, right, escaping from certain death, it slipped my mind!" Rodney yelled, turning back to the wall console.

John could see the Wraith moving around in the shadows, regrouping. Then Rodney said, "Got it!" and the hatch slid open.

They scrambled through into a big room, a couple of dim lights coming on inside as Ancient technology sensed their presence. Most of the chamber was lost in shadow, but there were low stone partitions and platforms at odd intervals, meant to hold equipment that wasn't there anymore. It looked a lot like an interior room in the installation in their reality, with dark blue stone walls with embossed abstract designs and the blue-green metal strips on the floor. Rodney hit the wall console to shut the hatch, pulling the panel open to rip the crystals out. His mouth twisted grimly, he said, "That's not going to hold them for long—I had to disconnect the security seal to get it to open."

"Crap." John started away from the door, flicking on the P-90's light to check the shadows, thinking, *if this is a dead end, it's going to be a literal one*. They needed to get further into the building, where they could pick the Wraith off in the endless maze of corridors.

Ronon, already ranging ahead and tall enough to see over the partitions, said, "Over here!"

John caught up with him, flashing the light over another door. It had the embossed panel in the center and no wall console; a security door like the one they had first found in the installation, locked to anyone without the Ancient gene. John reached for the panel.

"Wait!" Miko, holding tightly to Zelenka's arm to

keep him standing, was studying the detector. "Life signs, eight of them, fifteen yards that direction." She jabbed the detector toward the door for emphasis.

From behind them, something slammed into the outer hatch with a muted thunk. Rodney flung up his arm helplessly. "Eight versus, what, sixty or seventy? I vote for eight."

John said, "Here we go," and hit the panel. He ducked under the door as it started to slide up, Teyla and Ronon right behind him.

It was another big room, softly lit. In the center there were eight people gathered around a console, watching a holographic display of the Mirror platform. They scattered back at the sudden intrusion, some of them crying out in alarm. *No,* John corrected himself, seeing the dead white skin, the long silver hair, *not people.* They were Wraith or Eidolon, whatever they called themselves. All males, but some were smaller, slight enough to be teenagers. Instead of the black and silver the Wraith always wore, their clothes had colors, shades of dark red, purple, blue. They were unarmed, and John made a split-second decision. He snapped, "Hold your fire."

Ronon growled. He didn't lower his weapon, but he didn't shoot. The hatch was sliding shut behind them and Rodney was already pulling the crystals. There was another door on the far side of the room, sealed.

Beside John, studying the Eidolon with narrowed eyes, Teyla said, "They are like Trishen, I can't sense them."

The Eidolon were staring in astonished horror, exactly like...exactly like a bunch of bloody desperate armed-to-the-teeth aliens had just burst into the room. In utter astonishment, one of them said, "What are they?"

John raised his voice, saying harshly, "Just stay back, don't try to stop us, and nobody'll get hurt."

Behind him, Rodney said, "You sound like a bank robber."

John drew breath to tell him to hurry the hell up. Then a muted blast sent Rodney staggering back from the door.

John caught his arm as he reeled, hauling him away from the shattered hatch as Teyla turned to cover them. They didn't have time to run; they barely made it to the side wall, taking cover behind some metal crates. Ronon shoved Miko and Zelenka down behind him, just as armored drones swarmed into the room.

Some headed straight for them, others for the Eidolon. John opened fire, dropping three before one reached the first Eidolon. Too shocked to run away, the Eidolon just stared in horror as the drone grabbed him by the throat. The drone didn't hesitate at all, slamming a hand into the Eidolon's chest before a shot from Ronon's energy gun blasted it. Rodney recovered enough to lift his P-90, firing through the hatch with Teyla. Drone bodies were piling up out there, but more stunner fire struck the crates, the walls behind them.

John reached into his vest for a fragmentation grenade, but just then one of the older Eidolon rushed toward the hatch, slamming some device onto the wall beside it. A drone grabbed him, pinning him next to it and slamming a hand into his chest to feed. John fired a burst into its back, but the creature was oblivious to the bullets striking its body, to anything but its prey. The device lit up, then light rippled across the hatchway. The drones on the other side trying to push through the opening slammed into the light, staggering back as if they had hit a solid wall. *Force shield,* John thought, concentrating his fire on the drones still in the room. It was a portable force shield, like the one Trishen had used in her ship to hold them prisoner.

The remaining drones in the room finally fell, Ronon dropping the last one with a shot to the chest.

Teyla shook her head, sitting back with a gasp of relief. "I cannot believe we are still alive."

"When did you become a pessimist?" John stood, scanning the fallen drones cautiously.

"About five minutes ago," Teyla said grimly.

John didn't see any blinking self-destruct things on the drones' armor. Maybe they had been so distracted by the close proximity of dinner that they hadn't thought to activate them. Or they had been told not to, because the Wraith wanted at least a couple of humans alive to question.

Ronon stepped out from around the crates, looking over the fallen drones, shooting one that wasn't quite dead enough. John said, "Ronon, watch the other door." He gave Teyla a nod, and she shifted to cover the Eidolon now. Three of them were down, one stunned and two fed on, and the others were still huddled on the opposite side of the room.

John twisted around to check the rest of his team, gritting his teeth as his injured ribs protested the motion. Miko and Radek, crouched back against the wall, looked shell-shocked and sick. Rodney, more used to certain death, didn't look so good either. John asked, "Everybody okay?"

"Oh, we're fine," Rodney said, making a helpless gesture and rubbing his forehead. "Kusanagi, life signs? How surrounded are we?"

"Just us." Miko checked the detector, then jerked her chin toward the drones clustered outside the hatch. "And them. Nothing behind us, or to either side."

John thought, *breathing room, that would be nice*. He said, "Rodney, any chance the consoles in this room are what we need?"

"Oh, probably not." Not looking optimistic, Rodney turned to Zelenka. "Can you help or do you just want to sit there and nurse your concussion?"

Zelenka glared up at him from under his bloody bandage. "I'm fine, give me your hand, *prdelaty* bastard."

John circled around the crates, heading warily toward the force shield-sealed hatch, the P-90 ready. The drones on the other side stirred, straining against the field as John came near it, the faceless masks all turned toward him. He felt a chill walk down his spine; they were starving and he was a walking steak. But the field seemed to be holding.

He backed away, then twitched at nearby movement, jerking up the P-90. The Eidolon who had activated the force shield lay sprawled next to the dead drone that had fed on him; his eyes were still open, aware, and he was breathing in harsh gasps. It was harder to tell than with a human, but John could see the withered texture of the blue-tinged skin, the shrunken flesh around face and neck. It—He had sacrificed himself for the other Eidolon trapped in the room. Wraith just didn't do that.

"May I go to him?" a voice said.

John turned to see one of the Eidolon who had taken cover by the far wall, cautiously getting to his feet. He had spoken to Teyla and was pointing to the withered being at John's feet.

Teyla looked at John, brow lifted. He nodded, and she

told the Eidolon, "You may."

John backed away, out of arm's reach, as the Eidolon moved past him. It was one of the young ones, smaller than a mature Wraith, with more human features. Its voice hadn't been as deep, either. It threw him a frightened look, then went to kneel by the dying Eidolon.

Yeah, that was pretty much our fault, John thought. He mentally pushed that aside to deal with later and crossed back to the control area, asking, "What's the word, Rodney?"

Rodney shook his head, looking distinctly unhappy as he scrolled through the holographic display. Zelenka was leaning heavily on one of the consoles, his expression suggesting he was about to be sick. Miko was balancing the life signs detector and a tablet, holding it so Rodney could see it. Rodney said, "This is only monitoring equipment for the platform, I can't get good readings for the accretion surface with this, just the minor discharges it's still throwing off."

"Okay." John bit his lip, looking at the consoles. "That wasn't what I wanted to hear."

Rodney glared at him. "Yes, well, imagine how I feel." He took a sharp breath, threw a glance at the Eidolon still backed against the wall, watching fearfully. He lowered his voice. "There was monitoring equipment for the accretion surface in the pulse control room up on the roof. If that still exists in this reality, I should be able to see if the connection is stable enough to transport us back. If so, then we can try to steal a ship and make it through before the Wraith blow us up. And I know I'm simplifying it, but that's our best bet. Actually, it may be our only bet, unless we want to make a break for the mountains, learn to grow crops, and hide out for the rest of our lives on this moon."

Zelenka muttered, "I don't want to learn to grow crops."

That's a hell of a long way through this building, John thought, but he wasn't keen on the crops option either. He said, "Let's go."

The inner doorway led to a corridor, lined with square pillars that were set with milky crystal lights. Many of the lights weren't on, as if this section was only partially powered. John had Rodney pull the crystals from the door behind them; the Eidolon inside could still call for help, but John didn't want them ducking out to see which way the alien intruders had gone.

Once they were moving down the corridor, Teyla said, "What about the Wraith? We cannot leave them here, with access to this Mirror."

His tone clipped, Rodney said, "If—When—If we get back to our own reality, we have to destroy the pulse array immediately. That scout ship could raid this installation for technology, bring Eidolon prisoners back to our reality to teach them how to build it, render the Ancient cloaks useless, including the one we used to hide Atlantis, and be free to feed on everyone we know." He looked up, lips thin with anxiety. "Everyone, basically."

"We got that, Rodney," John said. Nothing had changed. They had the same problem as before, just less chance of surviving the possible solutions.

Moving quickly, they found a stairwell that only went up one level, then they cut through a dusty unused section with no power. Past it, they found a big room with partial power, and one of the triangular doorways that in their reality had marked the lift platforms.

But it wouldn't open at John's touch and Rodney swore, tearing the console off the wall. "What the hell?" he said, startled. "The crystals are gone."

Teyla looked up sharply, alarmed. John thought, *Crap.* Their time had just run out. "Back the other way, now."

They were almost to the door when Miko waved the tablet urgently. "Colonel, energy signature!" She turned back across the room, pointing to an empty section of the blue stone wall. "It's a transporter! Life signs!"

John turned with Teyla, covering the wall. A seam was already forming down it, splitting into doors. Then he heard a startled yelp behind him. He risked a look back, just in time to see a curtain of energy ripple across the open doorway. Rodney stepped back, his face horrified. "Force shield. We're trapped." Ronon tried to push a hand through anyway, flinching back when the field zapped him.

"Get behind us," John said, because this was it. He aimed the P-90 at the transporter, setting his jaw. "Ronon, don't fire, wait for my order." Rodney grabbed Zelenka, pushing him back with Miko, and Ronon stepped up beside John, snarling under his breath.

The transporter doors slid open and a male Eidolon stepped out, then another, until eight of them moved out of the bay. The two in front were unarmed, but the others in the back were holding long rifle-sized objects, with a shape suggestively like the Wraith stunners. *We can't get captured*, John thought. Even if Trishen wasn't lying, these were aliens. They had no idea what the Eidolon might want, how interested they would be in Atlantis' existence even in another reality, what they might want from humans. Obviously thinking along the same lines, Rodney whispered harshly, "They've never seen humans before, they could want anything from us. It's like the *X-Files* in reverse."

John grimaced. He hadn't even thought about medical experiments. "Thanks, Rodney, you had to bring that up."

Then the first Eidolon lifted his hands and said, "We mean you no harm."

Beside John, Teyla shifted uneasily, throwing him a worried look. It would be nice to be able to believe that. John swallowed the dryness out of his throat, and made his voice hard. "We don't want to hurt anybody either. We're just trying to get out of here."

There was a flicker of light from the transporter behind them, and then another Eidolon pushed out through the group, a smaller female. The male tried to stop her, saying something too low to hear.

Teyla whispered, "Is that Trishen?"

"I don't know," John murmured back. He still had no idea how this was going to go; it felt like they were breathing on borrowed time. "I could never tell Wraith apart."

"It's her," Ronon told them quietly.

"Of course it is," Rodney snapped. "Oh, this is just fantastic."

Trishen shook her head, pushing past the male and stepping out to face them. She said, "It's me, Trishen. Please put down your weapons."

John heard Ronon snort. That pretty much summed up his feelings. He said, "If you want to talk, we can do that just as well while we're holding our weapons."

Rodney said acidly, "Trishen. Your ship was pulled into the Mirror, too. How lucky for you, since I was locked out of the system before I could make the last adjustments to the pulse array."

"What? She did this?" John asked, startled, then thought, *oh come on, of course she did*.

His voice rising with anger, Rodney told Trishen, "The early activation caused a gravity well to form above the accretion surface, drawing in everything in range, including your new Wraith friends who in the interest of inter-species camaraderie are going to try to blast their way in here so they can feed on everything that moves!"

There was a murmur from the other Eidolon, a gentle stir. They were all staring, and the weight of those watching eyes made John's skin creep. In a weird way, it was worse than being stared at by Wraith. Wraith looked at you with that frightening combination of hunger and lust, the lust without any seeming awareness that the thing they wanted was a living sentient being. But at least you knew what a Wraith wanted from you. John had no idea what the Eidolon really wanted, except that considering the way things were going, it was probably worse.

Trishen stared, then said in helpless exasperation, "No, I didn't do it! I was as surprised as you. I——"

She stopped at another flicker from the transporter, as someone else beamed in. The males parted this time with no argument, and another female stepped forward. Every hair on the back of John's neck stood up in individual alarm. Her features were more distorted than Trishen's; further from human, closer to Wraith. She was taller than Trishen, and her long hair was a dark red. She was wearing something black and flowing that looked liquid against her dead white skin.

"Careful," Ronon said in a low-voiced growl. "That's a hive queen. She can get inside your head, if you let her."

"Yeah, we know," John said quietly, thinking of the Wraith caretaker, when he had found Colonel Sumner being questioned by her, as she slowly drained out his life.

The Queen looked at them with flat opaque eyes, and said, "This was not my daughter's doing."

Daughter? John exchanged a look with Teyla. Teyla rolled her eyes, exasperated. She whispered, "We were not negotiating with a scientist as we thought, but with a Hive Queen."

The Queen said, "We had been attempting to activate the Mirror, to retrieve her. When you made the adjustments to the pulse generator, it must have allowed the connection. With unanticipated results. It was not our intention to bring you, or the others, here."

"Well, whatever your intention, you brought them here. Any idea what you're going to do about it?" John asked. He was pretty sure he wouldn't like the answer.

But she said, "The few ships we have left here are scientific research vessels, unarmed. We've called for help, but it won't arrive for several days, and from what we have seen, that ship has weapons far superior to anything we can bring to bear." The Queen's eyes flicked from Rodney to John to Teyla, coldly thoughtful. "Does your ship have weapons?"

Maybe it was a legitimate question under the circumstances, but John didn't like giving the answer. It might be the only bargaining point they had. Trying to stall, he said, "Our ship is damaged, or we'd be in it right now."

She tilted her head, obviously picking up on what he hadn't said. "But if it was repaired, could it destroy the Wraith ship?"

John countered, "That depends. Can you activate the Mirror and send us back?"

She inclined her head. "Yes. We were able to activate it successfully once, we should be able to do so again."

John felt the others stir behind him, and he lifted his brows, exchanging a startled look with Rodney. He hadn't been expecting that concession; he was torn between more suspicion and relief at the first glimpse of an actual way out of this.

Trishen spread her hands, saying, "We had an alliance. We can still cooperate."

John felt he had to point out, "You know, every time you want to cooperate, we almost get killed."

Trishen gestured in helpless exasperation. "Yes, but it's not my fault!"

"We don't have a choice," Rodney whispered harshly. "If they have the right Ancient crystals, the jumper is repairable."

Teyla nodded. "I dislike this as much as you, but we must take the chance."

"Yeah, I know." John didn't see any other option. He looked at the Eidolon Queen, still watching them impassively. "Our ship is armed, but those weapons are only powerful enough to destroy the darts, the small fighters that are wrecked all over the platform. The scout ship has shields to protect it that we can't get through."

The Queen accepted that without argument. "I appreciate your candor." She looked thoughtful. "But there is a way?"

Rodney said briskly, "Yes, there's a way. But we'll need unimpeded access to our ship, some materials to repair it, the Quantum Mirror, and your beaming technology." He hesitated. "The Wraith shields may be configured to prevent anything from being beamed aboard. We'll also need a way to get around that."

The Queen just nodded. "I think I can provide that."

CHAPTER TEN

The Queen said, "There is a monitoring area nearby. We will continue this there." She touched a control on her wristband, and the force shield across the door disappeared.

"Well, that sounds...best," Rodney said, as she headed for the door, with Trishen and three of the males in tow. He added to John, "I suppose we should follow her."

"I suppose we don't have a choice." John lowered the P-90 as she passed.

Ronon dropped back to warily cover their six and they followed the Queen down the corridor, the other Eidolon trailing them at a careful distance. One of the males with the Queen spoke to her, his voice low and urgent. John had trouble reading his expression, but it was probably suspicious.

That didn't bother John; the suspicion, at least, felt normal under the circumstances, and he knew how to react to it. It was everything else he wasn't sure about.

"I don't like this," Ronon said, a growl under his voice.

Rodney snorted derisively, looking back at him to say, "No, really? Because the rest of us have always hoped something like this would happen."

Beside John, Teyla whispered, "They have not asked for our weapons. Even with the best of intentions toward an alliance, we would not let aliens walk our corridors armed."

"Yeah." That one was bothering John, too. He didn't know if it was meant to be a sign of confidence or a trap, or what.

Rodney muttered, "Thanks, yes, I needed something else to worry about."

Behind them, Zelenka whispered, "But what does that mean?"

"We don't know," John told him.

One of the other males with the Queen slowed to walk even with them, looking at them with open curiosity. It was a younger one with more human features, which for some reason creeped John out even more. Then the Eidolon asked Teyla, "Are you all the same species?"

"We are," she said, perfectly composed, though John could see the tension in her shoulders.

John rolled his eyes. He supposed it wasn't meant to be insulting. The Eidolon were like the Wraith; all the adult males here were close to the same height and build, with barely any noticeable variation in skin or hair color. But he still wanted to take it that way.

The Eidolon looked them over again, as if trying to decide if Teyla was serious. He asked, "Do they need medical attention?"

Ronon had black eyes and vivid discolored bruises on his face. Zelenka, leaning on Miko's arm, won the prize for most obvious concussion, and the cut on his forehead had bled through the quick bandaging job. John's knee was stiffening up again, his side hurt with every quick movement, and he and Teyla still had the bruises from their first encounter with the Wraith. But he didn't want any help from the Eidolon, no more than what it took to get them home. Especially help that involved physical contact. He said, "No, thanks."

The Eidolon looked from Teyla to John, startled and uncertain. "You are the leader?"

John flicked a narrow-eyed look at him. "Yes."

The Eidolon shook his head slightly, his white hair shimmering with the movement. "Our leaders are all female. It is...odd to see females in a subordinate role."

John gritted his teeth. "They're not subordinates."

Rodney frowned, pointing out, "Well, technically, as far as rank and pay grade go—"

John glared at him. "Yeah, technically, but not like he means."

Teyla broke in hastily, saying, "The leader of our... community is female. Colonel Sheppard speaks for her here."

Trishen dropped back, saying uneasily, "Edane, go back with the others."

Edane protested, "But I was only curious—"

"Perhaps there will be time for questions later," she told him.

John lifted a brow, exchanging a sour look with Rodney, thinking, *Hell, I hope not.* And he wasn't sure if Trishen had chased the young male off because she was afraid they would freak out and kill him, or because he might reveal something.

Two turns of the corridor and a security door took them into a large control room, lit by overheads and lights in the square pillars. There was a row of observation windows across the far wall, looking out onto the Mirror platform. A bank of consoles stood in the center, a couple of different holographic displays floating in the air above them. The Queen went straight to the consoles, passing her hand over a touchpad, and the windows turned to an opaque milky crystal.

One of the older males, the one who had been making the objections to their presence on the way here, had followed the Queen to the control board. Apparently the group skeptic, he said, "If this fails, they will attack in force, and we haven't had time to evacuate more than a few of our people."

Trishen turned to him impatiently. "Kethel, they will attack in force anyway. And you yourself said that our ships won't arrive for days; we have no choice."

The Queen didn't acknowledge either of them. Apparently the others were allowed to argue, but she wasn't under any obligation to even pretend to listen. She turned to regard John steadily. "First I will try to secure your ship. I assume you have materials aboard it that you can use to build some sort of destructive device, to be beamed aboard the Wraith vessel?"

John met her gaze steadily. "That's the idea."

Rodney added, "I may need more materials from you." He strained his neck to see the control station without going any closer to the Queen. "I won't be certain until I can evaluate what we already have."

"If we have the necessary materials, we will provide them." The Queen turned back to the console. She nodded to Kethel, who reluctantly began to hit the touchpads.

Zelenka leaned in between John and Rodney to whisper, "Rodney, there is enough C-4 for this?"

Rodney gave him an annoyed look. "Of course not. But combined with the energy drones—"

"Ah, I see." Zelenka nodded, then clutched his head

and winced in pain.

"Oh yes, Dr. McKay," Miko said, lifting her brows in comprehension.

"The energy drones?" John stared at him. He wasn't keen on the Eidolon getting a look at those. "Can't you just—"

"No, just shut up and trust me," Rodney whispered.

Then Kethel said, "The alien ship is accepting our communication."

"What?" John said, startled. "What are you telling them?"

Kethel gave him a glare. "Our vessels can't get close enough to lift your ship off the platform without being fired on."

John had thought the Eidolon meant to do something else to get the jumper off the platform. He didn't have a clue what that something else could be, but he hadn't thought it involved just asking the Wraith for it. "And they're just going to let you have it."

His skepticism must have crossed the cultural and species barrier just fine, because the Queen looked at him, her eyes a flat black. "They killed seven of our line when they destroyed our survey ship, which was unarmed and gave them no provocation, and three others when they invaded this installation. I do not wish them to have control of this Quantum Mirror, anymore than you do. I am prepared to negotiate for what I need to destroy them, nothing further. And I have no compunction against lying to them."

"Okay," John said slowly. That was sort of reassuring, except for what the Queen hadn't said. She hadn't commented on how the Eidolon in the control room had died, or what the Wraith were likely to do to any they caught. *She wasn't surprised,* John thought, realizing what else had struck him as wrong. Just like the other Eidolon who had witnessed it. *Nobody asked, nobody said 'what the hell is that?'* Maybe it was just a cultural miscommunication thing, maybe Trishen had told them what she had sensed from the Wraith back home, but John didn't think so. It was confirmation of what he had suspected about Trishen: The Eidolon might not need to feed on other sentient beings, but they weren't unfamiliar with the concept. Though he didn't have any intention of asking about it just at the moment. He said, "You sure they're going to listen to you?"

The Queen didn't answer. She stepped around the console, moving to the open area in front of the windows.

Trishen shifted closer to them, her arms folded and her shoulders hunched a little anxiously. "The holovid will only pick up the area immediately around her. They won't be able to see you."

"Oh, that's very reassuring," Rodney said in a sour undertone.

The blue glow of a holo-projection formed in the air a few steps in front of the Queen. Then a male Wraith appeared in it.

John tensed, tightening his hold on the P-90; he had been prepared for a hologram, and the image was translucent, but somehow that didn't matter much. Teyla stirred uneasily and Ronon shifted position, his hand flexing on his gun's grip. Rodney muttered, "This could go very badly."

The Wraith started to say, "You will comply with our orders—"

The Queen said, "Quiet." Her voice reverberated harshly, and John would have sworn she got taller. "Where is your mistress, or is she afraid to face me, even over this distance?"

The Wraith froze. In a different tone, it said, "She is not with us."

"Then return to her. Leave this place the way you came."

The Wraith hissed, recovering a little. "That is impossible."

"I can make it possible."

The Wraith hesitated again. John thought, *it didn't know that. It thought it was a possibility, but it wasn't sure.* The Wraith might have thought the Mirror's activation was an accident. *Or something we did.* Then the Wraith said, "We want the humans. They are of our feeding grounds, they belong to us. Return them and we will leave you."

John felt Rodney shift uncomfortably beside him. Teyla gave him a look, pressing her lips together. This was the part John was most worried about too.

But the Queen said, "You have destroyed one of my ships."

The Wraith hissed, open-mouthed, barring its teeth. The Queen lowered her chin, staring him down. Finally the Wraith said, "What do you want?"

She said, "The humans' ship."

It snarled. "Impossible."

"Then we have no further reason to speak."

It glared at her. The Queen gave the impression that she could stand there all day without blinking. *Oh, this is just great,* John thought incredulously. The Eidolon didn't have a card to play, except their Queen's ability to bluff the Wraith into temporary submission. And he had the feeling that if there had been a Wraith Queen aboard that ship, then things would be going a lot worse right now. Finally the Wraith said, "How do we know you have the humans?"

The Queen didn't move, but Trishen started, then turned to them urgently, whispering, "She wants one of you to come forward, to look as if you are a prisoner—"

John flicked a look at Teyla, saw they had both had the same thought. *The Eidolon have a mental communication thing going, just like the Wraith.* But that didn't change the fact that the Wraith needed to know that the Eidolon had something they wanted. Keeping his voice low, he told Trishen, "I'll do it." He unclipped his P-90 and pulled the 9mm out of his holster, handing both off to Miko and Radek. Teyla and Rodney looked like they wanted to object—everybody looked like they wanted to object—but if the Wraith got the idea there was a temporary human-Eidolon alliance, this plan was over before it had gotten started.

John stepped past Trishen to where Kethel was waiting uncertainly. John whispered, "Drag me over there and throw me down."

The Eidolon grabbed his arm and an instant later John hit the floor at the Queen's feet. He landed on his bad knee and went sprawling, unable to choke back a yelp. *Not that hard*, he thought, bracing on his forearm, unsteadily levering himself up a little. He heard a muffled protest and a scuffle behind him, and snuck a look under his arm. Teyla had stepped in front of Ronon, having planted an elbow in his chest to stop an instinctive surge forward.

Rodney looked like he was holding back a loud objection, and Miko and Radek both had expressions of startled sympathy.

John pushed up a little more, pressing a hand to his side as a cracked rib protested the movement. He squinted up at the holographic Wraith. It stared down at him, its face twisted into an avid expression.

The Queen said, "You see."

The Wraith didn't take its eyes off John. The Queen shifted and the hem of her skirts brushed John's arm; his instinctive flinch away from her was completely genuine. It must have looked convincing, because the Wraith said, "If I allow you to take the ship, you will return them to us."

"You will not interfere when I take the ship, and we will speak further." She lifted a hand, and the hologram vanished.

John breathed out in relief. The Queen stepped away immediately, turning to face the consoles. *You're welcome,* John thought sourly. He shoved himself into a sitting position, trying to get his good leg under him so he could stand.

Then somebody said, "Did I injure you?"

John looked up, startled, to see Kethel looming over him. For a moment he thought the Eidolon was being sarcastic. But Kethel kept staring at him like he actually expected an answer.

Then Teyla and Rodney and the others reached them. Ronon grabbed John's arm and hauled him to his feet, sneering at Kethel. Addressing everybody, John said, "Relax, I'm fine." Kethel seemed almost embarrassed, and the Queen was very clearly not acknowledging this little exchange. John almost wondered if this was some odd alien courtesy, that she was trying not to make Kethel's mistake worse by drawing attention to it.

Still facing away from them, the Queen said, "Are these creatures... Are all the Wraith like that one?"

John wasn't sure what she meant, if she was asking about the Wraith's appearance or violent tendencies. Rodney answered her, lifting his chin to say, "Actually, that one seemed a little more amenable to reason than usual."

Watching the Queen narrowly, Teyla said, "They think of nothing but feeding and culling, and hunting our people. It is their entire reason for existence."

The Queen tapped her long-fingered hands on the blue metal of the console. John wondered just how much she could sense from the Wraith, if they could sense anything from her. She said, "I believe you are correct. They seem...curiously unable to visualize anything outside the scope of their own concerns. What has caused that?" She turned to look at Teyla, tilting her head. "Is it genetic?"

Teyla wet her lips, hesitating, as if the idea that she was having an actual conversation with a Hive Queen was weirding her out as much as it was John. "We do not know. They have always been as they are. From what we have learned, even the Ancestors did not entirely understand them."

The Queen nodded, a flicker of something in her expression that was gone too quickly to read. She said, "On the top level there is a maintenance bay with a roof access, large enough for your ship. If they allow us to retrieve it, I will have it brought there." With that, she strode out of the room, sweeping Trishen and several of the males with her.

Kethel lingered behind, saying, "I will take you there when you're ready." He hesitated, then added, "I apologize for injuring you." He moved away to wait with the other Eidolon.

Everybody stared after him. Brow furrowed, watching the Eidolon with deep suspicion, Ronon commented, "That was weird."

John had to agree. Frowning, Rodney said, "Did a Wraith-like being just show remorse over almost knocking you unconscious?" He waved a hand beside his head. "The cognitive dissonance is causing my perception of reality to fade in and out, so I wasn't sure I heard right."

"Yeah." John was almost the same height as the adult Eidolon, and never having smacked a human around before, Kethel must have assumed John was just as strong as he was. *And now they know we aren't. Probably not a good thing.* He took his pistol and the P-90 back from Radek and Miko, saying, "Whatever. Let's get up there."

It's working so far, Rodney thought. At some frightening point in all this, that had become his mantra. Not that he believed in mantras. He actually hated mantras.

The Eidolon had sent another ship to get the jumper off the Mirror platform, intending to lift it with a tractor beam and ferry it over to the installation. Rodney and the others watched the process via one of the holographic screens in the maintenance bay, a big round room with two triangular hatches forming a square portal in the roof, easily large enough for a craft several times the size of the jumper. Various smaller chambers with work areas opened off several archways in the walls, and there was a raised platform with some kind of control station toward the back. The Eidolon were occupying it, so Rodney hadn't managed to get a look at what was up there yet. Safe from the Wraith, the Ancients who had fled here hadn't bothered to gut this installation the way they had the original version.

On the display of the Mirror platform, Rodney could see that the eclipse was starting to pass, the warmer light of the system's primary washing out the Mirror's silvery glow. The Eidolon ship stirred up dust on the platform as it moved to hover over the puddlejumper, which was still wedged awkwardly atop the crushed darts. The Wraith hadn't fired on it. Yet. If Rodney survived this, he was definitely coming out of it with another ulcer.

Kusanagi was chewing on her fingernails, Ronon was glowering at the screen, and Sheppard was doing his stoic manly calm act. Cradling her P-90, Teyla shifted uneasily and said, "If the Wraith fire now—"

"We're screwed," Zelenka finished darkly.

"There are degrees of screwed," Rodney said, wanting to disagree with Zelenka just to distract himself. But they had no idea how far the Eidolon's good will would extend, and if this didn't work... *Oh yes, ulcer.* He grimaced. *Maybe two.* Didn't that cause blood poisoning?

Zelenka began, "If one of those degrees of screwed is 'very—'"

Sheppard said, "They aren't firing." The stoic thing didn't quite conceal his relief.

The jumper was lifting off the platform in the Eidolon tractor beam, some debris from the smashed darts drawn up with it, glittering in the sunlight. The display's orientation changed, following the Eidolon ship as it headed up toward the installation roof. Overhead, the triangular hatches groaned and started to slide open. Rodney felt his ulcers unclench a little. He rubbed his hands together briskly. "Right, here we go."

While the jumper was being lowered gently into the bay, Trishen brought them a case of replacement crystals, asking, "Will any of these do?" They were in pristine condition, gleaming faintly in the light from the milky glass overheads. Rodney swallowed hard, controlled the urge to grab the entire case and run away, and managed to ask, "Did you manufacture these?"

"No, we don't know how yet," she said, regarding the case regretfully. "We gather them from sites left behind by the Creators." Looking up at Rodney with sudden hope, she asked, "Do you know how to—"

"No." Glumly, he chose a selection of replacement crystals.

Then he gathered everybody on the jumper's ramp, saying, "Two teams, one works on repairing the power train, the other removes the drones and builds the bomb. Our time is extremely, one might say fatally, limited, so everybody works. Everybody except Ronon; we don't want him touching anything delicate or potentially explosive."

Ronon contemplated Rodney in silence, then said, "I'd rather stand watch."

"It's better if I do crystals," Zelenka said, poking cautiously at his new bandage. Kusanagi had changed the dressing but now that his bruises were starting to turn greenish-black, he looked, if anything, worse. "If I pass out in the middle, nothing will explode. You had better take Miko, and perhaps the Colonel. Teyla can help me."

Rodney sighed in annoyance. "No, actually, the Colonel is the last person we want handling the drones."

Sheppard actually looked offended. "Why not?"

Rodney rolled his eyes, and considered mentioning various reasons, such as Sheppard's belief that all the jumpers were his property, leading him to stand around looking personally violated whenever anyone made absolutely necessary but tricky adjustments to vital systems, not to mention his habit of demanding to know how long it was going to take at ten second intervals. To save argument, Rodney decided to go with the real point of concern. "As we discovered in Antarctica, the drones don't have to be mounted in a launching device in order to activate. Carson, the most incompetent natural gene carrier that we have, managed to fire one with the weapons chair right off Peter's work bench. It may be impossible for you to set them off just by direct physical contact, but I'd rather not make the experiment while I'm sitting next to a pile of C-4. Neither Kusanagi nor I have ever had much luck with the chair, so we should be safe. Fairly safe. Marginally safe."

Sheppard's brow furrowed. "Oh."

They got to work.

The energy drones were only accessible from outside the jumper, tucked into the hull below the drive pods, so Rodney and Kusanagi had to pull the housing, then carefully remove each drone from the launch rack. Detaching connections on one end of the rack, Rodney did a double-take as Kusanagi lifted out a drone. They were bullet-shaped, with trailing tentacle-like filaments; in flight, they looked like glowing squids. He asked tightly, "Did that just...quiver?"

"Um, no, Dr. McKay. I'm shaking," Kusanagi admitted, gently lowering the drone to the floor.

Rodney relaxed. "Well, stop it. Do you have low blood sugar?" He felt his vest pockets, looking for a power bar.

"No, it's...fear." She winced, pushing her glasses back up on her nose.

"Oh." They stared bleakly at each other for a moment, and he knew it wasn't handling Ancient energy missiles that made her afraid. If she wanted reassurance, he was aware he had limitations in that area; he would have to send her to talk to Sheppard or Teyla. But she didn't ask for it, just smiled wanly. Rodney nodded, letting out his breath. "Yes, well, that's a rational response to the situation."

When they had most of the drones out, Rodney crawled out from under the drive pod, intending to go inside and check Zelenka's work. Some of the Eidolon were watching from a safe distance, including Edane, the young one who had tried to talk to Teyla. They seemed to be more curious about the technology than anything else, and spoke among themselves in a perfectly ordinary way. It was still incredibly unnerving.

As Rodney was heading around the bulk of the jumper toward the hatch, Edane stepped forward, saying, "Please let me help. Our technology is different, but I think I know enough that I could assist you."

"Oh, no, I appreciate the offer, but you know, classified material, regulations—" Rodney backed toward the ramp where Ronon had stationed himself. "We just can't—"

"He means 'no, thanks,'" Ronon said, with an unfriendly grin, and Rodney bolted inside.

Just inside the hatchway, he almost ran into Sheppard, who demanded, "What happened?"

Rodney shook his head, waving it aside. He was a little annoyed at himself for overreacting. "Nothing, nothing." Inside the rear cabin, they had the lower side panel open and Teyla was crouched beside it, removing the drained crystals from the matrix. Rodney scanned their work with a frown, while Sheppard glared suspiciously out the hatch. "I'm going to make sure Zelenka isn't about to short out the main bus."

Rodney went forward to the cockpit, where Zelenka was crouched under the console. "What was that?" Zelenka asked, blinking up at him worriedly.

"One of the Eidolon asked to help." Rodney waved a hand, dismissing it. "Seems to mean well, but..."

"Large 'but,'" Zelenka agreed fervently. "Working in close quarters—"

"Yes, huge enormous 'but.'" Being in a small enclosed space with an alien who might be able to suck the life out of you with a touch wasn't exactly Rodney's notion of an ideal work environment either. Maybe the uncertainty of not knowing whether the Eidolon could feed on them—*No, no, the certainty would definitely be worse*. Rodney sat on his heels to look inside the console, taking the light away from Zelenka to flash it over the crystals. "How is this going? You've got the polarity aligned properly?"

"No, I thought I'd ignore such fine details so we could explode when drive pods engage." Zelenka clutched his head, wincing. "It's almost done."

"Good, good. Ah..." Rodney threw him a look, his mouth twisting uneasily. He was responsible for getting Zelenka and Kusanagi into this, admittedly way out of their depth and normal working conditions. And it was a different situation, but it still gave him some unwilling insight into how Sheppard felt about losing Ford.

Rodney didn't like thinking about Ford, especially that last encounter on P3M-736. The glimpses of the real man under that enzyme-driven insanity had been more disturbing than anything else, making you think it was somehow still possible to reason with him, to bring him home. But at least Rodney had accepted that he was gone, and wasn't sublimating his issues by trying to adopt Ronon, Conan the Barbarian's less progressive cousin, like certain Air Force Colonels he could mention. Whatever, he felt the need to apologize to Zelenka, and he hated that. "I'm...ah. Sorry."

"What?" Zelenka stared, then peered into the console. "What did you do?"

Rodney made an impatient gesture. "About this. Before we left base camp, Sheppard asked me if I was certain I wanted to bring you and Kusanagi, and I said yes, that you needed the experience." He let out his breath. "This wasn't the experience I meant."

Zelenka frowned. "I admit, I do not like crashing in jumpers, or shooting, or fear, but... It was very fine to see the spaceport, and the giant Quantum Mirror, before it tried to kill us."

Rodney lifted his brows. "So you're okay with all this."

"No, no, I still blame you for bringing me here, but..." Zelenka shrugged. "This is our lives now."

"Right." It was, sadly, true. Rodney pushed to his

feet, going back to work.

John didn't kiss Zelenka when the jumper powered up, but he felt a little like it. They weren't free and clear yet, but he didn't feel quite so much at the mercy of the Eidolon's whims. He put the board on standby and pushed out of the seat, stepping into the rear cabin. "Good job, Radek."

"Yes, Dr. Zelenka," Teyla added with relief. "That was very well done, especially under these circumstances."

Zelenka nodded, sinking down on the bench. "Yes, very good. I'm going to lie down now." Then he slumped over.

John lunged forward to catch him, easing him down to the padded bench, while Teyla lifted his legs up onto it. John tried to check his pulse, but Zelenka just batted at him without waking and snored. John said, "I can't tell if he passed out or fell asleep on his feet." He straightened up, wincing as his own injuries reminded him that abrupt movements weren't a great idea. "I guess the snoring is a good sign."

Watching Zelenka with concern, Teyla gave John a quick nod. "I will stay with him."

"Just make sure he doesn't fall off the bench. That'd be about all he needs."

John walked down the ramp, noting that there were only five male Eidolon watching them now. There were a few others up on the raised platform where there seemed to be another control area.

Rodney received the news that the jumper was working again with a preoccupied grunt and a "Hello, didn't I say stay away from the bomb!" From what John could tell at a distance, Rodney and Miko were almost done: the currently inert energy drones were wired together in a bundle, with C-4 packed in. They were carefully attaching the detonators now. The theory was that when the C-4 exploded, it should simulate an impact on a target, which should cause the energy drones to detonate. Rodney kept saying it had worked in the lab with a single test drone a few months ago, so it should work on this larger scale. Rodney also freaked out every time John so much as looked at the thing, so John stayed over near the ramp with Ronon.

He was waiting there when Kethel approached. The Eidolon stopped a cautious distance away, and said, "The Matriarch wishes to speak with you."

"The what?" John said, then realized he must mean the Queen. "Okay." He looked around at Rodney and Miko, who were watching uneasily. "I'll be back." *I hope.*

As John started away, Ronon followed him, looming at John's elbow. John stopped to tell him, "Stay with the jumper." By that he meant, "guard the others." Teyla was the only one not distracted by a delicate task at the moment, and she was occupied with Zelenka.

Ronon's expression said he got the message, but he didn't look happy. "That a good idea?"

John looked up at him, narrowing his eyes. "That's an order." Having to glare Ronon into submission all the time was going to give him a crick in the neck.

Ronon looked sullen, gave Kethel a look that promised death at some point soon, and went back to the jumper.

John followed Kethel to the back of the maintenance area, through an archway into one of the smaller control rooms. The Queen was standing at a console, and when

John approached she touched a panel. A holographic display sprang to life, showing a 180 degree view of the Mirror platform. There was a group of drones and a few male Wraith moving along the Mirror's giant frame. *Looking for the controls,* John thought, frowning at the display. The scout ship was still hovering dangerously near the Mirror. If this Mirror had been as unstable as the one in their reality, it would have been erupting continuously.

The Queen said, "They have been trying the lower level entrances into the complex. Fortunately, we have had time to block all the passageways with containment fields, and the evacuation of our personnel is nearly complete." Trishen had told them that the Eidolon were evacuating the installation through the underground passage to the spaceport. In this reality it had never been blocked by a collapse. The Queen added, "The Wraith have attempted to contact us three times, with increasing impatience." She didn't sound particularly worried, more as if she considered the Wraith's impatience as a sign of incompetence on their part.

John tried to look like it didn't worry him, either. "We're nearly done with the bomb. It shouldn't be much longer." At least, that's what he thought she wanted to know. He wondered if the Eidolon were so used to doing the mind-to-mind thing that they didn't communicate very well without it.

"Then I will answer their next call, and suggest that there may be an arrangement soon." She turned to another display, one that was all abstract shapes and blips and dots. John thought it must be a life signs detector screen, though the distance measurements were all different from the Ancient version. "They do not seem to be venturing out past the installation."

"They want control of the Mirror, they're not going to leave the platform." He shrugged. "That's going to make this easier." Marginally easier.

"It wouldn't matter if a few escaped. It is only the ship that confounds us." She turned off the display. "I will wait for your word that the device is ready."

John thought that was a pretty clear dismissal, except he realized he had a question. "Why are you helping us?" It was probably a bad idea to bring this up, but he just had to know. He was starting to wonder if Trishen hadn't given them the whole story, about why the Ancients' attempt to seed humans in this reality had failed. If some of them had survived the plague, but the early Eidolon had fed on them to extinction, before figuring out another way to survive. If by helping them now, the Queen was working off some kind of weird species guilt.

Instead, she looked directly at him, her flat dark eyes expressionless. "Why did you help my daughter?"

John hesitated, then gave her the truth. "I didn't know what else to do with her."

He might have been imagining it, but he thought he saw a faint trace of amusement in her expression. She said, "I am aware that if I had waited only a few more minutes to enact my plan for her return, none of this would have happened."

She turned away again, and John had the feeling that that was the best answer he was going to get.

CHAPTER ELEVEN

John returned to the jumper; he hadn't really expected to find anything wrong, but it was good to see Ronon standing on the ramp, warily keeping watch.

At Rodney's urgent wave, John halted, keeping what Rodney evidently considered to be a minimum safe distance from the bomb. Rodney jumped up, heading for the jumper's hatch, saying in passing, "I'm putting together the remote detonation control now."

Miko stood up, taking off her glasses to rub her eyes. She looked dead tired. "You okay?" John asked her.

She nodded, fumbling her glasses back on as she walked over to him. "Yes, it's just...we were attaching the detonators for the C-4. It was very...tense."

John nodded, eyeing the bomb. "McKay and touchy explosives are always a fun combination." There were seven drones wired together with the C-4 blocks, the drones' tentacles hanging out every which way. He just hoped it worked like Rodney thought it should.

Then a rumble shook the stone floor underfoot. "Oh, hell no," John said under his breath. Miko stumbled as the rumble escalated suddenly and the whole building seemed to sway. John caught her arm to steady her. On the ramp, Ronon swayed, but stayed upright. The few Eidolon left working on the other side of the bay looked around, startled. Dust trickled down from the seam of the giant hatch overhead. Just as John was about to grab Miko and run for the jumper, the rumble died away. Thinking, *don't let that be what it sounded like*, he asked, "Earthquake? Or moonquake?"

"Oh no," Miko said, looking anxiously at the bomb. "Mirrorquake."

Then Trishen leaned over the railing of the upper control area, calling urgently, "Dr. McKay, we think the Mirror is destabilizing again!"

Rodney ducked out of the jumper, harried and angry. "Yes, the quake that shook the entire surface of this moon would possibly indicate that there just might be a problem! Did you make the adjustments to the array? Because the wrong sequence—"

Trishen shook her head, making a helpless gesture. "It's not working anymore."

"What do you mean 'not working?' The array or the adjustments—" Rodney bolted for the stairs.

John told Miko, "Stay with Ronon," and ran after him.

John reached the top of the steps right behind Rodney, bumping into him when he stopped abruptly. Rodney said, "Oh, now, fine, look at this." He flung both arms in the air, annoyed. "This, this is what we couldn't find in our reality."

In the middle of the dais was a big round console, with an ornate silver rim inset with blue crystal panels. The air above it was alive with glowing diagrams, scrolling data, curves and graphs and figures in Ancient. In the center was a glowing silver pool, some sort of holographic miniature of the Mirror itself. Looking at it, John felt prickles of unease climb his spine. The surface was disturbed, rippling continuously, like a puddle in the rain. If the Mirror was actually doing that... *That just can't be good*. The holographic readouts seemed to agree; most of them were blinking in alarm.

A few Eidolon were watching the displays, and Kethel was carefully manipulating a set of touchpads on the console's rim. With a harsh tension in his voice, he said, "It's still not responding. This is the same sequence that worked earlier."

Trishen moved to the console, pointing toward one of the graphs. She told Rodney, "The accretion disk field has changed radically from—"

Rodney moved forward, half around the console, as John trailed after him. His expression grim, Rodney said, "Yes, this is about the cap to my day." He rounded on Trishen, making an abrupt gesture. "The connection to the Mirror in our reality is effecting this Mirror, and accelerating the destabilization. The singularity is detaching."

Kethel turned to him, face twisted into the expression Wraith made when they hissed in anger. Instead, he said, "It can't be."

"Oh, but it is!" Rodney snarled. "Check your figures!" He turned urgently to John. "I've seen this before, on the equipment we were using to monitor the Area 51 Mirror as it was being melted down. When the outer rim was destroyed, the singularity detached, closed in on itself, and vanished. Fortunately, we were expecting it, and all it took with it was a small concrete bunker and a naquadah generator." Rodney grimaced at the Mirror display. "This one's going to take this entire installation with it."

Trishen hit more touchpads on the console's edge, bringing up different data displays, enlarging others. The Queen came up the stairs, stopping at the top, her cold eyes narrowed slightly.

"Rodney." John kept his voice tightly controlled. "What does that mean for us, exactly?"

Rodney's jaw was set as he glared at the blinking displays. "It means we need to hurry. We need to do this now."

So there's still a chance to do it at all, John thought, relief undoing a few of the knots in his spine.

The Queen glanced at Kethel, who nodded sharply, saying, "Even if he's wrong—"

"I'm right!" Rodney shouted.

"—nothing can be served by delay." Kethel waved a hand toward the holographic image of the Mirror, which rippled like it was experiencing a rip tide. "This will surely only get worse."

The Queen's dark gaze turned to John. "The explosive?"

John flicked a glance at Rodney, and in response got a nod and hand-wave combination that he hoped meant "yes." John told her, "We're ready."

First, the Queen had to contact the Wraith and get them to lower their shield. John wasn't looking forward to that part. Hell, he was worried about all the parts, but at the moment, mostly that one.

One of the work stations toward the back of the maintenance bay had the comm equipment, and Kethel was using it to set up the contact with the Wraith ship. He was wearing a weird organic headset device, frequently using it to speak to the Eidolon ships in orbit. John, Rodney, Teyla, and Ronon watched from a short distance. Miko and Radek were in the jumper, ostensibly so they could run a few last diagnostics on the repair. John also wanted

Miko in there as a little extra insurance. She and Rodney hadn't removed all the drones, and if the Eidolon changed their minds about cooperation at the last moment, the armed jumper would be a powerful deterrent.

Standing nearby, Trishen shifted uneasily, saying, "This is my fault. If they hadn't activated the Mirror again to get me back, none of this would have happened."

John folded his arms, keeping his eyes on the displays that Kethel was manipulating. One held a real-time image of the Wraith scout ship where it hovered above the platform. He was starting to get used to Trishen's voice, but it was easier to talk to her if he didn't look at her. He said, "We're not in any position to point fingers." He didn't really care whose fault this was or wasn't at this point; as long as they could get back home and permanently disable their Mirror, he was fine with it.

Rodney was standing next to John, arms folded, rocking back and forth on his heels impatiently. "Besides," he said, "This is a far more effective method of destroying the Mirror in our reality. And by far more effective, I mean incredibly dangerous."

John and Teyla exchanged a bewildered look, and John frowned at him, asking, "What? I thought when we got back we'd still have to destroy the array."

Rodney shook his head at the ceiling, as if asking it to witness what he had to deal with. He said pointedly, "The two Mirrors are still connected, that's what caused that minor discharge, and yes, compared to what's coming, that was minor. As long as that connection lasts, they are the same Mirror. Actually, they're always the same Mirror, all the Mirrors are the same Mirror, but that's too complicated to explain to you. But right now, because of the connection and the continued destabilization, they're more one than usual."

Teyla eyed him worriedly. "You are saying that when this Mirror destroys itself—"

Rodney waved an impatient hand. "The singularities are sharing the same reality. It's good for us in that the destination can't be reset, so there's no possibility of losing the connection for our reality. It's bad for us in that when this Mirror goes, the other one will go, except there is no other one, they're both one. It's a form of quantum entanglement."

John just stared at him, brow furrowed. Maybe he was missing the point here, but this sounded bad. "Rodney—"

Kethel said, "They are accepting the transmission." The Queen stepped smoothly into position in front of the communications console.

John tensed, shifting his grip slightly on his P-90. Teyla had her arms folded over her weapon, outwardly casual, but like John she was holding it so her finger was near the trigger. Ronon was watching the other Eidolon, who were all gathered near Kethel.

A moment later the hologram appeared in a haze of blue static. It resolved into a male Wraith, possibly the same one that the Queen had spoken to earlier. It bared its teeth, demanding, "Why did you refuse to speak with us?"

She inclined her head and, with a faint trace of amusement in her voice, said, "I had nothing to say." Before the Wraith could react, she added, "I have decided to comply with your request. One of my ships will move into position above this structure, to beam the humans to you. Lower your shield and send coordinates."

This was the other part that John was worried about. From what the Eidolon had said, their transporter was more similar to the Asgard beam than it was to the Wraith culling beam. A quick test had shown that it couldn't get through the Wraith's shielding, anymore than the Asgard beam could. Since the *Daedalus* had destroyed a few hiveships by beaming aboard nuclear warheads, all the Wraith they had encountered had been extra careful about making preventative adjustments to their shields.

The Wraith stared at her, unblinking. Then it said, "Send them outside, we will take them."

"If I open a passage in or out of this facility, you will attack."

It hissed at her. "We have an agreement."

There was something in the Queen's tone that suggested she was talking to a somewhat backward child. "Then lower your shield and send the coordinates."

The Wraith snarled. The Queen stepped out of pick-up range, and Kethel cut the transmission, the hologram disappearing in an angry flash of light. The Queen eyed the spot where it had been, as if an afterimage of the Wraith's form still lingered. All emotion gone from her voice again, she said, "They will comply. Their limitations make their actions easy to predict."

"Yeah, that's what we've noticed," John said, and thought, *so far, so good*.

Rodney grimaced, saying in a low voice, "They'll give us coordinates for a hold area. If we could get the device closer to the main drive, it would be more effective, but what's she supposed to say? 'Oh, give me the coordinates to your weapons and shield control compartment too; no reason, just curious.'"

Since Rodney's idea of a low voice wasn't all that low, Trishen heard him anyway. She said, "We can get those coordinates with a sensor sweep."

Rodney's eyes lit up. "Wait, your sensors can get past their hull plating?"

She nodded, explaining, "One of the ships in orbit has special equipment for scanning ruins and underground structures left behind by the Creators. Once the Wraith shield is down, its sensors should be able to get a partial schematic."

Kethel looked up from his control board, telling the Queen, "We're received the information, and they have lowered their shield."

Trishen went forward to one of the consoles, picking up another headset and speaking quickly into it. After a moment, she set it aside, saying in relief, "Yes, it worked. They've managed to get the data."

A schematic started to form above the console, next to the real-time view of the scout ship. It rotated, offering alternate views, but there wasn't much detail, just blots and blurs of energy, dark spaces apparently indicating large compartments.

Rodney nodded. "Good, good. We're going to want to beam it right here." He pointed to a spot on the schematic, one of the brightest red blots. "Right where all these high-output energy signatures are, the drive, shield generators, and weapons."

Kethel looked at the Queen, and she gave him a nod. "Beam the device."

With everybody else, John looked at the bomb where

it sat near the jumper, but he kept one eye on Trishen. All the Eidolon had been careful to keep a non-threatening distance, but she was standing only a few paces away, close enough for easy conversation. If the Eidolon were going to screw them and send them instead of the explosive to the Wraith, it would be now. And if that happened, John intended to take Trishen with them.

A haze of light sparkled around the bomb, and it vanished with an audible pop. *Okay, still not screwed,* John thought, the tension in his shoulders relaxing just a little. He heard Teyla exhale in relief, and saw Ronon shift his stance slightly; he hadn't been the only one tensing for a last-second double cross.

"Give it a minute," Rodney muttered, his gaze on the overlapping images of the Wraith ship.

Kethel put a hand on his headset, apparently listening to a communication from the ship that had done the beaming. "Confirmed arrival." He pointed at the schematic of the scout ship. "It should be in what we believe to be the main engine compartment."

"Perfect." Rodney pulled something the size of a radio base-unit out of his vest pocket. It looked like it had started life as some other kind of handheld control device, but had recently undergone some major alterations. There was a small readout screen with Ancient characters and a couple of touchpads. "Signal is good. And here we go." Rodney pressed a touchpad.

John looked at the image of the scout ship. It didn't appear to be exploding. He had a bad feeling about this.

"No," Rodney said under his breath. "No, no, no." He pressed the touchpad again. John looked at the detonator, saw that the Ancient characters were now blinking an error code. Rodney said through gritted teeth, "Nothing's happening."

"What do you mean 'nothing's happening?'" John demanded. "What happened?"

"I don't know!" Mouth twisted with angry despair, Rodney popped the cover off, studied the weird combination of Ancient and Earth technology inside, and shook his head. "It should be working, but it isn't. If there's some sort of interference with the signal—I can try to boost it—" He turned away, heading for another empty console, ignoring the Eidolon who scrambled out of his way.

Kethel looked from the schematic to his section of the control board, his face set in a frustrated snarl. "It may have been the transport beam. If our coordinates were off—"

John knew they didn't have time for a post-mortem on why the frigging remote detonator wouldn't work. "In a minute, they're going to find it—" They were going to find it, open fire on the Eidolon ships, then break into the installation. John turned to Kethel. "Can you beam us over there, to the corridor where you beamed the bomb?"

Kethel stared. "To set it off directly?" He shook his head, looking at the screen again. "It's too dangerous for living beings. If our coordinates were off enough that the device was beamed inside a bulkhead—"

Fine, John got why that was a bad idea. "What about here?" He pointed to another more open area, only one level up from the bomb.

"The bridge?" Kethel asked, astonished and sounding like he thought John was completely crazy. "But—"

"Sure, there's probably only a couple of them in there right now." John thought it was a great plan. Okay, not a great plan, but a plan. The only plan he could think of.

"I agree," Teyla said, looking urgently from Kethel to the Queen. "It is our only choice."

Ronon just shrugged. "Sounds good to me."

John added, "Look, you beaming us in there to take them on is the last thing they'll expect." He did a quick inventory of his tac vest, making sure he had ammo and grenades. Teyla was doing the same. Ronon just checked the set of his knife in its scabbard.

"He's correct." The Queen's gaze was fixed on the image of the scout ship. "This must be done."

Kethel looked at the screen again. He shook his head slightly, as if he meant to refuse. Then he said, "Once on their bridge, I might be able to activate their self-destruct."

John stared at him. "Wait, you, what?"

Edane, the younger Eidolon that kept wanting to talk to them, stepped forward. "I'll go too." He looked around at the few remaining Eidolon. "Surely I'm not the only one."

Rodney came back from the console with the detonator, his expression caught between horror and incredulity. "This is insane, we can't possibly get through the ship to the bomb. And how are we getting back?" he demanded.

"You're not going," John told him. "You need to stay here to deal with the damn Mirror." If they didn't succeed, the scout ship might be too occupied with shooting at the installation and the Eidolon ships to worry about the Mirror or the cloaked jumper, and Rodney might still have a chance to get himself, Radek, and Miko back home. But Rodney did have a point. John eyed Kethel. "How are we getting back?"

Trishen had been hurriedly digging into one of the equipment cases stacked up to be transported out, and now came back with a handful of little silver buttons, each set with a flat green stone. "We have emergency transponders. Simply touch this crystal and it will signal the ship to beam you back here." She looked at the image of the scout ship, adding worriedly, "As long as their shield remains down, these should work."

Famous last words, John thought. He just said, "So let's go."

With a few moments of scrambling, they were ready. Kethel was bringing two other young male Eidolon, Edane and Caras; John wasn't happy about it, but Kethel might be able to activate the ship's self-destruct and render the bomb unnecessary, so he was willing to put up with it. Kethel also had a handheld scanning device that would help them locate the engine compartments where the bomb had been sent, just in case the self-destruct proved elusive. The Eidolon also had weapons, long elegant silver-gray devices about the size of sawed-off shotguns.

"Those are stunners?" Teyla asked Kethel. John had assumed they were just a different model of the Wraith version.

"No." Kethel glanced at her, distracted. "They are energy weapons, the blast is fatal. Stunners are forbidden."

Teyla lifted her brows, obviously not getting it anymore than John did. *So shooting to kill is fine, stunning and asking questions later is forbidden,* he thought. John just said, "Okay. That's handy."

Rodney came back to shove the detonator into John's vest pocket, saying, "I tried boosting the signal, still nothing. Hopefully you won't need this. And if you do need it, the damn thing probably won't work, but there it is."

"Great. Wait for us in the jumper," John told him, taking the detonator out of that pocket and putting it in a more convenient one.

Rodney shook his head impatiently. "I need to monitor the array—"

John glared. He didn't want Rodney out here alone, distracted with the Mirror, with no one to watch his back. "Rodney, jumper, now."

Rodney glared back, unimpressed. "Yes, because I respond so well to that sort of thing. What are you going to do, threaten to shoot me in the foot?"

John just stared at him, narrowing his eyes. "You want to stay out here alone with the folks who look like Wraith?"

Rodney looked around, apparently realizing it was just going to be him, the Queen, and the scatter of other Eidolon left in the room. "All right, fine," he snapped, and started toward the jumper.

John told Kethel, "We're ready." Kethel signaled to the Eidolon who had taken his place at the control console. White light flashed.

Abruptly another room shimmered into existence around them, John's ears popping at the sudden transition to a pressurized space.

They were in a large dimly-lit chamber with dark walls of a rubbery black substance. There was a raised center dais, with three consoles each supported by weirdly organic-looking stalks. John spun around, opening fire on two surprised Wraith standing in front of a large irregularly-shaped viewport. Ronon and Teyla fired at the same time, and both Wraith jerked and twitched under the combined onslaught. They dropped, sprawling on the deck.

John pivoted, checking the room, as Ronon moved around the dais to watch the door. Teyla finished her own survey of the chamber, saying, "We are clear."

John pulled the detonator control out of his vest. "Let's see if this is going to be easy." He hit the touchpad. The readout did the same thing that it had before, blinking the error code. And he hadn't heard anything, either. "Anybody hear an explosion?" he asked, hoping against hope.

"Nothing," Teyla said with a grimace. Ronon and the Eidolon shook their heads.

Kethel was already stepping up onto the dais, examining the consoles. "I'll look for a self-destruct. Perhaps something onboard is still interfering with the detonation signal." Edane and Caras were warily looking around the control area.

John shoved the detonator back in his pocket and pulled out the life signs detector. There were blips moving on the level immediately below, but none coming toward them. The Wraith probably didn't realize anything had been beamed aboard yet, and were still waiting for the Eidolon. That wasn't going to last long.

Looking around, Caras asked, "What is that smell?" John had barely noticed it; the air had that sour taint common to every Wraith ship John had been in, the sick stench of death and rot.

Ronon sneered. "Their supplies."

Caras stared at him, uncomprehending, and Ronon didn't elaborate.

Kethel frowned down at the console, his hands flat against the surface. From his expression, the news wasn't good. John knew the Wraith systems weren't anything like the Ancients' or what he had seen of the Eidolon's. The interfaces weren't touchpads or buttons, but thin membranes that the Wraith apparently manipulated by passing their hands over them. John asked, "Any luck?"

Kethel shook his head, wiping his hands off on his coat, as if disgusted by the contact. "It's not responding to me. If I had time—"

The blips John could see were starting to move rapidly. "No time, we've got to get down there." He headed for the door, checked the detector again, and hit the slimy control-thing on the wall. The door membrane folded open, revealing a long curving corridor, the dark ceiling arching overhead, draped with shrouds and strands of web. As Teyla led the others out, John hung back with Ronon, pulling out a fragmentation grenade. When the others were all out in the corridor, he gave Ronon a nod and they both tossed their grenades onto the dais, Ronon landing his directly atop one of the consoles. John hit the control, closing the hatch. The muted thump from inside didn't sound destructive enough, and he asked Kethel, "Can you jam this door?"

"Yes." Kethel pulled out a tool that looked like a scalpel, slit open the bulbous control panel, and stuck his hand into it, manipulating the slimy things inside.

John figured that would slow the Wraith down, but the ship had to have alternate controls for the shields, and they had to move fast. He looked deliberately at the

Eidolon, saying, "Any time you want out of here, if you get separated, cornered, whatever, just hit your transponder. If you fall behind, we're not going to have time to come back for you."

Kethel looked at Edane and Caras, giving them a sharp nod to reinforce the order. Life signs detector braced over the P-90, John headed down the corridor.

They found the first cocooned body only a few paces along, crammed back into a cubby in the wall. John glanced at it only long enough to see it was dead, withered to a husk, with the gaping wound of the feeding mark in its chest.

"What is that?" Edane asked, in what sounded like horrified fascination. He tried to stop, but Kethel took his arm and pulled him into motion again.

"What do you think it is?" Ronon countered.

John really didn't want to get into this just now. He said, "Just keep moving." They passed two more desiccated bodies webbed to the wall, then a dozen more, all dead. More passages led off the first corridor, dim and web-draped. Kethel guided them with his scanner, finding a path toward the big blot of energy signatures where the ship's drive was located. John caught some blips off the detector, but most of the Wraith seemed to be down below. His headset came on and Rodney's voice suddenly demanded, "Can you hear me?"

John flinched, startled. "Yes, dammit."

"I had to boost the gain before I could get through," Rodney explained impatiently. "Did you try the detonator again? The signal might have—"

"Tried it, didn't work. Are you in the jumper?"

There was a hesitation. "I'm near the jumper."

John swore. "Rodney—Later." John signed off, his eyes on the life signs detector. Four strong blips, coming up toward them from the lower level, moving rapidly. *That's an elevator.* He held up a fist to signal the others to stop, ignoring the slight scuffle behind him as the Eidolon belatedly realized what that meant. *Where the hell is—Hah, got you.* The corridor had widened a little and there was a membrane stretched across an indentation in the bulkhead.

Ronon stepped forward with John as Teyla covered the corridor. The membrane slid open, and four more surprised Wraith died in the elevator doorway. With a wary glance at the bodies, Kethel stepped forward. "The drive area is one level below."

Teyla told him, "We cannot take this elevator, they could shut it down and trap us."

John tried the detonator, just for luck, and got the error code again. *Son of a bitch.* He shoved it back in his pocket and checked the life signs detector. As he expected, the blips on this level were moving their way. The level below, at least in this area, still looked clear. "We need another way down, now."

Kethel nodded, eyes on his scanner. "I'm reading a maintenance passage...this way."

They found it around the corner, in another intersection of passages. It was a ribbed shaft like something's gullet, with multiple ladder rungs down the sides, leading down into a chamber lit with dim red light. John exchanged a wince with Teyla and grabbed for the first rung.

Halfway down, Rodney's voice burst into John's headset again, almost making him lose his grip on the slick material of the ladder. "The Queen says the Wraith know you're there."

"We know they know that, Rodney," John said through gritted teeth. The rungs had been spaced for adult male Wraith only, and Teyla and the two younger Eidolon were moving slowly, having to awkwardly stretch to reach them. Kethel slowed down, waiting for Edane and Caras, and John waited for Teyla, motioning Ronon to go ahead. "Rodney, what the hell are you—"

Rodney said in annoyance, "I'm entering the last codes for a pulse array adjustment. The detachment of the singularity started to accelerate, but this should—Oh, oh, that's...unusual. Hold on a minute."

Ronon climbed around John, then swung down, dropping to the bottom of the shaft and landing in a crouch. As the others caught up, John climbed down the rest of the way, remembering at the last moment not to drop the last few feet; his knee just wouldn't take it right now.

The shaft opened into a wider corridor that curved out of sight just past a couple of membrane-sealed hatchways. John pulled out the life signs detector.

Kethel checked his scanner, nodding toward the first hatchway. "It should be there—"

That was about the moment John's screen registered a dozen or more blips headed straight for them. He yelled a warning, ducking across the corridor and hitting the control to open the hatch. Ronon and Teyla moved instantly, taking cover with John in the hatchway, but the Eidolon were slow to react.

Kethel and Edane reached the hatchway just as the first group of drones burst around the corner, but Caras was still in the middle of the corridor. He took a stun blast in the face, dropping his own weapon before falling to the ground in a limp sprawl. Edane ran for him, as John and the others fired on the drones, driving them back.

Edane reached Caras, stooping to touch the transponder. The Eidolon's body vanished in a flash of blue-white light. More drones poured into the corridor, and in a moment Edane would be hit, with no one to trigger his transponder. John yelled, "Go, go! Get out of there!"

Edane looked at the drones, wide-eyed. Then he touched his transponder and vanished.

John and Teyla kept up steady bursts of fire, with Ronon using his energy gun, and the first few drones dropped. The others retreated back around the corner, a few leaning out to take shots. John had time to notice the membrane sealing the hatch still hadn't opened. "What the hell is—" John reached around, hitting the door control again, a narrow miss from a stun blast making his fingers go numb for an instant. "It's locked! Kethel—"

Kethel stepped past him, slashed open the control surface, and shoved his hand inside. John leaned out to cover him.

Abruptly the door membrane folded open. As Teyla turned to cover the room inside, a stun blast hit Kethel in the side. John made an instinctive grab for him but Kethel staggered backward, away from the hatchway, and fell, sprawling on the deck.

John stepped back into cover as more stun blasts hit the wall near him. Ronon leaned out, took several shots, and the blasts abruptly stopped. John could see Kethel wasn't unconscious, his eyes were open, but his hands were twitching helplessly. The Eidolon couldn't lift his arm to reach the transponder on his shoulder.

John swore and ducked out into the corridor, leaning

over Kethel. He grabbed the scanner where it had fallen on the deck, tossing it back to Ronon. Then he pushed the transponder on Kethel's shoulder. It pulsed blue, and John flinched back as Kethel's body dissolved in a sudden blue-white flash.

As he started to stand, a drone barreled around the corner, almost on top of him. It lunged for him and John fell backward, firing the P-90 almost point blank. Then a blast from Ronon's energy gun took the drone in the face, and Ronon grabbed John's arm, yanking him back through the hatchway.

Teyla hit the door control, but just as the membrane was folding down, another drone reached the hatchway, leaning down to fire his stunner under it. Ronon caught a burst in the leg and staggered, dropping his gun. He went to one knee, reeling. John lunged for Ronon's fallen gun, grabbed it and fired at the door control. The burst of energy fused the organic components just as the membrane sealed. The burned area steamed, releasing a sickening smell like fried meat.

Wincing at the odor, John said, "I hope that worked." He turned to Ronon. "You okay?" Ronon didn't look okay. He was trying to stand, but one arm hung limply and he struggled to move his leg; he looked like he was having a stroke. Teyla grabbed his arm, just managing to keep him upright. "How many hits did he take?" John asked incredulously.

"At least two," Teyla said with a sympathetic wince. Ronon tried to lurch to his feet and almost fell over. She set her jaw and held onto him. "Send him back?"

John nodded. "Do it."

Ronon growled an incoherent protest, glaring at them,

but Teyla let go of his arm and pressed his transponder. She stepped away as Ronon disappeared in the flash. John keyed his radio, "Rodney, you got Ronon?"

"What? Hold it, wait—Yes, yes, he's here!" There was a slurred grumbling protest in the background. Rodney came back on, sounding sour, "He's not happy about it, but he's fine."

"Get him to the jumper." John signed off as he looked around. The dimly lit chamber was packed with pulsing membranes and bizarre organic shapes that looked like the internal organs of something huge, all shrouded with web. He could hear thumping and a high-power hum from just outside the closed membrane, a pointed reminder that they didn't have much time before the Wraith cut their way in here.

Teyla pivoted, flashing her P-90's light into the dark corners, her face grim. "I do not see it. Will Kethel's scanner work for us?"

"Good question." John studied the little device, brow furrowed. The screen showed the same schematic that Kethel had used to pick a spot for the damn bomb, and according to it, these were the coordinates it had been beamed to. John turned, surveying the chamber again. "It's working, and it looks like we're in the right spot, but where the hell is—" Then his eyes fell on a set of small familiar-looking tentacles sticking out of the bulkhead. They were near one of the pulsing organ-things, a foot or so above the deck. *The energy drones. Oh, crap.* The bomb was melded to the organic material of the ship's wall. "That can't be good."

Teyla followed his gaze, shocked. "Kethel was right, it was beamed into a wall." She shook her head, her brow creased. "Can it still work like that?" She threw a look back at the door membrane; a glowing spot was forming in the center, letting off steam and smoke as the Wraith outside burned their way through. "There is no time for anything else."

There was only one way to find out. "Get ready to hit your transponder." Just for luck, John closed his eyes, concentrating the way he did in the puddlejumper or the weapons chair, thinking about the energy drones, thinking about launching, targeting, impact. He pressed the detonator touchpad again.

There was a muted thump. John opened his eyes to see the heavy bulkhead around the bomb bulged out, like it was a misshapen helium balloon. He exchanged a desperate look with Teyla. "Okay, that's—"

Across the room, the door membrane exploded outward, sending them staggering back, showering the room with slimy debris. John ducked, raking the doorway with a burst of fire from the P-90, driving back the first two drones to step inside. Teyla opened fire an instant later, shouting, "We must go! It is not going to—"

Suddenly the distended bulkhead started to glow white, a high power whine filling the chamber. *That did it*, John thought. He yelled, "Go, go now!"

Two drones forced their way through the shattered door membrane, just as Teyla hit her transponder. She vanished and John pressed the crystal in his. The drones lifted their stunners, then the chamber disappeared in a haze of white light.

CHAPTER TWELVE

John sat down hard, but the floor he landed on was the floor of the maintenance bay in the installation. The abrupt change to brighter light and warm clean air was a shock. Next to him, Teyla was sprawled on the floor, just pushing herself upright.

Kethel and Caras were lying on the floor nearby, a couple of older Eidolon checking them out with some sort of medical scanner. John didn't see Edane, but nobody was acting worried. There weren't many Eidolon left in the room anymore; Edane might have been sent away to evacuate already. Across the room, the Queen and the others were still gathered around the console, watching the realtime sensor image of the scout ship.

Rodney hurried over from the jumper, crouching down beside John. He demanded, "Did it work? We need to get out of here as soon as possible."

Teyla pushed her hair back, starting to say, "It looked as if—"

At the console, one of the Eidolon said, "I'm reading an energy surge—"

Then lines of red and black crept through and across the ship's image, growing out from the center. John heard a reverberating roar from outside, and the glowing hologram image tipped sideways, drifting downward, the angle changing as the sensors followed it down. John slumped in relief. "It worked."

"That was...uncomfortably close," Teyla said ruefully,

and drew her fingers through her hair, combing out a handful of door membrane with a disgusted expression.

"That's our specialty," John told her. The adrenaline was wearing off, and he had time to notice just how much he hurt. Knee, side, the occasional shooting pain down his back. And he had a big splat of door membrane goo on his shirt.

"Seriously, we have to move," Rodney persisted. "The Mirror's accretion surface is building up to a major discharge and from my readings, it'll be the last one before the singularity collapses."

"Yeah, we're leaving now." John looked back at the jumper. Ronon was sprawled on the open ramp, Miko anxiously patting his hand. "How's Ronon?"

Rodney snorted, making a throw-away gesture. "He's fine, he's just sulking because he can barely move."

Then John saw the Queen coming toward them, her dark skirts sweeping the floor. Before John could try flailing to his feet, Rodney and Teyla got a grip under his arms and they all stood up together. The Queen stopped a few paces away, and said, "The Wraith ship is completely disabled. We thank you."

"You're welcome." John watched her warily. They had fulfilled their part of the bargain, and if the Eidolon wanted to screw them over, now would be the time. But the Queen just said, "The singularity is close to detaching, so we must retreat to our ships now. The others have already evacuated." She paused, as if weighing what to say, and it was odd to see her show even this much uncertainty. "If the Mirror does not function as expected—"

"It'll work," John said, because he didn't want to think about the alternative. Not until he had to.

The Queen eyed him, apparently deciding not to argue with the crazy human. She said, "Good luck."

John backed away with Rodney and Teyla as the blue-white transport beam outlined the Eidolon's bodies. In another instant the whole group vanished. He let his breath out in relief, shoving a hand through his hair. "Right. Rodney, what do we need to do?"

Rodney bolted for the stairs that led up to the Mirror control platform. "I need to make a last adjustment, then we go." He waved a distracted hand overhead. "The ceiling hatch will open automatically for the jumper, so that's not a problem."

John told Teyla, "I'll stay with him."

Teyla nodded and started for the jumper. "I will get Ronon inside and make sure the others are strapped in."

John followed Rodney up the stairs to the platform, keeping himself going mostly by force of will. He reached the platform to see Rodney at the big console, carefully manipulating a set of touchpad controls. Then he saw the miniature Mirror in the center.

He forgot his exhaustion, and limped forward for a closer look, circling around the console. From what this was showing him, the Mirror was an angry swirling cloud, throwing off jagged sparks of light. And he was going to take the jumper into it and hope it got them back home. Rodney glanced up and saw his expression. His mouth twisted in grim agreement, he said, "We've only got one shot at this."

"Yeah, well." John hadn't been expecting anything better.

John heard footsteps and looked at the stairs, expecting to see Teyla. But the figure standing at the top of the steps was Edane. The Eidolon halted, one hand on the railing, staring blankly at them. "I thought you guys were gone," John said, puzzled, though maybe the Queen had sent him back for some reason.

Edane said, "I stayed behind to help."

Occupied with the Mirror, Rodney barely glanced up. "I don't need help. After this last sequence engages, we'll be set to go."

Edane was looking at John, his alien eyes unreadable. That was when John knew why he was here.

John jerked the P-90 up but Edane threw himself across the small platform, slapping the weapon aside and slamming John backward into the floor. John caught Edane's arm before his hand could hit his chest, held it off inches away from him, the P-90 trapped between their bodies.

The bizarre thing was that Edane still didn't look that much like a Wraith. His features were still smooth and human, and his yellow eyes intent, lost in concentration; he was focused on his task and completely oblivious to the fact that John was pinned under him and fighting for his life.

Past Edane's shoulder John caught a glimpse of Rodney scrambling up, dragging out his sidearm and taking aim. *Take the shot, Rodney,* he thought, teeth gritted, all his strength concentrated on holding Edane back. He knew to his bones that he would rather take a stray bullet than be fed on.

Then Edane twisted, abruptly pulling away from John to slam the pistol out of Rodney's hand. It went off, flying across the platform. Rodney stumbled sideways, knocked off balance, and John tried to wrestle the P-90 up again.

Edane grabbed it, tore it off the strap, and backhanded John. John's head bounced off the floor. Stunned for an instant, he saw Edane leaning over him.

Then somebody fired a 9mm, emptying the clip.

Dazed, John watched Edane stagger sideways and fall.

Trishen was standing beside the Mirror console. She set Rodney's pistol down on the edge with a shaking hand. She said, "We realized he was missing. Mother sent me back to find him."

Rodney dropped to his knees beside John, patting his shoulder anxiously. "You said you didn't feed on sentient beings!" he shouted at Trishen, furious and afraid. "What the hell was that?"

She shook her head. "I lied to you. That was the only lie."

John lifted a hand to his jaw. *That really hurt*. He managed to say, "Yeah, we figured that out."

John heard someone charging up the stairs, saw Teyla jerk to a sudden halt at the top, P-90 ready. John lifted a hand, signaling her not to fire. She nodded an acknowledgement, eyes wide as she took in the scene.

Trishen glanced back at Teyla and said, "It isn't—We aren't like the Wraith. We don't need the life force of sentient beings, but we can take it, and some are tempted. Some of us go all our lives without ever feeling that temptation, others feel it and resist. But there are always a few who give in." She looked at Edane's body sprawled on the platform, and pressed a hand to her mouth. After a moment she continued, "They try to resist, but eventually they give way, and they take a life. A sibling, a friend, a child. It's terrible, and we punish them as the criminals they are."

"You have to kill them," Rodney said, sounding shell-shocked. And now John understood what Kethel had said, about stun-weapons being forbidden. *Of course they're forbidden.* If you wanted to feed on someone, you needed him immobile but conscious, not dead. Rodney's throat worked and he shook his head. "Of course, you have to kill them."

Trishen nodded. "Yes. Once one of us succumbs, there is no turning back. Edane would have been dangerous to everyone he encountered." She made a helpless gesture. "We have tried to discover why, to stop it, but there's no answer. We can't tell if it's genetic, and there are no other signs of insanity or criminal acts. When we find places left behind by the Creators, that is the answer we desperately search for." She looked up, and this time John had no trouble reading the bleak misery in her expression. "My mother believes that the Creators were dying from the plague when they gave us life, and that they didn't survive long enough to finish what they had started. Some of the others here wanted to ask your assistance, thought that perhaps you could help us."

Rodney nodded, eyeing her. "Then we told you that we didn't know very much about the Wraith."

"Yes. And we knew the Creators didn't begin work on our race until long after they came here, so the chances of our solution even existing in your reality seemed small. My mother thought it safer for all of us if you left as soon as possible, then we realized the singularity was detaching and that there was no other choice. But we have the bodies of the Wraith killed inside the complex for our doctors to examine, and perhaps that will help us."

Watching her with a furrowed brow, looking torn between sympathy and disgust, Teyla said, "You were not afraid of us. You were afraid of what you might do to us."

Trishen turned toward her. "I was afraid of you because I knew you had every reason to kill me. The longer I was around you, there was something...strangely compelling. I was afraid that there would be those here who, though they weren't tempted by members of their own species, would be tempted by you."

John grabbed Rodney's arm, dragged himself into a sitting position. He said harshly, "We've got to go."

Trishen nodded, her face set in what might have been regret. "I'm sorry. I hope...that you will be safe." She touched her transponder and an instant later the blue-white light took her.

Teyla came forward hurriedly. "Are you all right?"

"Yeah, just help me up." John held back a yelp as they hauled him upright. Once there, he thought he was fine; it was just that transition from sprawled on the floor to standing that he was having trouble with.

"Well, that was fun," Rodney said, grimly determined, picking up his side arm from where Trishen had left it and holstering it again. "Now let's go give the giant Quantum Mirror another shot at us, shall we?"

They got down to the jumper, and while John managed to fold himself into the pilot seat, Rodney secured the ramp. Rodney came forward to the shotgun seat to strap himself in, while Teyla stayed in the back. Powering up the board, John heard her quietly telling Miko and Ronon what had happened. Radek was only semi-conscious, strapped in on the bench with a couple of pillows from the sleeping bags to help pad him.

As they lifted off the bay floor, the ceiling hatch started to open, the triangular partitions sliding out of the way, letting in wan daylight and a strong breeze that carried dust all through the empty chamber. His voice tight with anxiety, Rodney said, "There's a chance of a strong concussion wave when we hit the accretion surface. Not hit. Pass through. I meant pass through the accretion surface."

John stared at him. "Right." He lifted the jumper up through the hatch.

As soon as they cleared the roof, the jumper registered a strong pull forward. Down on the platform, past the far side of the Mirror's frame, the Wraith scout ship was in pieces, smoke swirling up from it. But the lighter dart wreckage was stirring, lifting up as if pulled by a tractor beam. "Gravity well?" John asked.

"Yes." Rodney studied the platform, eyes wide. "It's going to pull some of this wreckage in. And us too."

"Here we go," John said, and directed the jumper straight for the Mirror.

The silver surface grew larger and larger in the port until there was nothing else. Then everything went black.

Carson felt he was half-mad from waiting. The *Daedalus* had been scanning the system for hours now, with no result. He couldn't fault their efforts; Hermiod and Dr. Novak had come up to the bridge to assist, and the little Asgard was at one of the consoles now, fine-tuning the sensors to better search for the jumper.

"It doesn't look good, Doc," Lorne said. He leaned

on the bulkhead, watching the activity at the forward section of the bridge, his face set with concern. "If they had to land somewhere on this moon, they would have come out by now."

Carson knew Lorne was trying to prepare him for the worst. But Carson knew just how many times Rodney, Sheppard, and Teyla had survived the worst, and they had some good people with them. "Then it's either the Wraith or the Quantum Mirror, Major." Both possibilities were fairly terrible. He folded his arms, shaking his head. "I'd rather it was the Mirror. At least then we'd have a chance of finding them."

Lorne frowned. "They wouldn't have gone into that thing voluntarily. McKay knows just how dangerous it is." He threw an uncertain look at Carson. "Would they?"

Carson had to admit, "No, I don't think so either, lad. Not voluntarily."

An alarm went off somewhere forward. Carson saw Caldwell stride over to look at Hermiod's screen. He decided to hell with patience. He hurried forward, demanding, "What is it?"

Caldwell glanced up from the screen to say, "The Mirror's apparently activated. It's spitting out Wraith darts, and pieces of a ship."

"A ship?" Carson looked from Lorne to Caldwell, wishing the man would just say what he meant. "Is it—"

Caldwell clarified, "A Wraith ship, Doctor. We can't tell what class yet."

"Colonel!" Novak called from her console. She flailed excitedly. "I'm picking up an energy signature from Ancient technology. I'm not sure if it's a cloaked puddlejumper, it doesn't quite match the pattern—"

Hermiod interrupted in his dry laconic voice, "It is a gate ship signature, possibly altered to avoid interfering with the Mirror's destabilized quantum field."

"It's them," Carson said. It had to be them.

"Open a channel." Caldwell sat down in the command chair.

"Oh, this isn't good," Novak muttered. "Sir, the Quantum Mirror—"

"The singularity is detaching from the Mirror's matrix and collapsing," Hermiod overrode her. "It will close, destroying the Mirror's physical structure, and causing a massive disruption to the area around it."

Caldwell shifted impatiently, leaning forward. "Can you raise the jumper?"

At the forward control board, Major Meyers glanced up, her brow furrowed in concentration. "No, sir, it's not responding. And it's just heading straight up from the surface. It could be on automatic pilot."

Caldwell grimaced. "Life signs?"

"There's too much interference from the Mirror, sir," Lieutenant Hawkins answered him.

"They must be unconscious, that's why they aren't answering the comm," Carson said. He wasn't sure how much Caldwell knew about the puddlejumpers' ATA interface. "The jumper wouldn't still be flying if there wasn't someone with the Ancient gene alive inside it."

"He's right, Colonel," Major Lorne added quickly. "The jumpers only have a limited unmanned autopilot function, and that's only for dropping out of the Atlantis jumper bay and going through the gate. If it's under power and maintaining a heading, it's got a gene carrier pilot, whether he's conscious or not."

Hermiod's voice grated, "The singularity is detaching now. It will cause a gravitational well to form temporarily over the area. The gate ship is not powerful enough to pull free. If you intend to retrieve it—"

Caldwell sat back in his chair. "Full power, take us down into tractor range."

The starfield wheeled as the *Daedalus* dove down toward the moon's surface. Though the deck felt rock steady under his feet, Carson's stomach did a psychosomatic dip anyway.

"We're nearly in range." Captain Kleinmann, on the other forward console, made some careful adjustments to his controls.

The ship started to shake. "The gravity well is forming," Hermiod informed them, probably unnecessarily.

Carson couldn't see a damn thing through the port. He stepped forward, looking at the screens, but it was all just blips.

Hawkins said urgently, "Sir, we have a hiveship on longrange sensors, just entering the system."

Carson's stomach clenched but Caldwell just muttered dryly, "Of course we do."

"We've got it!" Novak called, "We've got the jumper, sir."

"Pull up, bring it into the bay, and get us out of here," Caldwell said, watching the screen with narrowed eyes. "It looks like the Mirror isn't going to be a problem anymore."

The screen was displaying a sensor schematic of the giant structure around the Mirror. The collapsing singularity had taken a good portion of the ground around it when it had vanished. The remaining structure was slowly crumbling into the crater it had left behind. Carson didn't stay to watch further; he and Lorne hurried to the elevator, making for the F-302 bay.

John came to feeling like someone had punched him in the head. A lot. "Not again," he muttered. He managed to get his eyes open. The HUD was fuzzy and flashing error codes, but it was the view through the jumper's port that made him grip the armrests, the sudden jolt of adrenaline clearing his head. He wasn't looking at a starfield, but a set of enormous ship bay doors that were just starting to slide open. "What the hell—?"

"Giant Quantum Mirror of death," Rodney groaned from the co-pilot's seat. He was leaning forward on the control board, his head pillowed on his arms. "Does that ring any bells? The concussion wave must have knocked us out. If the jumper's inertial dampeners hadn't—" Rodney lifted his head, saw what was happening, and froze, gaping. "Oh, you meant 'what fresh hell is this?'"

But as the opening grew wider, John spotted the familiar racks of F-302s. They weren't being tractored into an alien spaceship, this was a rescue. "It's the *Daedalus*," he said in relief. He tried to twist around in his seat, gritted his teeth as pain stabbed through his midsection. He fumbled at the straps, calling, "Teyla, Ronon, you guys okay back there?"

Sounding shaky, Teyla's voice answered, "I believe...ow."

John managed to get himself out of the chair and stagger into the back cabin. Everyone was stirring, except for Zelenka, who hung limply against the straps. John limped over to him and felt his pulse. It was there, and he seemed to be breathing normally. "Is he all right?" Teyla asked, pushing unsteadily to her feet. Ronon was gripping the bench seat for support, still moving sluggishly from the stun blasts. Miko was fumbling to unbuckle her safety straps, watching Zelenka anxiously.

"He's alive," John told her. Rodney, standing in the cabin doorway, swore in weary relief. *Alive*, John repeated to himself. They were all alive. *And apparently in the right reality*. It was just starting to dawn on him that they had really made it.

By the time they got Zelenka unstrapped and laid out on the bench, the jumper had thumped softly to the deck of the bay and someone was banging on the hatch. Rodney hit the ramp release and it lowered, letting in the *Daedalus'* filtered air. A group of SFs were warily waiting, aiming weapons. John understood the necessity, but at the moment it just exasperated the hell out of him. He said tightly, "Yeah, it's us. Get a damn medical team in here, now."

Then Major Lorne pushed forward, stepping onto the ramp as soon as it touched the deck. He was already on his radio, saying, "Dr. Beckett, we need a medical team for Dr. Zelenka immediately. Everybody else looks pretty beat up, too."

"And we were actually pretty beat up before the concussion wave," Rodney added, slumping down on the bench in relief.

Beckett came up the ramp, saying, "Thank God." He turned, waving to someone across the bay. "Get those gurneys over here!"

John ended up debriefing Caldwell from a gurney in the sick bay, in one of the private treatment compartments with a lot of esoteric unrecognizable medical equipment built into the bulkheads and people in *Daedalus* medical uniforms walking in and out.

John gave Caldwell the brief outline while a nurse scanned him and took blood. With a grimace, Caldwell said, "This was a close one. If the Wraith had managed to return with an Eidolon ship, this war would be over."

"I don't think they were there long enough to figure out what the Eidolon could do." On the way down to sick bay, before Beckett had chased him off, Lorne had managed to tell John about the hiveship that had arrived. The *Daedalus* had entered hyperspace before it could scan them, and there hadn't been anything left of the Mirror installation for it to find. "And none of the Wraith in the other reality made it out alive." John frowned, realizing he didn't actually know that for certain. The scout ship had been in pieces, and he didn't think any of the darts had managed to get in the air. "Did they?"

Caldwell shook his head. "Our scans didn't pick up anything coming out of the Mirror but debris and your jumper."

That was a relief. John winced as the nurse jabbed the needle for the IV into his arm. "I need to send a report to Dr. Weir." Lorne had said that Atlantis hadn't gotten any of the transmissions sent to the base moon after the Wraith had arrived, and John knew Elizabeth would be worried.

"As soon as we're well clear of the hiveship, we'll drop out of hyper and I'll send her an initial report." With a restrained flash of humor, Caldwell said, "Your team got lucky, again, Sheppard."

"Yeah, we usually do," John told him.

Caldwell left, and John meant to get up and check on the others. But this was the first time he had been able to rest in hours and the IV was taking the edge off the pain; he fell asleep before the nurse finished scanning him. He woke up with someone leaning over him, and he almost punched Beckett before he realized who it was. Beckett, used to this after more than a year in Pegasus, just dodged like a pro boxer and said, "Easy now." An unfamiliar doctor in *Daedalus* coveralls retreated hastily. Unperturbed, Beckett ran an Ancient handheld medical scanner over John. "You've banged yourself up this time, Colonel."

"I think I knew that." John rubbed his eyes. He had cold packs jammed into various places and his bad knee was propped up on a couple of pillows. Whatever was in the IV must be working, because the pain felt floaty and distant. Not unlike his head. "Where's my team?"

"They're all fine," Beckett assured him. "Just get some rest."

Beckett left with the other doctor, but John still wanted to check on everybody. He unhooked the IV bag from the stand and climbed carefully to his feet, shedding cold packs. Then he had to hold onto the table to steady himself, head swimming. Okay, maybe getting up wasn't such a great idea, but he was here now, and he still wanted to see how the others were doing.

The corridor was quiet now, empty except for Ronon,

who was sitting in a chair, holding an IV bag in his lap. He looked like he had been in a bar fight involving chairs and broken bottles. John was pretty certain he looked the same. "You okay?" John asked.

Ronon nodded. John was a little too woozy to wonder why Ronon was out in the hall instead of in a treatment room, and just checked the next compartment.

He found Teyla and Miko there, both curled up asleep on the narrow beds that doubled as examination tables. Miko still had her glasses clutched in one hand. Teyla woke enough to squint blearily up at him, asking, "All is well?"

"Yeah. Go back to sleep," John told her softly, trying not to wake Miko.

John went out to the corridor again, noticing he now had Ronon trailing along after him. "Where's Rodney and Zelenka?" John asked him.

"Down there." Ronon nodded toward the end of the corridor.

John found the right cabin, stepping in to see a very pale Zelenka in the bed, hooked up to IVs and monitors, with a nurse making notes on a tablet. He asked, "How is he?"

"He's going to be fine," she told him, giving him an odd look. "Are you supposed to be—"

Rodney appeared in the hatchway, a laptop tucked under his arm. He was pale, bruised, and looked like he had a hangover. He frowned. "What are you doing up? Carson said not to bother you."

The nurse tried again, "You really need to—"

Zelenka stirred and tugged at the blankets, then he blinked, managing to focus on them. His voice hoarse, he asked, "Am I dying?"

"Don't be an idiot," Rodney told him, before John or the nurse could reply.

Zelenka frowned, waking up a little more. "Where are we?"

"The *Daedalus*," John said. "Everything's fine."

"Oh." Zelenka squinted up at them uncertainly. "You all look terrible."

The nurse made herding motions, saying, "He really needs to rest now. So do all of you."

She was probably right, so John left, prodding Rodney in front of him.

Outside, Lorne was just coming up the corridor. "Colonel—"

"Did Caldwell send a message to Elizabeth?" John asked him.

Lorne nodded sharply. "Yes, sir. While we were out of hyper."

"Great." John rubbed his eyes, swaying a little. That was one thing he didn't have to worry about. Maybe going back to his treatment table and the ice packs wasn't that bad an idea.

Then Lorne said, "I'm sorry I left you there, sir."

John blinked at him. "Left me where? Sorry, there's been drugs. What?"

Lorne hesitated, and started to back away. "Maybe I should do this later."

"No, it's fine." John fought back a yawn. "What were you saying?"

Lorne fixed his gaze on the wall past John. "The Wraith showed up at base camp, sir, and I evacuated the teams. I should have—"

"That was your job, Lorne." John was too tired and drugged and in pain to put this any other way but bluntly. "If you'd done anything else, I would've been really pissed off."

Lorne looked relieved. "Thanks, sir, I—"

Then Beckett stepped out of a cabin down the corridor, spotted them, and waved his PDA in exasperation. "Bloody hell, will you lot get back in your beds?"

Rodney turned toward him. "Oh, I'm sorry, I thought this was the sick bay, but obviously it's the brig."

While Rodney and Beckett were arguing, John decided lying down again wasn't such a bad idea. He was halfway to his room when he realized why Ronon was following him around. He stopped, looking up at him. "Ronon. You don't have to guard us here."

Ronon looked away, fixing his eyes on some invisible point down the corridor. "I've heard the others say the commander of this ship doesn't like you."

"Uh." John stared at him. The corridor was currently empty, but this wasn't a good place for this conversation, or to explain John and Caldwell's personal issues. And John wasn't thrilled to realize there were rumors about it. "That's kind of complicated. But it's not like—It doesn't mean you have to stand guard here. It doesn't work like that, with us."

Ronon shrugged a little. "I don't mind." He looked down at John finally, and he looked tired and young. "Even if you don't think there's a need."

"Look, just find somewhere to get some rest." This was a little too complicated for John to deal with right now, and he wasn't going to stand here and argue with Ronon until somebody overheard them. "We'll talk about it later, okay?"

Ronon shrugged again. Deciding to take that for an assent, John went down the corridor. He found his treatment room, and started the lengthy process of climbing back onto the narrow bed.

Rodney came in, dropping into the only chair and opening his laptop. He said briskly, "Carson wants a full debrief on the Eidolon when you're all more conscious."

"We don't have that much information." John eased down, propping his knee back up on the pillows. Yeah, this was a much better place to be. He had forgotten to hang the IV bag on the stand, and it was too much trouble to do it now, so he just left it on his chest.

Rodney huffed in annoyance, got up, hung the IV bag back on the hook, then sat down again. "I think he thinks that there's some kind of clue there for a weapon against the Wraith."

"Weapon?" John frowned at the metal ceiling. "Like what?"

"Something chemical, that stops them from being able to feed." Rodney made a vague gesture, frowning at the laptop's screen. "I have no idea. I don't listen to his medical babble."

"Yeah, but the Eidolon had been looking for that for years," John pointed out. "Centuries. And their technology was pretty good."

"Whatever. It's an area that needs further research anyway," Rodney said, or something like that. John was already falling asleep again.

MARTHA WELLS

Martha Wells is the author of seven fantasy novels, including *Wheel of the Infinite*, *City of Bones*, *The Element of Fire*, and the Nebula-nominated *The Death of the Necromancer*. Her most recent novels are a fantasy trilogy: *The Wizard Hunters*, *The Ships of Air*, and *The Gate of Gods*, all currently out in paperback from HarperCollins Eos.

She has had short stories in the magazines *Realms of Fantasy*, *Black Gate*, *Lone Star Stories*, and *Stargate Magazine*, and in the Tsunami Relief charity anthology *Elemental* from Tor Books. She also has essays in the nonfiction anthologies *Farscape Forever* and *Mapping the World of Harry Potter* from BenBella Books. Her books have been published in eight languages, including French, Spanish, German, Russian, Polish, and Dutch, and her web site is www.marthawells.com.

STARGATE
SG·1™

STARGATE
ATLANTIS™

**Original novels based on
the hit TV shows,
STARGATE SG-1 and
STARGATE ATLANTIS**

AVAILABLE NOW

**For more information, visit
www.stargatenovels.com**

SNEAK PREVIEW

STARGATE SG-I: ROSWELL

by Sonny Whitelaw and Jennifer Fallon

This had to have been McKay's bright idea, Sam decided. Only he would have been so conceited. "I'm going to beam us down well away from the crash site. We have to do everything possible to minimize our impact on this time."

"Oh, we're gonna impact, all right," Cam yelled back. "In about one hundred and fifty thousand feet!"

"C'mon Jack, snap out of it!" Daniel implored.

Sam glanced aft. Teal'c was applying a pressure bandage to a ragged gash on Vala's thigh. Her BDUs were stained dark with blood, but it wasn't enough to have caused her to pass out like that. It must have been the cumulative effort of her own wounds and dealing with the General's injury. Sam knew from personal experience how draining using a handheld healing device could be. If Teal'c could wake her, Vala may yet be able to bring O'Neill around. "How is she?"

"Unresponsive," Teal'c replied, tying off the bandage.

"Coming up on one hundred thousand feet." Cam was scrambling to collect additional items that had floated out of the First Aid kit. Every one of them, even Teal'c, needed medical attention as soon as possible.

Assuming they weren't dead in the next few minutes, or so.

Sam glanced outside, but the jumper's spin was still erratic. Lightning bolts and watery sheets fanning out across the windshield told her that they were coming down in the middle of a storm, while data from the HUD confirmed they were now over New Mexico, thankfully well clear of any major towns. Abandoning the jumper would maroon them in this time, but they were fast running out of options. She reluctantly turned to the Asgard transport controls and locked onto their signals.

And then a not-so muted curse alerted her to the fact that the General was coming around.

"Jack!" Daniel patted him on the cheek none-too gently, adding green gunk to the blood already there. "Listen to me. You have to think about getting us out of here."

Glazed eyes half opened. "Where…?"

"Not where, sir. When," Sam amended. "You came back in time to get us but something went wrong. I think you ran into an Asgard ship."

"Carter?" O'Neill's face screwed up. His voice was slurred. "Distinctly recall you being against time travel."

"Jack!" Daniel shook the General's shoulders in frustration. "We don't have time for a discussion. Just get us out of here!"

"Fifty thousand," Cam called, grabbing Sam's discarded pack and the P-90s. Cam was getting ready bail. He obviously didn't share Daniel's optimism that the General would recover in time to save them from crashing.

Cam was wrong, however. The jumper's flight systems suddenly powered up, the HUD flickered into full color and a remarkably well-rendered set of images appeared. Sundry floating debris dropped to the floor as the inertial dampeners and artificial gravity both kicked in.

"That's it, Jack," Daniel said encouragingly. "You're doing it."

"Woulda been a great game," O'Neill mumbled.

"Ten thousand," Cam announced. "Plus or minus, but the minuses are catchin' up real fast."

"Yes, yes I'm sure it would have been a wonderful game." The words tumbled out of Daniel's mouth. "Jack…listen to me. Can you concentrate on getting us into orbit?"

"Eight thousand!" Cam grabbed the back of her seat. "Sam? It's time to get outta here!"

"Just a minute. He's doing it." Sam scanned the controls, hoping she wasn't imaging things. She really, really did not want to abandon the jumper.

"We don't have a minute!"

O'Neill blinked again and shook his head as if to clear it. "Carter said…gotta go back four hundred years, first."

"Five thousand feet and that ground is coming up damned fast—Sam!"

"Or was it three hundred, then forward two hundred?"

From the cargo bay she heard the time machine's consol hum to life, and something rippled over them. Surprised that the General had actually read her report on the jumper's log and time travel capabilities, Sam looked around in wonder at the stars. "It's working!"

She barely had time to register the relief of the faces of her companions before another ripple passed over them—and the jumper slammed sideways and began tumbling again, this time, end over end.

The inertial dampeners compensated a moment too

late, throwing Sam out of the copilot's seat and into Cam. Bright blue, early morning sky filled the windscreen before the ground spun into view long enough to tell her that they were now at least fifty thousand feet above a densely forested landscape. The HUD flicked wildly through a dozen images, but O'Neill seemed coherent enough to straighten out the jumper's erratic flight path. As they leveled off, Sam glanced up to discover a Ha'tak plummeting towards the ground, a fiery tail in its wake.

Sam's head reeled with the implications. Two time jumps and five seconds earlier it had been the wreckage from an Asgard ship, and the jumper had been less than five thousand feet from impact. Now they were at fifty thousand feet, looking at a damaged Ha'tak?

"We must have hit the Ha'tak when we jumped forward to our time!" Cam remarked unnecessarily.

Ignoring the pain from the dozens of stinging slices down her legs and arms, Sam disentangled herself from him, grabbed her chair and awkwardly pulled herself upright relative to the Asgard transport device. They were not out of danger, yet.

"Oh, that's bad," Daniel declared. "That's going to upset the Jaffa."

Although he still appeared to be half-out of it, the General was struggling to bring the jumper under control, but at least the inertial dampeners and gravity were working at maximum efficiency, giving them a considerably more stable ride.

"Like they're not already pissed enough." Apparently satisfied they were no longer in imminent peril of crashing, Cam pushed past the still unconscious Vala to check on Loki, who'd been all but squashed beneath Teal'c's considerable bulk.

"That's the least of our problems. When the Ha'tak hits, it's going to explode with the force of a mid-yield nuke." Sam glanced at O'Neill. He was blinking and shaking his head, trying to focus. "Sir, are you okay?"

"What the hell was a Ha'tak doin' skulking around the place, anyway?"

"The mere fact that it did not reveal itself," Teal'c observed with a scowl, "indicates it should not have been there."

"Got a point, there, T." With Daniel's help, Jack pulled himself upright and grabbed the controls. "Base, this is Jumper One, do you copy?"

There was no response.

"Base, this is Jumper One. We've recovered SG-1, but we've got a little problem, here."

The jumper continued to fly erratically. Sam peered at the HUD. The detail was exceptional, and somewhat reassuring. The region they were flying over was sparsely populated, which meant casualties from the impact of the Ha'tak would be minimal. A glance at the map coordinates confirmed why: 60°55N 101°57E. They were over Siberia.

But that Ha'tak was going in fast and she hadn't been exaggerating when she'd predicted the result of the explosion. Intending to beam the ships' crew to safety, she turned to the Asgard transport controls, but the screen was dead. One look inside the access panel beside her, told her why. She stared in dismay at the shattered crystals. "Sir, we—"

Without warning, the interior of the jumper was flooded with a searing light. Sam caught a glimpse of O'Neill lifting his hands to shield his face, but the photo-sensitive windscreen had already compensated, protecting them from a burst of light as intense as the sun. Had it got through to their eyes, it would have seared their corneas and blinded them permanently. The Ha'tak had either self-destructed or the engines had blown moments before impact.

"General!" Cam called in a voice that indicated he clearly understood the danger. "We have to get—"

"Doing it!" O'Neill was already angling the jumper into a near vertical climb. "Hang on."

Even at maximum power, Sam wasn't confident the shields could deal with such a close proximity to the equivalent of a nuclear detonation. A high-pitched whine diverted her attention to the cargo bay. Sparks were arcing out of the time machine.

The shockwave hit the jumper with the force of a giant fist slamming her back into the seat, momentarily overriding the inertial dampeners. She'd lost count how many times that morning her vision had started graying out from erratic g-forces, but surprisingly, the dampeners rapidly compensated.

Something else from inside the jumper wasn't faring so well, though, because acrid smoke was billowing into the cockpit. She heard a fire extinguisher, and, trusting her teammates to do whatever was necessary, blinked away the white spots before her eyes and turned her attention back to the Asgard transport scanner.

They may yet need to abandon the jumper.

COMING MAY 2007

STARGATE ATLANTIS: EXOGENESIS

**by Sonny Whitelaw &
Elizabeth Christensen**
Price: £6.99 UK | $7.95 US
ISBN: 1-905586-02-7

When Dr. Carson Beckett disturbs
the rest of two long-dead Ancients,
he unleashes devastating consequences of global proportions.

    With the very existence of Lan-
tea at risk, Colonel John Sheppard
leads his team on a desperate search for the long lost Ancient
device that could save Atlantis. While Teyla Emmagan and Dr.
Elizabeth Weir battle the ecological meltdown consuming their
world, Colonel Sheppard, Dr. Rodney McKay and Dr. Zelenka
travel to a world created by the Ancients themselves. There
they discover a human experiment that could mean their salvation...

    But the truth is never as simple as it seems, and the team's
prejudices lead them to make a fatal error — an error that could
slaughter thousands, including their own Dr. McKay.

The team battles the Hounds of Hell.

STARGATE ATLANTIS

ATLANTIS

HALCYON

James Swallow

Based on the hit television series created by
Brad Wright and Robert C. Cooper

Series number: SGA-4

STARGATE ATLANTIS: HALCYON

by James Swallow
Price: £6.99 UK | $7.95 US
ISBN: 1-905586-01-9

In their ongoing quest for new allies, Atlantis's flagship team travel to Halcyon, a grim industrial world where the Wraith are no longer feared — they are hunted.

Horrified by the brutality of Halcyon's warlike people, Lieutenant Colonel John Sheppard soon becomes caught in the political machinations of Halcyon's aristocracy. In a feudal society where strength means power, he realizes the nobles will stop at nothing to ensure victory over their rivals. Meanwhile, Dr. Rodney McKay enlists the aid of the ruler's daughter to investigate a powerful Ancient structure, but McKay's scientific brilliance has aroused the interest of the planet's most powerful man — a man with a problem he desperately needs McKay to solve.

As Halcyon plunges into a catastrophe of its own making the team must join forces with the warlords — or die at the hands of their bitterest enemy…

STARGATE ATLANTIS: THE CHOSEN

by Sonny Whitelaw & Elizabeth Christensen
Price: £6.99 UK | $7.95 US
ISBN: 0-9547343-8-6

With Ancient technology scattered across the Pegasus galaxy, the Atlantis team is not surprised to find it in use on a world once defended by Dalera, an Ancient who was cast out of her society for falling in love with a human.

But in the millennia since Dalera's departure much has changed. Her strict rules have been broken, leaving her people open to Wraith attack. Only a few of the Chosen remain to operate Ancient technology vital to their defense and tensions are running high. Revolution simmers close to the surface.

When Major Sheppard and Rodney McKay are revealed as members of the Chosen, Daleran society convulses into chaos. Wanting to help resolve the crisis and yet refusing to prop up an autocratic regime, Sheppard is forced to act when Teyla and Lieutenant Ford are taken hostage by the rebels...

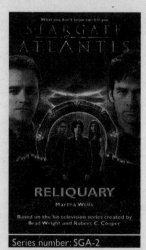

What you don't know can kill you

STARGATE ATLANTIS

RELIQUARY
Martha Wells

Based on the hit television series created by
Brad Wright and Robert C. Cooper

Series number: SGA-2

STARGATE ATLANTIS: RELIQUARY

by Martha Wells
Price: £6.99 UK | $7.95 US
ISBN: 0-9547343-7-8

While exploring the unused sections of the Ancient city of Atlantis, Major John Sheppard and Dr. Rodney McKay stumble on a recording device that reveals a mysterious new Stargate address. Believing that the address may lead them to a vast repository of Ancient knowledge, the team embarks on a mission to this uncharted world.

There they discover a ruined city, full of whispered secrets and dark shadows. As tempers fray and trust breaks down, the team uncovers the truth at the heart of the city. A truth that spells their destruction.

With half their people compromised, it falls to Major John Sheppard and Dr. Rodney McKay to risk everything in a deadly game of bluff with the enemy. To fail would mean the fall of Atlantis itself — and, for Sheppard, the annihilation of his very humanity…

STARGATE ATLANTIS: RISING

by Sally Malcolm
Price: £6.99 UK | $7.95 US
ISBN: 0-9547343-5-1

Following the discovery of an Ancient outpost buried deep in the Antarctic ice sheet, Stargate Command sends a new team of explorers through the Stargate to the distant Pegasus galaxy.

Emerging in an abandoned Ancient city, the team quickly confirms that they have found the Lost City of Atlantis. But, submerged beneath the sea on an alien planet, the city is in danger of catastrophic flooding unless it is raised to the surface. Things go from bad to worse when the team must confront a new enemy known as the Wraith who are bent on destroying Atlantis.

Stargate Atlantis is the exciting new spin-off of the hit TV show, Stargate SG-1. Based on the script of the pilot episode, Rising is a must-read for all fans and includes deleted scenes and dialog not seen on TV—with photos from the pilot episode.

Order your copy directly from the publisher today by going to www.stargatenovels.com or send a check or money order made payable to "Fandemonium" to:

<u>USA orders:</u> **$10.82 ($7.95 + $2.87 P&P). Send payment to: Fandemonium Books, PO Box 2178, Decatur, GA 30031-2178.**

<u>UK orders:</u> **£8.30 (£6.99 + £1.31 P&P).** <u>Rest of the World orders:</u> **£9.70 (£6.99 + £2.71 P&P). Send payment to: Fandemonium Books, PO Box 795A, Surbiton KT5 8YB, United Kingdom.**

Or check your local bookshop – available on special order if they are out of stock (quote the ISBN number listed above).

STARGATE SG-1: ALLIANCES

On the book cover:

STARGATE
SG·1

Karen Miller

ALLIANCES

Based on the hit television series developed by
Brad Wright and Jonathan Glassner

Series number: SG1-8

by Karen Miller
Price: £6.99 UK | $7.95 US
ISBN: 978-1-905586-00-4

All SG-1 wanted was technology to save Earth from the Goa'uld ... but the mission to Euronda was a terrible failure. Now the dogs of Washington are baying for Jack O'Neill's blood—and Senator Robert Kinsey is leading the pack.

When Jacob Carter asks General Hammond for SG-1's participation in mission for the Tok'ra, it seems like the answer to O'Neill's dilemma. The secretive Tok'ra are running out of hosts. Jacob believes he's found the answer—but it means O'Neill and his team must risk their lives infiltrating a Goa'uld slave breeding farm to recruit humans willing to join the Tok'ra.

It's a risky proposition ... especially since the fallout from Euronda has strained the team's bond almost to breaking. If they can't find a way to put their differences behind them, they might not make it home alive ...

STARGATE SG-1: SURVIVAL OF THE FITTEST

by Sabine C. Bauer
Price: £6.99 UK | $7.95 US
ISBN: 0-9547343-9-4

Colonel Frank Simmons has never been a friend to SG-1. Working for the shadowy government organisation, the NID, he has hatched a horrifying plan to create an army as devastatingly effective as that of any Goa'uld.

Series number: SG1-7

And he will stop at nothing to fulfil his ruthless ambition, even if that means forfeiting the life of the SGC's Chief Medical Officer, Dr. Janet Fraiser. But Simmons underestimates the bond between Stargate Command's officers. When Fraiser, Major Samantha Carter and Teal'c disappear, Colonel Jack O'Neill and Dr. Daniel Jackson are forced to put aside personal differences to follow their trail into a world of savagery and death.

In this complex story of revenge, sacrifice and betrayal, SG-1 must endure their greatest ordeal…

Aris Boch is back – and he's after Daniel Jackson!

STARGATE
SG·1

SIREN SONG

Holly Scott & Jaimie Duncan

Based on the hit television series developed by
Brad Wright and Jonathan Glassner

Series number: SG1-6

STARGATE SG-1: SIREN SONG

Holly Scott and Jaimie Duncan
Price: £6.99 UK | $7.95 US
ISBN: 0-9547343-6-X

Bounty-hunter, Aris Boch, once more has his sights on SG-1. But this time Boch isn't interested in trading them for cash. He needs the unique talents of Dr. Daniel Jackson — and he'll do anything to get them.

Taken to Boch's ravaged home-world, Atropos, Colonel Jack O'Neill and his team are handed over to insane Goa'uld, Sebek. Obsessed with opening a mysterious subterranean vault, Sebek demands that Jackson translate the arcane writing on the doors. When Jackson refuses, the Goa'uld resorts to devastating measures to ensure his cooperation.

With the vault exerting a malign influence on all who draw near, Sebek compels Jackson and O'Neill toward a horror that threatens both their sanity and their lives. Meanwhile, Carter and Teal'c struggle to persuade the starving people of Atropos to risk everything they have to save SG-1 — and free their desolate world of the Goa'uld, forever.

STARGATE SG-1: CITY OF THE GODS

by Sonny Whitelaw
Price: £6.99 UK | $7.95 US
ISBN: 0-9547343-3-5

When a Crystal Skull is discovered beneath the Pyramid of the Sun in Mexico, it ignites a cataclysmic chain of events that maroons SG-1 on a dying world.

Xalótcan is a brutal society, steeped in death and sacrifice, where the bloody gods of the Aztecs demand tribute from a fearful and superstitious population. But that's the least of Colonel Jack O'Neill's problems. With Xalótcan on the brink of catastrophe, Dr. Daniel Jackson insists that O'Neill must fulfil an ancient prophesy and lead its people to salvation. But with the world tearing itself apart, can anyone survive?

As fear and despair plunge Xalótcan into chaos, SG-1 find themselves with ringside seats at the end of the world…

• *Special section: Excerpts from Dr. Daniel Jackson's mission journal.*

O'Neill faces a nightmare from his past

STARGATE SG·1

A MATTER OF HONOR
Book One
Sally Malcolm
Based on the hit television series developed by
Brad Wright and Jonathan Glassner

Series number: SG1-3

STARGATE SG-1: A MATTER OF HONOR

**Part one of two parts
by Sally Malcolm**
Price: £6.99 UK | $7.95 US
ISBN: 0-9547343-2-7

Five years after Major Henry Boyd and his team, SG-10, were trapped on the edge of a black hole, Colonel Jack O'Neill discovers a device that could bring them home.

But it's owned by the Kinahhi, an advanced and paranoid people, besieged by a ruthless foe. Unwilling to share the technology, the Kinahhi are pursuing their own agenda in the negotiations with Earth's diplomatic delegation. Maneuvering through a maze of tyranny, terrorism and deceit, Dr. Daniel Jackson, Major Samantha Carter and Teal'c unravel a startling truth — a revelation that throws the team into chaos and forces O'Neill to face a nightmare he is determined to forget.

Resolved to rescue Boyd, O'Neill marches back into the hell he swore never to revisit. Only this time, he's taking SG-1 with him...

STARGATE SG-1: THE COST OF HONOR

**Part two of two parts
by Sally Malcolm**
Price: £6.99 UK | $7.95 US
ISBN: 0-9547343-4-3

In the action-packed sequel to *A Matter of Honor*, SG-1 embark on a desperate mission to save SG-10 from the edge of a black hole. But the price of heroism may be more than they can pay...

Returning to Stargate Command, Colonel Jack O'Neill and his team find more has changed in their absence than they had expected. Nonetheless, O'Neill is determined to face the consequences of their unauthorized activities, only to discover the penalty is far worse than anything he could have imagined.

With the fate of Colonel O'Neill and Major Samantha Carter unknown, and the very survival of the SGC threatened, Dr. Daniel Jackson and Teal'c mount a rescue mission to free their team-mates and reclaim the SGC. Yet returning to the Kinahhi homeworld, they learn a startling truth about its ancient foe. And uncover a horrifying secret...

Terror stalks the team at night

STARGATE
SG·1

SACRIFICE MOON
Julie Fortune

Based on the hit television series developed by
Brad Wright and Jonathan Glassner

Series number: SG1-2

STARGATE SG-1: SACRIFICE MOON

By Julie Fortune

Price: £6.99 UK | $7.95 US
ISBN: 0-9547343-1-9

Sacrifice Moon follows the newly commissioned SG-1 on their first mission through the Stargate.

Their destination is Chalcis, a peaceful society at the heart of the Helos Confederacy of planets. But Chalcis harbors a dark secret, one that pitches SG-1 into a world of bloody chaos, betrayal and madness. Battling to escape the living nightmare, Dr. Daniel Jackson and Captain Samantha Carter soon begin to realize that more than their lives are at stake. They are fighting for their very souls.

But while Col Jack O'Neill and Teal'c struggle to keep the team together, Daniel is hatching a desperate plan that will test SG-1's fledgling bonds of trust and friendship to the limit…

Order your copy directly from the publisher today by going to www.stargatenovels.com or send a check or money order made payable to "Fandemonium" to:

<u>USA orders</u>: $10.82 ($7.95 + $2.87 P&P). Send payment to: Fandemonium Books, PO Box 2178, Decatur, GA 30031-2178.

<u>UK orders</u>: £8.30 (£6.99 + £1.31 P&P). <u>Rest of the World orders</u>: £9.70 (£6.99 + £2.71 P&P). Send payment to: Fandemonium Books, PO Box 795A, Surbiton KT5 8YB, United Kingdom.

Or check your local bookshop – available on special order if they are out of stock (quote the ISBN number listed above).

STARGATE SG-1: TRIAL BY FIRE

By Sabine C. Bauer
Price: £6.99 UK | $7.95 US
ISBN: 0-9547343-0-0

Series number: SG1-1

Trial by Fire follows the team as they embark on a mission to Tyros, an ancient society teetering on the brink of war.

A pious people, the Tyreans are devoted to the Canaanite deity, Meleq. When their spiritual leader is savagely murdered during a mission of peace, they beg SG-1 for help against their sworn enemies, the Phrygians.

Initially reluctant to get involved, the team has no choice when Colonel Jack O'Neill is abducted. O'Neill soon discovers his only hope of escape is to join the ruthless Phrygians — if he can survive their barbaric initiation rite.

As Major Samantha Carter, Dr. Daniel Jackson and Teal'c race to his rescue, they find themselves embroiled in a war of shifting allegiances, where truth has many shades and nothing is as it seems.

And, unbeknownst to them all, an old enemy is hiding in the shadows...